FIRST THERE WAS *On the Beach*,
THEN THERE WAS *Fail-Safe*—
A CLASSIC THAT MUST BE READ BY
EVERYONE CONCERNED ABOUT NUCLEAR
WAR AND THE FUTURE OF THE PLANET.

"Chilling, shattering, a multimegaton wallop!"
—*Chicago Tribune*

"A terrifying tale of our time."   —*Book Week*

"Excruciatingly tense!"
—*The Wall Street Journal*

"An exciting story."   —*The New Republic*

"This book leaves the reader defenseless. . . . It is his
life that is directly involved in the outcome. He will be
chilled to his cortex by the awareness that the prime
elements of this cosmic horror story exist in real life."
—Norman Cousins, *Saturday Review*

F. J. BRENNAN
ENGLISH DEPT.

QUANTITY SALES

Most Dell Books are available at special quantity discounts when purchased in bulk by corporations, organizations, and special-interest groups. Custom imprinting or excerpting can also be done to fit special needs. For details write: Dell Publishing Co., Inc., 666 Fifth Avenue, New York, NY 10103. Attn.: Special Sales Dept.

INDIVIDUAL SALES

Are there any Dell Books you want but cannot find in your local stores? If so, you can order them directly from us. You can get any Dell book in print. Simply include the book's title, author, and ISBN number, if you have it, along with a check or money order (no cash can be accepted) for the full retail price plus $1.50 to cover shipping and handling. Mail to: Dell Readers Service, P.O. Box 5057, Des Plaines, IL 60017.

FAIL-SAFE

by EUGENE BURDICK
and HARVEY WHEELER

A DELL BOOK

Published by
Dell Publishing Co., Inc.
1 Dag Hammarskjold Plaza
New York, New York 10017

For Carol and for Peggy

Dell ® TM 681510, Dell Publishing Co., Inc.

ISBN: 0-440-12459-X

Reprinted by arrangement with McGraw-Hill Book
Company, Inc.

Printed in the United States of America

Two Previous Editions

December 1987

10 9 8 7 6 5 4 3 2 1

WFH

CONTENTS

PREFACE

The people in this novel are our contemporaries and they deal with a problem that is already upon us. It is being discussed daily in Washington, Moscow, London, and elsewhere by heads of state, diplomatic and military experts. Men of good will and ill have been agonizing over the problem for years. They have found no solution.

Although science and technology have been harnessed to the American defense system in a miraculous way, most people are unaware of even those portions of the miracle which have been declassified and discussed openly in technical books and journals. Thus, paradoxically, a fictional portrayal employing declassified information may seem like science fiction to the layman and ancient history to the expert.

The authors have not had access to classified information but have taken some liberties with what has been declassified. Usually this amounted to attributing improved or more powerful performances to control and weapons systems. Modified or fictional names have been given to the improved equipment. The events in this story are thought of as taking place in 1967.

This book is not an exposé. It does not purport to reveal any specific technical flaw in our defense system. Perhaps our charge may be considered even more grave. For there is substantial agreement among experts that an accidental war is possible and that its probability increases with the increasing complexity of the man-machine components which make up our defense system. Hardly a week passes without some new warning of this danger by knowledgeable persons who take seriously their duty to warn and inform the people. In addition, all too often past crises have been revealed to us in which the world tottered on the brink of thermonuclear war while SAC commanders pondered the true nature of unidentified flying objects on their radar screens.

Thus the element in our story which seems most fictional—the story's central problem and its solution—is in fact the most real part. Men, machines, and mathematics being what they are, this is, unfortunately, a "true" story. The accident may not occur in the way we describe but the laws of probability assure us that ultimately it will occur. The logic of politics tells us that when it does, the only way out will be a choice of disasters.

Eugene Burdick
Harvey Wheeler

ch. 1

THE TRANSLATOR

Peter Buck walked up to the Pennsylvania entrance of
the White House. It was one of the hard, deceptive,
crystal days of early spring. The obelisk of the Washington Monument was white and glittering. Tourists
hurried rather than shuffled past the White House.
Official limousines went by with their windows rolled
up and their back-seat occupants thumbing through
papers, their chesterfield collars up. The air was mar-
velously clear and full of sun, but it was cold.

Often Buck had the desire to mingle with the
crowds, to wander down the Mall, to loiter in the
Smithsonian, actually to visit the capitol and sit in the
Senate gallery, to visit the Supreme Court on Monday
when decisions were rendered, to regain the innocence
he had felt years ago when he first came to Washington. With a soft poignancy Buck realized he had become a new victim of an old malady: he saw less of his
city than the tourist. But today he was glad to reach
the White House sentry box and looked forward to
his warm steam-heated office.

The Pot was on duty in the small wooden guardhouse. The Pot was a thin wiry man, but sixteen years
of White House guard duty had given him a hard
round belly. He never exercised, but by some odd law
of physiology his arms and face remained skinny.
Looking out the window of the sentry box he seemed

a frail and almost undernourished figure. The moment he stepped outside the impression vanished. He looked precisely as if he had swallowed an ancient cannonball.

Buck did not know his real name. This was part of the White House drill: the guards *had* to know everyone's name, but the other employees seldom knew the names of the guards. The Thin Man, the Pot, the Indian, Scar Face, Chief, the Grunt, the Sphinx, were some of the names which the civilian staff had given to the guards. Buck had never heard one of the guards called by a proper name.

The Pot stepped out of the guardhouse and nodded at Buck. His eyes flicked over Buck's leather attaché case and he grunted.

"Ham and cheese?" the Pot asked.

"Wrong," Buck said and grinned. He opened the attaché case. It contained two apples, a carton of yogurt, and a chicken leg wrapped in wax paper.

"Pay up."

The Pot reached in his pocket and took out a nickel. He dropped it in Buck's hand.

"O.K., I lose today," the Pot said. "You know where we stand now, Mr. Buck? After 932 bets I have won 501 and you have won 431. What do you think it means?"

"Who knows?" Buck said. He smiled at the Pot and walked on, but the Pot's question irritated him. For over three years he and the Pot had had this small running bet. It was uncanny how the Pot could estimate when Buck was picking up weight and would start to bring a reducing lunch to the White House. Long ago they had jokingly established categories of food and the Pot would guess what Buck had in his lunchbox. Gradually it had hardened into a bet, had become somewhat serious and, finally, a major part of the day for each of them. Today was the first time that the Pot had lost a bet in almost a week. In his efforts to deceive the Pot, Buck had become very ingenious in his preparation of lunches. He had instructed his wife, Sarah, to seek out exotic sausages, salad-stuffed eggs, sometimes caviar sandwiches. Once as a joke he had even gone to one of the more expensive delicatessen stores in Washington and purchased a small can of kangaroo meat, but when he produced the kangaroo sandwich, and saw the look on the Pot's face, he realized he had gone a bit outside the rules. The Pot paid the nickel but his eyes were icy.

Buck went into the East Wing, nodded at the Indian, and then turned left. He entered his small office.

He opened his attaché case, quickly deposited his lunch in the left-hand bottom drawer of his desk, took a copy of the *Washington Post* from the case and put it on the desk. He closed the case and put it in the corner behind the coat rack. He sat down to the desk. Squarely in the middle of his desk, put there a half hour before by a messenger, were the usual copies of *Pravda* and *Izvestia,* plus a monthly Russian literary magazine.

Buck began to read the Russian newspapers. He read with an incredible speed. As he read, repeating a task he had done hundreds of times, he was aware of a slight thrill of pride. He knew, quietly and competently, that he was among the three best Russian translators in the United States. Ryskind at Berkeley might be a hair better on accent, but that was all. Buck was sure that he was better than Watkins over at the Pentagon. After the three of them there was a big gap before one came to the fourth best American-born Russian-language expert. Probably Haven at Columbia.

Buck remembered with a stab of malice that at the

last meeting of the Slavic Language Association Haven had misused the Russian word for "popery" twice in the same paper. Only Ryskind and Watkins and Buck had been aware of the error. They had smiled across the room at one another and shaken their heads slightly. No one else had noticed it.

Buck had become a Russian expert quite by accident. In the 1950s when he was twenty-two years old he had been called up for military duty just as the Korean War started. He was a junior in college at the time, but had no special interest in languages. He intended to be an engineer. When the Army tested him, however, he placed very high on language aptitude and found himself at the Army Language School at Monterey.

What followed bewildered Buck. By the end of the first week of instruction he was at least two months in advance of the others in the class. The instructor, a Russian immigrant from Kazakstan, was astounded. Not only did Buck learn the Russian alphabet and syntax and peculiarities of grammar quickly, but he could instantly speak back in whatever dialect was being spoken. In two weeks he was something of a celebrity. The Russians on the staff of the Language School would bring him into a room and start to speak Russian to him. Promptly he would respond with the same accent in which he was addressed. If the Russian was Georgian, Buck came back with a Georgian accent, if from Leningrad, the peculiar light inflection of the Leningrad area. The instructors watched him intently, occasionally smiling as he reproduced an obscure accent. At the end of three weeks they took Buck from his class and explained that his presence there was demoralizing to the other students.

From then on he lived a dual existence at the school. Half of his day was spent in an accelerated course in

Russian, in which he was exposed to everything from ancient forms of Russian literature to contemporary Russian scientific writing. The other half of the day he was the subject for a group of psychologists who tried to discover why he learned Russian so easily. They put him through an endless series of aptitude, intelligence, personality, and physical tests. The results were a strange nullity. Buck had the I.Q. of an average college student, around 122. He was somewhat high on the tests that measured verbal facility, but his memory was not especially good nor was his eye-hand reflex better than the average student's. His hearing was actually subnormal. His tone, frequency, and pitch discrimination were phenomenal, but correlated with nothing else. The psychologists were both puzzled and suspicious. They harbored the lingering doubt that Buck was holding back something. One psychologist had the theory that Buck had been exposed at an early age to someone who spoke Russian; to expound it he even wrote a paper called "A Case Study in Infantile Language Imprinting." He was quite unmoved when no one could discover a Russian-speaking person in Buck's background.

After a time, the psychologists, sensing Buck's indifference, began to talk in front of him about their test results. He knew precisely how his Rorschach inkblots were interpreted, the results of the MMPI, his I.Q. on eight different tests, the results of his Strong Vocational Guidance Inventory, his index of neuroticism, how tolerant he was of ambiguity. In everything he came out close to dead center.

Buck smiled indulgently at the psychologists. He was fully aware that his capabilities were quite average. For his exceptional language skill he had no explanation. It worried him very little.

At the end of a year Buck could speak Russian, in

most of its dialects, as well as any of the instructors at the school.

His first assignment was to a division in the Pentagon which translated the more important Russian military documents. Sometimes the articles were said to have been stolen by American espionage agents or purchased from the spy hives of Hong Kong and Berlin and Tangiers. Sometimes they were merely long articles from Russian military journals.

Buck did his work in the Pentagon quickly and efficiently. Even the old hands were startled at the rapidity with which he could translate obscure phrases. "Sergeant Buck is something of a phenomenon in this division," his superior wrote in evaluating his work. "Not only does he know the Russian language flawlessly, but when it comes to interpreting a new colloquial phrase, in which Russian abounds, Buck's interpretation is invariably correct." After several paragraphs of praise the letter closed by recommending him for training as an officer in rather negative terms. "This person should be sent to OCS because his virtuosity in the language makes it somewhat embarrassing for his superiors to treat him as an enlisted man."

Buck was aware that others in the division had reservations about him, and he knew why. Everyone else in the division was deeply interested not only in the Russian language, but in Russian politics, personalities, weaponry, economic conditions, and even Russian gossip. Buck did not conceal the fact that he was enormously bored with Russia. He was much more interested in a small red MG which he had brought to a high pitch of mechanical perfection, a soft-spoken girl from Georgia with the name of Sarah, and cool jazz.

There would be days when everyone in the division was in a paroxysm of excitement because some member of the Soviet Presidium had been demoted. They spent hours trying to tease out the significance of this. When they asked Buck his views, he shook his head and said, "No comment." He was not rude, he was simply not interested. The division traced the rise and fall of obscure Russian bureaucrats, they speculated on Russian agricultural production, they argued bitterly about whether Stalin had been a Marxist or an opportunist. Buck's very sense of noninvolvement was at first puzzling and then finally unbearable. His sheer flawless ease in translation, the fact that he was the only person in the division who never needed a dictionary, did not make him popular.

At the end of a year of Pentagon duty Buck was ordered to OCS. He emerged a second lieutenant with orders to report to an infantry division in Germany. He sold the red MG with regret, but left the Pentagon with pleasure. He was relieved to escape the tyranny of his strange and unwanted Russian skill. He liked the long war games in which he and his platoon crept through the dark German forests, their rifles tipped with eight inches of bayonet, the rumble of tanks just ahead of them, the occasional crashing sound of a simulated land mine giving the maneuver an element of excitement.

Occasionally he went with other members of the platoon into a nearby town and got drunk on the excellent German beer and ate huge quantities of various German sausages. His spare time was devoted to the care and maintenance of a Porsche coupé which he bought because it was incredibly cheap for an American soldier and he loved its lines. He also wrote a letter a day to Sarah. The Porsche was a miracle of mechanical perfection. Buck tuned it to an exquisite level of adjustment. Occasionally he would take it for a workout on the beautifully intricate forest roads of the nearby mountains. He thrilled to the dangers of the abysses which underlay each hairpin turn, but never pushed the car to its ultimate capacity. After such trips he carefully washed the car, wiped the leather with saddle soap, retuned the motor, and covered the coupé with a red parachute.

After two years of duty, Buck was discharged from the Army. He and the Porsche were returned to America on the same ship. Two weeks after he arrived in New York he married Sarah and took a job as translator at the United Nations. Two years later only two things had changed in Buck's life: they had a four-months-old son, and Buck had discovered the law.

He had started to read a casebook on the law of torts that someone had left in the translators' room at the UN building and did not stop until he had finished the whole book. It was a stunning discovery. There was something so symmetrical and neat and perfect about the organization of the law, it seemed so logical and majestic, and so awesome in its certitude. It was like a new complex foreign language with its own special vocabulary, grammar, and syntax. Buck found it irresistible.

Sarah, a girl who combined a low metabolic rate with a rare sweet face and a gentle nature, encouraged Buck in his enthusiasm for the law. The only problem was how to support his family and go to school at the same time. Through the network of translators, he heard of an opening on the White House staff for a Russian translator. The job was reputed to make very little demand upon the translator's time. He merely had to be there in the unlikely case that the President needed to speak directly to a non-English-speaking Russian. The last man who had the job had held it for five years, had not seen the old President and quit out of boredom when the new President took office. Buck had applied for the job and in the competitive examinations had been 14 points ahead of his nearest competitor.

He and Sarah and the child and the Porsche made their way to Washington. Sarah set up housekeeping in Arlington. Buck began to go to Georgetown Law School at night. During the day he spent his time reading law books in his office and occasionally glancing through the heap of Russian documents which were automatically circulated through his office.

A hard-driven student could have gotten through Georgetown Law School in four years while occupying an outside job, but Buck was in no hurry. He loved his law courses and worked at them carefully and patiently, much like a jeweler determined to give a lapidary finish to a rare stone. His law-school professors regarded him as intelligent, hard-working, a perfectionist for detail, and completely lacking in what they called "legal imagination." Once Buck had asked a professor why he was given only a *C* on a paper in which he had answered a very long and involved question in the most specific detail.

"Mr. Buck, I agree with you that your answer to that question probably deserved an *A*," the professor said, leaning back in his chair and rubbing his eyes. "But we are in the business of training practicing lawyers who will be able to think on their feet and in a constantly changing legal context. Your answer was the perfect textbook reply. I could not have done better. But it lacked any flair, any feel for anything outside of the law. Perhaps, Mr. Buck, it is your vocation to be a professor of law rather than a lawyer."

Buck was thrilled by this answer. He would like nothing better than to spend his life immersed in the intricacies of legal scholarship. Slowly, methodically, with the pure pleasure of the utterly committed, Buck learned the law. The classes came and went but Buck stayed on year after year. He knew that at some point he would finish his legal education and would then become a law professor. Until that time he found life very full.

The White House job took very little time. Over the years he came to regard the White House as a place where he went to study, a kind of refuge which also gave him an income. It was true he had seen the President, but never on business. In the first month after the new President took office he had wandered into Buck's room, introduced himself, and sat down. Buck was impressed by the President's youth, his relaxation, the way in which he put his feet up on Buck's desk and rambled over Buck's background. It was only later that Buck realized that behind that boyish manner and seeming relaxation was a tough and analytical mind. The pleasant informal meeting had really been a disguised examination. Buck knew he had passed. The President had coolly lopped a half-dozen old-timers from the White House staff and told them bluntly it was for incompetence. He had told them face to face, not through another person.

Despite the President's toughness Buck had a lingering doubt about the man. Being the scion of a wealthy family, having easy access to politics, and marrying a beautiful woman did not, Buck thought, really equip him to deal with his adversary in the Soviet Union. The Russian leaders, Buck had gathered, were hard to the point of ferocity, committed to a degree that was unbelievable to an American—especially a wealthy American.

Buck's doubts about the President's capacity made his own slow-paced and easy job somehow more justifiable to himself.

This particular morning Buck had finished his

quick scanning of *Pravda* and *Izvestia* and was turning
with pleasure to one of Maitland's essays on the corporation's personality. He opened the book, began to
make careful marks on the margin and entries in his
notebook.

Buck was so absorbed in Maitland that the shrill
sound pierced through the office for several seconds
before he was aware of it. He had never heard the
sound before, but instantly he knew where it came
from. In the second drawer of his desk there was a red
telephone. When he had been given the office and his
instructions, he had been told that this telephone
would ring only in case of emergency and was never to
be used for ordinary communications. The black telephone on top of the desk was to be used for normal
business. He had also been told that when the red
phone did ring it would not give the short intermit-
tent rings made by an ordinary telephone, but would
give off a steady sharp sound until it was answered.

Someone at the White House switchboard had made
a mistake, Buck thought. He had been in this office for
three years and the red telephone had never rung.
Buck was convinced it never would. He pulled open
the drawer and instantly the sound of the telephone
became more shrill.

Once he saw the red phone something began to nag
at his memory; he felt a sharp sense of unease. Then
he remembered: the official who had installed him in
the office had also given him a logbook labeled "Red
Phone Log Book" with instructions to log the precise
time that the red phone rang . . . if it ever rang. Buck
had not seen the logbook for over a year. It had become mixed in with the law books, old copies of *Izvestia,* Russian magazines, notebooks. With both hands
Buck pawed through the debris of paper on his desk,
pulled open the top drawer, yanked at the three draw-

ers on the left side of the desk. He could not find the logbook. He calmed himself. The call was sure to be a mistake. Nevertheless, he took a clean piece of paper and then looked at his watch. He wrote the time in big black figures in the middle of the white rectangle: "10:32 A.M."

With relief he picked up the phone.

"Mr. Buck, this is the President speaking," a voice said. There was no mistaking the voice. It was calm, New England accented, nasal. "Would you please make your way to the White House bomb shelter as soon as possible?"

"Yes, sir, I . . ." Buck said and then stopped. As soon as he had said the word "Yes" the President had hung up.

ch. 2

THE WAR ROOM, OMAHA

The War Room of the Strategic Air Command at Omaha was not immense. Not in terms of what it had to do. It was no bigger than a small theater. The pools of darkness in its corners, however, gave the sensation of immensity, almost of a limitless reach. The only illumination in the War Room came from the Big Board. It covered the entire front wall and resembled a gigantic movie screen, except that it was made of a kind of translucent plastic. At that moment the Big Board showed a simple Mercator map of the world. The continents and the oceans were familiar, as were the lines of latitude and longitude. But there the similarity to ordinary Mercator maps disappeared. The map was covered with a strange flood of cabalistic signs. Arrows, circles, squares, numbers, triangles were strewn across the screen, sometimes came up bright and clear, sometimes dimmed, and occasionally a sign notation would fade entirely and leave only a phosphorescent glow that persisted for a few seconds.

Even in the uncertain light it was possible to see that there were only a half-dozen men in the War Room. In the dimness the men looked doll-like and diminutive. This added to the impression of vastness.

"I expected a little more action," Congressman Raskob said. "This is just like a second-rate theater. Where are the ushers?"

Lieutenant General Bogan, United States Air Force, glanced down at Congressman Raskob. The Congressman's reaction was not uncommon among people who were seeing the War Room for the first time, but General Bogan also knew that he was being baited. He had been briefed on Raskob's background.

"Right now, sir, we are at our lowest condition of readiness," General Bogan said. "Right now everything is routine. The moment that something starts to happen there is plenty of action."

"In a few minutes, sir, your eyes will get adjusted to the light and we can show you some of the more interesting things in the War Room," Colonel Cascio said. Colonel Cascio was General Bogan's deputy.

The Congressman grunted. He stood at the raised runway at the back of the War Room, his feet wide apart, his short stocky body held in a posture that was almost arrogant.

He's going to be a tough one, General Bogan thought. He looked over at the other guest, Gordon Knapp, the president of Universal Electronics. No trouble there.

Knapp was one of the new breed of scientists who, after World War II, had become a scientist-inventor-businessman. Although he was almost six feet tall, Knapp's body was hunched over as if he had just finished a long and desperate race. In fact it was his habitual posture. Ever since he had discovered science Knapp *had* run with a zestful enthusiastic desperation which had no element of anxiety. It had taken Bogan some months to realize that Knapp's adversary was scientific problems. He threw his physical and intellectual power against problems and his record of successes was unbroken. He had become an expert on miniaturization, solid-state physics, semiconductors, and, more recently, problems of data storing. In the process he had become a millionaire and had achieved a high reputation. Both of these facts he forgot constantly. He was oblivious of everything except unsolved technical problems. In the process of mastering them he had ravaged his body, learned to exist on five hours of sleep a night, and was an extremely happy man. He was a man of black coffee, hurried airplane flights, phone calls, technical drawings, intuitions about amperage and voltage, a vast unanswered correspondence, harassed secretaries, rumpled suits, and a burning attention for only one thing: his scientific problems. His wife once said—entirely in jest for she loved and admired him—that she would have divorced him long ago but he was never home long enough to discuss the matter.

This was Knapp's first visit to the War Room and General Bogan could see that he was quivering with excitement. Many of the mechanisms that he had invented and manufactured were used in the room, and his eyes glittered as he tried to identify the machinery in the gloom.

"It may look simple, Mr. Raskob, but this is one of the most complicated rooms in the world," Knapp said in a whisper.

"And one of the most expensive," Raskob said.

General Bogan resisted the tendency to sigh. Raskob was a tough and intelligent man. He came from a congressional district in Manhattan which was made up partly of new and expensive apartment houses and partly of old tenements gradually being taken over by Puerto Ricans and Negroes. The first time he had been elected it was by a narrow margin and Raskob had known he must work out some formula of political appeal which would be equally attractive to the new and poor and to the old and wealthy. His political reputation was as carefully hewn as the work of a master sculptor. On every welfare and civil-rights issue he voted liberal and made sure that this fact was widely disseminated among the Puerto Ricans and Negroes. On military appropriations he was invariably critical, stating that they were inflationary, were expended by shortsighted generals and admirals, and only added to the tax burden. This posture benefited him in two ways: his constituents in the big expensive apartments saw him as anti-inflation and pro-lower taxes; his working-class constituency, too poorly skilled to qualify for entry into the big unions or for work in the large armaments industry, saw him as antimilitarist, and thus attractive. He had been reelected eight times, each time by a higher plurality.

Raskob's squat figure was somewhat reminiscent of La Guardia and Raskob played on the similarity. He wore a wide-brimmed fedora hat and when he made speeches he constantly banged the fedora against the podium. Whenever he spoke before a foreign-speaking group he had at least a few lines which he could render in the language of the group. In the wealthy part of his constituency his speeches were calm, deliberate, short, and concerned with the future. In the working-class district he was more flamboyant and talked of pay checks and pork chops. In hard fact his voting record was almost straight Democratic but few in his district knew that. Nor did they care. Raskob was a personality.

"Where are you from, son?" Raskob asked Colonel Cascio. His eyes were still peering, not yet adjusted to the thin light. His words were an automatic political response to fill vacant time.

"New York City, sir," Colonel Cascio said.

Raskob's head swung around and he stared at Colonel Cascio. His interest now was real.

"What part of the city?" Raskob asked.

Colonel Cascio hesitated a moment. "Central Park West," he said, "in the Seventies."

"Probably in the Twentieth District," Raskob said speculatively. "You're getting some Puerto Ricans in there now. It's one of those swing districts. Might go either Democrat or Republican. In a few years it will be solidly Democratic."

"Actually, Congressman Raskob, my family moved over to the East Side some years ago," Colonel Cascio said. He turned his head sideways and glanced quickly at General Bogan. Then he added as an afterthought, "As a military man I really don't follow politics very closely."

General Bogan felt a slight sense of unrest, a barely recognizable sense of protectiveness. Then he recalled the carefully buried memory. It was during one of the frequent visits that General Bogan and Colonel Cascio made to New York City. One night General Bogan had been called and told that SAC was staging one of its endless surprise drills. He must be back in Omaha by morning. An Air Force car was already outside of his hotel and General Bogan ordered it to the address where Colonel Cascio was "visiting his family."

The address was an old apartment house, aged with wind and soot, but respectable. There was, however, no CASCIO on the long line of door bells. Impatiently General Bogan pushed the MANAGER button and a neat, hard-faced and stocky woman appeared at the door.

"I'm looking for the Cascio apartment," General Bogan said. "It's rather urgent."

"He in trouble again?" the woman asked. "You from the police?"

She squinted, made her watery blue eyes come to a focus, but could not distinguish the uniform.

"Cascio's got no apartment here," she said. "He lives

in the janitor's quarters down the steps to the left. If it's a police thing you can tell him for me it's the last time. He can just clear out." She leaned forward, sharing a confidence in a faintly whining voice. "Officer, I'd of fired the sonofabitch a long time ago, but janitors are hard to keep."

General Bogan went down the steps two at a time and rapped on the door at the bottom. There was a shuffle inside and he heard a Southern-accented voice say, "You got no right, son, to barge in and start in on us like this. Damn it, I won't stand for it."

The door swung open and the light from four naked bulbs in an old brass chandelier caught everything in the room in a pitiless and hard illumination.

The man at the door was unquestionably Cascio's father, they had the same features. But the man was drunk, his face slack, his eyes bloodshot, his pants baggy. He had the pinched, furtive, crabbed look of the long-time drunkard. He looked like an older, ruined version of his son.

Colonel Cascio was sitting behind a table covered with a linoleum cloth. He sat straight in the chair, an untouched plate of barbecued spare ribs and black beans in front of him. Leaning against a stove was Colonel Cascio's mother. She had a waspish look and was very thin and wore an old cotton dress and black felt slippers which were too large for her. General Bogan realized that she also was a drunkard . . . and not only because she held a pint of muscatel in her hand. It had to do with the posture, the beaten face, the suspicious eyes.

"Sir, I am General Bogan and I am calling for Colonel Cascio," General Bogan said. Standing in darkness he realized that his aide had not yet recognized him. At his words Colonel Cascio came half out of his chair, a look of pure agony on his face.

"Let the gennelmun in, Walt," Colonel Cascio's mother said. Her face spread into a mask of welcome, so broad it was grotesque. She stepped toward the door, her feet spread, balancing carefully. An amber thread of muscatel flowed from the bottle onto the floor.

The father, cued on some deep level, bowed to General Bogan. He muttered some extravagant words of welcome. "Son always speaks well of you, sir . . . honored have ya' eat with us . . . or anything . . . just anything."

There was a long moment of silence, a moment in which General Bogan understood something which he had never bothered to analyze before. Colonel Cascio's parents had Tennessee accents; they were hill people who never adjusted to the city life. And they were the reason that Colonel Cascio never spoke with a Southern accent, never drank, and was unmarried. His military career was everything.

Colonel Cascio had broken the squalid tableau. He stood straight, walked to the doorway and saluted General Bogan.

"Yes, sir," he said, and he was under perfect control. "I gather we're needed for a drill."

"That's it, Colonel. Sorry to break up your time at home."

Colonel Cascio smiled thinly at him. He turned and, deliberately and heavily, as if he were swinging shut a bank vault, closed the door. Behind the thin panels his father's voice yelped, "Ungrateful damned snot-nosed kid. So damned uppity."

They got quietly in the car and neither of them had ever spoken of the episode.

General Bogan himself came from a Tennessee family with a strong military tradition. They had always lived in the high hills of Tennessee and the land had never been able to support all of the sons. The military had been the only acceptable nonfarming occupation for Bogan's family. Ever since colonial days at least one Bogan had been in the armed forces of the United States. Some had been enlisted men, some officers. During the Civil War, Bogans had fought on both sides. Bogan's grandfather had been a naval captain and an aide to Admiral Mahan. His father had been a sergeant in the infantry and had been decorated twice in World War I with the Silver Star. General Grant Lee Bogan's first and middle names came to him, not because his father had a sense of humor, but because he thought that General Grant and General Lee were the greatest generals in American history. The fact that they had fought on opposite sides did not appear to him to be ironic. Grant Lee Bogan was the first of the Bogans to be a general officer.

Bogan's attention snapped back to the War Room. It was Knapp's voice saying, "It's almost like working in a submarine, isn't it, General?"

"Only the air lock reminds me of a submarine," General Bogan said. "After a while you get used to being four hundred feet under the surface and it's just like any other job."

General Bogan was not telling the complete truth. In fact he had disliked the War Room when he was first assigned as its commander. He had joined the Air Force back in the 1930s for one specific reason: to fly planes. For almost thirty-two years he had done precisely that. He had flown the early biplane fighters, later the P-38, the P-51, and after the war he had moved into the jet bombers. He flew "by the book" and had a reputation for being more methodical than imaginative. But to his methodicalness there was also added courage. These two things had earned him the Distinguished Flying Cross during World War II.

He had been flying a P-38 escorting a group of B-17s

on a day raid over Germany. It was early in the war and the fighter pilots could not resist temptation. Some of them made passes at Focke-Wulfs which were still at a considerable distance. Others could not resist joining in a dogfight which was already being amply handled by other fighters. General Bogan flew a perfectly mechanical and orthodox flight. He stayed with the bombers he had been ordered to defend, he nursed his fuel supply, he fired only in short bursts. The result was that every other one of the escorting fighters had reached its fuel range fifty miles before the target was in sight. One by one they swung away for the flight back to England. When the B-17s came over target General Bogan was the only fighter with them. He stumbled into a perfect setup. The Focke-Wulfs, thinking that all the fighters had left, became careless. A long string of eight fighters came up from below to strike at the bellies of the B-17s. Bogan put on additional speed and methodically began to clobber the line of German fighters. He came in on the blind port quarter of each of the Focke-Wulfs, gave a short burst directly into the cockpit hoping to kill the pilot before he could give a warning. Neatly, following the instructions he had been given during months of training, Bogan shot down six of the eight Focke-Wulfs. In avoiding the exploding debris of the six planes he pulled back quickly on the yoke and gained several hundred feet of altitude. In that moment the seventh and eighth planes saw him and instantly put on speed and began to loop back toward him. Again Bogan followed the book. Using the slight speed advantage which the P-38 had he kept just far enough ahead of the two German fighters to be out of cannon range. They followed him almost to the English Channel, tantalized by the prospect of a kill, made reckless by the death of their six comrades. Bogan had calmly called ahead on his radio and twenty miles from the English Channel a group of P-38s were circling high in the sky waiting for him. They came screaming down, every advantage on their side, and thirty seconds later the last of the Focke-Wulfs were destroyed.

Bogan always felt guilty about receiving the Distinguished Flying Cross. All he had done was follow instructions. Like everyone that flew in combat he had felt fear, deep and rooted and unending, as long as he was in action. But on the operation which earned his decoration he felt no special danger or risk—only the same familiar fear.

The last plane which General Bogan had flown in operation was the B-58, the Hustler. Then he had almost failed a physical examination. It was not clearcut. The flight surgeon had hesitated, evaded his eyes, talked about the kinesthetic atrophy and its correlation with age, eye-hand reflex and reaction times. The discussion had been general but they both knew what it meant. If General Bogan insisted on flying the Hustler he would be labeled physically unfit. If he would content himself with flying the slower bombers or fly as a copilot he could stay in the air. It had been a hard moment. Then General Bogan had mentioned, quite casually, that he'd been thinking of turning his efforts away from operations and more to strategy. "Flying is a young man's game," he lied. "We oldsters have to accept the responsibility for the big picture."

In the end the two men wordlessly agreed. Bogan would shift to a ground assignment provided he could occasionally fly T-33s, "to keep his hand in."

In two weeks General Bogan had been promoted to lieutenant general and assigned as commanding officer of the War Room.

General Bogan looked sideways at Raskob. He understood something of the disappointment that Raskob felt. He could recall his own initial impression of the War Room all too sharply. General Bogan had hated the elevator. The elevator shot downwards in one long sickening 400-foot drop. The last five feet of deceleration gave him a sharp sense of leaden helplessness. Then, after the elevator doors closed, the small room in which one stood became a compression chamber. The air pressure in the War Room was kept a little higher than normal atmosphere so that no dust could filter in to foul the machinery or atomic fallout to contaminate the humans.

Another thing that General Bogan had disliked was the smell of the room. All of the dozens of desks on the long sloping floor of the War Room were in fact electrical consoles, which contained thousands of electrical units each coated with a thin layer of protective shellac. When all of the consoles were warmed up the smell of shellac became thin and acrid, slightly sickening.

It had taken General Bogan a long time to forget the old familiar smells of airplanes. These were the muscular and masculine odors of great engines, the kerosene stink of jets, the special private smell of leather and men's sweat which hung in every pilot's cockpit.

For months the War Room had seemed effete and too delicate and also quite unbelievable. With time General Bogan had changed. He came to realize that the desks, small and gray, were incredibly intricate. The quiet, low-pitched, gray and trim room was enormously deceptive. Simplicity was its mask. Its primness hid an intricacy and complexity that, when fully apprehended, was almost an artistic concept. By radio, teletype, message, written report, letter, computers, memory banks, card sorters, conveyors, tubes, telephones, and word of mouth, information came to the War Room. It came in the form of calculations, fear, courage, intuition, deduction, opinion, wild guesses, half-truths, facts, statistics, recommendations, equivocations, rumor, informed ignorance, and ignorant information; all were put through a rigorous procedure with one of two conclusions. Either a statement was a fact or it was expressed as a probability of fact.

General Bogan looked at Raskob and wished he could communicate his secret vision. The War Room had become a ship, a plane, a command, a place of decision. Although locked in hundreds of tons of concrete and millions of tons of earth the room gave him a curious sense of motion. Perversely, the descent by elevator came to have something of the excitement of the take-off. From his desk, in the front center of the room, he had the impression of flying, and flying entirely on instruments. He also came to respect the crew of this strange vehicle of his imagination. They were professional, every bit as professional as any air crew he had ever commanded. He was not the faceless servant, an automatic cog, in an elaborate machine. The War Room was the most delicate of man-machines. Most of the time the machines received, analyzed, and made the decision. But just often enough it had been made clear to him that he was the commander. He was still in the profession of making decisions.

General Bogan knew that his visitors' eyes were probably now adjusted enough so that they could walk down the incline to the Command Desk.

"Colonel Cascio, will you project the naval situation in the Pacific on the Big Board?" General Bogan said, starting to walk down the slight incline.

"Yes, sir," Colonel Cascio said and walked briskly ahead of the party. By the time they reached the big central desk he had pressed down a lever labeled PA-CIFIC, NAVAL. Instantly the picture on the Big Board began to dissolve. The Mercator projection of the world disappeared. For a moment the screen was blank. Then in sharp strong outline the entire screen was covered by a map of the Pacific Ocean. Colonel Cascio looked up at General Bogan. "Would you like to start with the Russian submarine layout?" Colonel Cascio asked.

General Bogan nodded agreement. Colonel Cascio pushed two levers. Suddenly the map of the Pacific contained sixteen red blips. At the same time a small machine at a nearby desk began to click and a tape poured out of its side. One of the red blips seemed to be only a few inches off of Los Angeles. Another was a foot or so due west of Pearl Harbor. The remainder were scattered around the Pacific.

Raskob went rigid. Unthinkingly he jammed his fedora on his head.

"Well, sweet Jesus, you don't mean to tell me that all those little things are Russian submarines?" Raskob asked. "That one there looks like it's almost in Los Angeles harbor."

"Sir, that Soviet submarine is approximately fifty miles from Los Angeles harbor, and in or under the high seas of the Pacific," General Bogan said quietly. "Unless they come within the three-mile limit or give signs of acting in an aggressive manner all we can do is observe them."

"Look, General, this looks dangerous to me," Raskob said. "What the hell are they doing with submarines that close to our shores?"

"I would presume they are doing the same thing that we do when we send U-2 planes and surveillance satellites around and sometimes over the Soviet border or set up radar stations in Turkey. They are scanning us."

It was the kind of explanation that Raskob understood. He relaxed slightly. When he spoke his voice had a new hardness.

"How do you know that those submarines are Russian and that they are really there?" he asked.

"Sir, the Navy has spread a pattern of sonobuoys around the Pacific," Colonel Cascio said. "They are extremely sensitive instruments and they pick up any kinds of sounds that are made any place in the Pacific. The information is transmitted to Kaneohe Bay in Hawaii and interpreted by a sailor-specialist there. The specialists are so good that they can tell the difference between a whale breaking wind and a submarine blowing tanks."

Colonel Cascio turned to the machine on the adjoining desk and tore off the tape. He handed it to Raskob. "When the Big Board is switched to a specific projection a signal is tripped and simultaneously the various memory banks which store millions of bits of information are automatically searched for bits which are keyed to the projection. These come out on the tape."

The four men bent over the tape which was stretched out on the desk. The first sentence read, "Soviet submarine *Kronstadt*, two torpedo tubes, operated radar equipment for 30 seconds at 1820 slant line 18 slant line 00. Submerged depth 120 feet, proceeded northwest to point WLDZ at 6.5 knots." The tape went on to give estimates of the fuel level in various Soviet submarines in the Pacific, the number of messages they had transmitted, the time they had been on patrol.

"If we wanted we could tap another memory bank and get the complete strategic information on the Russian submarine situation around the entire world," General Bogan said. "That would include the percentage of their national steel product that has gone into submarines, how many of them are nuclear powered, how many have atomic missiles. Almost anything."

"I'll be damned," Raskob said. "That's a nice gadget."

"That gadget and the other gadgets in this room cost over a billion dollars, Mr. Raskob," General Bogan said, carefully keeping any irony out of his voice. "There is another room like this at the Pentagon and another at Colorado Springs. There are also several smaller versions at other locations around the world. There are also a number of planes, one of which is in the air at all times, which give a miniature version of this same information."

"Where are all these other rooms?" Raskob asked.

"I'm sorry, sir, but I cannot give you that information except on orders from my superiors or the President," General Bogan said. He hesitated and then went on, warned by the flush on Raskob's face. "It's what we call 'top secret for concerned eyes only.' That means that only those people who have a need for the information and can demonstrate that need have access to the information."

Suddenly Raskob smiled. "That rules me out," he said. "The only use I could have for the information would be to sell it to the Communists or use it to beat hell out of the military people at an appropriation hearing. What other kind of stuff can you show up on that board?"

Colonel Cascio leaned toward the levers on the desk. Before he touched them, however, a blue light began to flash over the Big Board. It flashed quickly a half-dozen times and then glowed steadily. The levers on the desk snapped back to neutral position without being touched by Colonel Cascio's fingers. General Bogan and Colonel Cascio stared at the Big Board. Already it had gone into another dissolve. A ticker machine at another desk-console started to stutter. The screen went blank and then steadied down on a large projection of the area between Greenland and Canada. From a door at the side of the room six officers entered and moved to various desks. As instruments and scopes at the desks went on the illumination began to brighten the room.

Both Raskob and Knapp were staring at the board and glancing around the room with fascination.

"What's happened, General?" Raskob asked.

"I don't know yet," General Bogan said. Nothing in his manner indicated there was any cause for concern. "All I know is that we have gone to Condition Blue, which is our lowest position of readiness." He glanced at Colonel Cascio.

Colonel Cascio turned and walked over to the machine that was stuttering. He looked at the tape and then tore it off. By the time he returned to the desk the map had steadied down and a tiny bright red blip showed between Greenland and the eastern coast of Canada.

"Gentlemen, that is an unidentified flying object which has been picked up by our radar," General Bogan said, his eyes fastened to the Big Board. "Until we identify it positively it will remain a red blip and we will regard it as hostile."

The two visitors stared, mesmerized, at the red blip. It moved slowly across the projection. General Bogan knew precisely what was going through their minds. There was a possibility that they were viewing a real enemy, a plane or a missile, which was flying toward the United States with a hostile intention.

"What are you going to do about it?" Knapp asked. Since he had entered the War Room his voice had never been raised above a whisper. Now the whisper was almost hoarse.

"That information, Mr. Knapp, is not classified," General Bogan said with a smile. "The Soviets can make a good guess about what we are doing. We always have a certain number of SAC bombers in the air. They have been informed of the Condition Blue and will start to fly toward their Fail-Safe points," General Bogan said.

"Fail-Safe?" Raskob asked.

"The Fail-Safe point is different for each group," General Bogan explained. "They also change from day to day. This is a fixed point in the sky where the planes will orbit until they get a positive order to go in. Without it they must return to the United States. This is called Positive Control. Fail-Safe simply means that if something fails it is still safe. In short, we cannot go to war except by a direct order. No bomber can go in on its own discretion. We give that order."

"They must get the order to 'go' by radio," Raskob said. "Is that right?"

"That's right, Mr. Raskob," General Bogan said. "Actually they do not receive the order verbally but it is transmitted to a small box which we call the Fail-Safe box, which is aboard each plane. That box is operated by a code which changes from day to day and can be operated only at the express order of the President of the United States. You have probably read that he is accompanied everywhere by a warrant officer from the Air Force who has the current code that would operate the box."

"Why don't you just give them a direct verbal yes or no and save yourself all this trouble?" Raskob asked.

General Bogan could tell Raskob was becoming restless. His eyes were fastened on the red blip and its inexorable progress.

"Actually we do both. But an enemy could easily come up on the same radio frequency and give whatever message it wanted just by imitating the voice of the President or one of our commanding officers," General Bogan said. With a smile, he added, "Remember that our President has a rather distinctive regional accent which can be easily imitated. Also, when people talk over the radio there is often a misunderstanding of what is said, especially if there is any radio interference. But there can be no interference with the Fail-Safe box. It can be activated in only one manner and at the express order of the President."

The Congressman turned from the board and spoke sharply to the General. "And what if someone up there —or down here—cracks?"

"You will probably remember, Congressman Raskob, that last July, the Air Force testified before your committee on our program to give a psychological screening to any airman who had anything to do with nuclear weapons," General Bogan added, trying to keep the irony from his voice. "From generals down to privates."

"Yes, sir, there are a number of people who believe that the Air Force has a high incidence of madmen among its air crews," Colonel Cascio said with a smile. "A few years back there was a lot of upset about whether or not an individual madman, ranging from a general down to the pilot of a plane, could start a war. With this procedure we may still have the madmen around but there is nothing they can do to start a war."

Raskob's eyes were back on the Big Board. Now he licked his lips. When he spoke his voice had something more than the rasp of irritation in it.

"Well, what else are you doing?" he asked brusquely. "Jesus Christ, that could be an ICBM or a Russian bomber and as far as I can tell you aren't doing very much about it."

General Bogan could not resist. "We are doing a good deal right now. Fighter planes are flying toward

the unidentified object, ICBMs are going through the
initial stage of preparation for launching, whole
squadrons of bombers are being fueled and armed in
case it really is an enemy vehicle that is coming toward
us," he said. "But, Congressman Raskob, if we went
full out every time an unidentified object appeared on
the screen we would need four times the appropriations that we now get from Congress. All-out safety is
a very expensive thing."

Raskob missed the irony. "What do you mean 'every
time that this happens'?" Raskob asked. "How often
does this happen?"

"About six times a month," General Bogan said.
"And if we went straight to Condition Red each time
it would probably cost around a billion dollars."

Instantly Raskob's face relaxed, his whole posture
became easy. He laughed.

"O.K., General, you win," Raskob said. "I got that
bit about the congressional appropriations. But you
should have told me that it happened six times a
month. It can't be very dangerous if it happens that
often."

"Sir, we never take a chance," Colonel Cascio said.
His voice had an odd sharp inflection to it, almost re-
proving. "Right now we don't know what that object
is. We treat it exactly as if it were an enemy vehicle of
some sort. If we cannot identify it in a few more minutes or it acts suspiciously we will go to Condition Yellow. If we still are unsatisfied or things occur that complicate the picture we might even go to Condition
Green. The last condition, as you know, is Condition
Red. We have never gone to Condition Red, for that
would mean that we actually considered ourselves at
war and would launch weapons, all of our weapons, at
the enemy. What all of this machinery assures is that
if we do go to war it is not by accident or because of

the act of some madman. This system is infallible."

Colonel Cascio was wrong.

Branching off from the War Room is a warren of powerfully built and beautifully orchestrated rooms. Each room has a function. Each is protected by sheaths of reinforced concrete and a layer of lead. Each is air-conditioned. Each is linked to the War Room by alternate methods of communication. The whole thing is as symmetrical, efficient, and orderly as the mind and muscle of man can make it.

One room in the warren about the War Room is labeled Presidential Command Net. *The door is guarded by an Air Force man twenty-four hours a day. Within the room—of classified length and classified breadth—there are six low, gray, squat machines. Above them is a sign which reads* Fail-Safe Activating Mechanisms. *Below that sentence and in heavy raised red letters are the words* To be used only at express Presidential order. *There are two desks in the room. One of them is in front of the bank of six machines. The other is behind the bank of machines.*

Seated behind each of the desks is an enlisted man whose sole duty is to check the mechanical condition of the activation machine. The machines are deliberately not covered. All of the operating parts must be visible to the two inspectors. The air which is forced into the room is triple-filtered so that it is dustless.

At about the moment that Colonel Cascio said the word "infallible" a sergeant sitting at one of the desks stood up and walked around the bank of machines.

"Frank, how you fixed for cigarettes?" the sergeant asked. "I'm out."

Frank tossed him a pack of Chesterfields. The sergeant reached to catch them. At that moment in Machine No. 6 a small condenser blew. It was a soundless event. There was a puff of smoke no larger than a walnut that was gone instantly.

The sergeant sniffed the air. He turned to Frank. "Frank, do you smell something?" he asked. "Like something burning?"

"Yeah, that's me," Frank said. "You bumming cigarettes all the time and then not paying me back, that burns me."

They grinned at one another. The sergeant returned to his desk. Things returned to normal . . . almost. A small shield hid from the sergeant's view the tiny knob of burnt carbon on top of the disabled condenser. No instruments on the table indicated a malfunction.

Congressman Raskob was a tough man. He regained his composure quickly. Now he was even enjoying the situation. It had something of the elements of politics in it.

"Can you project the fighter planes that are flying toward the unidentified object onto the Big Board?" Raskob asked.

"Certainly, sir," Colonel Cascio said.

He moved some levers. A few feet from the red blip a phosphorescent worm began to glow, became more distinct, and then broke itself into six separate blips, all black. They were diminishing the distance between themselves and the red blip at a rate which was perceptible to the human eye.

"Those are Canadian fighters. They are probably subsonic planes so they will close the unidentified object in a half hour or so."

"Colonel Cascio, what information do we have on the UFO?"

Colonel Cascio walked over to the machine and tore off a piece of tape. He handed it to General Bogan. It read, "UFO at Angels 30, speed 525, heading 196."

"That means that it's at 30,000 feet going 525 miles an hour on a compass heading of 196," General Bogan said.

"Just suppose, General, that the planes get there right on schedule, what are they likely to find?" Raskob asked.

"Usually it is a commercial airliner that has neglected to file a flight plan or has been blown off course by high winds," General Bogan said. "But keep in mind, sir, that there is a big blank space over the Atlantic where neither the radar sets from Europe nor America have the range to pick up planes. This wasn't much of a problem with slow-flying planes at low altitudes, but with jets going at high speeds and altitude they can drift a couple of hundred miles while they are 'in the gap.' Occasionally the radar itself makes a mistake and gets a blip off the moon or a swarm of geese or gets a false echo from a satellite. But the radar mistakes have pretty well been eliminated since 1960."

"Suppose it just looks like a commercial airliner but has actually been loaded up with thermonuclear bombs and is trying to sneak through, masquerading as a commercial plane?" Raskob asked.

"It's possible, but not likely," General Bogan shrugged. "The fighter pilots would raise the plane on radio and ask where it had started from and what its destination was and this would then be checked out with Federal Aviation Agency operators to make sure it was a legitimate flight. Also the fighter pilots, if they are the least suspicious, get close enough to the plane to give it a good inspection. If there were seams and hinges that indicated a bomb bay on what looked like a DC-8 that would change the situation. Plenty."

"What would you do in that case?" Knapp asked. "I mean that even after the fighters see the plane they still have some suspicions?"

"Probably not a great deal," General Bogan said. "The fighter pilots would order the plane to land or to turn around and if it ignored orders then we would have a tough decision. We would probably go to Condition Yellow and would start to launch more fighters and also bring up some of the bombers to a higher degree of readiness. But just a single unidentified plane by itself, still over a thousand miles from any Canadian or American city, doesn't constitute a very great danger. Any conceivable enemy would be launching a number of planes at us. What we would do is make sure that the single plane did not have a runaway pilot who wanted to commit hara-kiri on New York or Montreal."

"General, can you add the SAC bombers that are flying toward their Fail-Safe point to the board?" Raskob asked.

"Yes, sir," General Bogan said. He nodded at Colonel Cascio. Colonel Cascio started to move some levers. "What you will see is a fuller projection of the Northern Hemisphere. It's something like looking down at the earth from directly above the North Pole and at an altitude of about one hundred miles."

Again there was a slow dissolve on the Big Board. When it had firmed up, the longitude lines came together at a neat point in the center of the board. The unidentified flying object and the six fighters were now tiny and because the scale was much greater they were closing at what seemed a much slower pace. Six large green blips, fragmented into small dots of luminosity, swam into clear visibility. Even to the unaccustomed eyes of Raskob and Knapp it was clear that these blips were moving at a much higher speed than either the fighters or the unidentified flying object. Each of the green fragmented blips was moving toward a green cross which in each case was well outside the Soviet boundaries, but which formed a rough circle around her borders.

"As you can see, the bombers are moving much faster than either the fighters or the UFO," Colonel Cascio said. "Those are Vindicator Bombers and they fly at over 1500 miles an hour. You also notice that some of them, such as the group based on Okinawa, can get to their Fail-Safe point very quickly so they jink around a good deal. The idea is to have all of the planes arrive at the Fail-Safe point at the same moment. The one which has the farthest distance to travel is Group Six, which is the one over the Bering Strait. As you can see, it is moving fast and straight toward the green cross over St. Matthew Island, which is just about at longitude 80 degrees. That is its Fail-Safe point."

"Seven minutes to Fail-Safe," a loud clear voice suddenly said in words that could be heard throughout the whole War Room. It was a tape-recorded voice that was geared to one of the calculating machines.

"That is a recorded voice and it goes on automatically at seven minutes and starts a countdown," General Bogan said. "It is very unlikely that the planes will actually get to the Fail-Safe point. That happens very rarely. Usually the UFO or the radar disturbance is identified well before the bombers get to the Fail-Safe point. When that happens we simply raise the Vindicators on a predetermined radio frequency and order them back to their bases, or to a refueling point. I would say that in only one in twenty Conditions Blue do the planes reach the Fail-Safe point."

"But assume that they reach the Fail-Safe point and the unidentified object is still unidentified, then what?" Raskob asked.

"Just one helluva lot," Knapp said unexpectedly.

All three of the men looked at him.

"Mr. Knapp's firm manufactures some of the equipment that goes into operation at that point," General Bogan explained. "The first thing that happens is that automatically we go to Condition Yellow. Even if the situation has not changed materially, the passage of time constitutes a danger. Secondly, a number of supporting light jet bombers equipped with defensive gear and groups of fighter planes would start to fly toward the Fail-Safe point in support of the entire operation."

"Six minutes to Fail-Safe," the mechanical voice said.

One of the doors in the side of the War Room opened and four officers walked in and sat down at various desk-consoles.

"Actually you are seeing a pretty unusual Condition Blue," General Bogan said. "Usually we have the situation analyzed and solved well before this. Just as a precaution, once we get to six minutes to Fail-Safe we start to man the various machines in the War Room."

Both General Bogan and Colonel Cascio were looking steadily at the UFO. The two blips seemed almost to have merged. For a few seconds the larger fragmented blip of the fighter plane obscured the blip of the UFO. General Bogan nodded his head at Colonel Cascio. Colonel Cascio walked to a machine and pulled off a piece of tape. He handed it to General Bogan.

At this moment the UFO disappeared from the screen.

"The unidentified object is now over the Nenieux Islands off Baffin Bay," General Bogan read. "The UFO is losing altitude rapidly. Our fighters overflew and are now making a visual search. No visual contact as yet. The radar signal is erratic."

"Five minutes to Fail-Safe," the mechanical voice said. "From now until Fail-Safe, time will be given in half minutes."

"General, what the hell happened to that thing?" Raskob asked. "It's gone."

"Colonel Cascio, let's go to Condition Yellow," General Bogan said briskly.

Raskob and Knapp both swung about and stared at General Bogan. He did not take his eyes from the Big Board.

"There is nothing to worry about, gentlemen, this is fairly orthodox," General Bogan said. "The UFO is not acting in the characteristic way and I have the option to go to Condition Yellow. I have taken that option, because the UFO has dropped from 30,000 feet and disappeared in the grass. 'Grass' is the fuzz at the bottom of a radarscope which is caused by interference from hills, some inherent defect in the tubes, and other things we don't quite understand. But once the plane is 'in the grass' it is lost to radar. It may be a plane with mechanical trouble about to crash, but it is conceivable that it is an enemy plane taking evasive action."

General Bogan turned and looked at the two visitors. Both of them had a look which he had come to recognize. It was a look compounded of excitement, horror, and malice. It was not a pleasant look to see, but General Bogan had learned long ago that even for experienced airmen there was a morbid fascination with plane crashes.

"Four and one-half minutes to Fail-Safe," the voice said.

On the Big Board the six Vindicator blips were

drawing close to the Fail-Safe crosses. It was an elegant maneuver, possessing all of the grace of ballet dancers positioning themselves on a stage. Each group was precisely the same distance from its Fail-Safe point and each was now moving at maximum speed.

"Four minutes to Fail-Safe."

One of the desk-consoles started to chatter. A major tore off the tape and handed it to General Bogan. He did not even have to think about the words.

"Go to Condition Green," General Bogan barked. "And project the light bombers, the Skyscraper support, and the jet tankers on the Big Board."

"What the hell—" Raskob started to say, but stopped in mid-sentence as General Bogan raised his hand.

The light over the Big Board went green. There was a sharp, piercing klaxon sound that cut through the room. Doors began to open and in thirty seconds every desk-console in the room was manned.

"Three and a half minutes to Fail-Safe," the voice went on relentlessly.

Strange shapes were blossoming all over the Big Board. Behind each of the Vindicator groups appeared a large single blip. These were air-borne tankers. Two fragmented blips appeared on the port and starboard quarter of the Vindicators and began to angle toward them. These were the support fighters which are always activated in a Fail-Safe maneuver but which had not been projected on the Big Board until that moment.

Colonel Cascio quickly explained the situation to the two visitors, but without taking his eye from the board.

"Three minutes to Fail-Safe."

"Can you tell us why you went to Condition Green?" Knapp asked, in a whisper.

"No, sir, I cannot tell you, for the reason which I gave earlier," General Bogan said without looking at them. His voice was flat and imperative. "Colonel Cascio, will you come with me to the 413-L desk?"

He looked at Raskob and Knapp as he turned, felt an impulse to explain, and then felt a sudden pressure of anxiety.

When they reached the desk General Bogan handed the slip of paper to Colonel Cascio. It said, "Extended DEW Line Station No. 4.6 on UFO. Some atmospheric interference, but UFO is not air-breathing vehicle."

"Two and a half minutes to Fail-Safe," the mechanical voice said. Now the voice was not as loud, for the dozens of machines in the room gave off a low collective hum which toned down its harsh clarity.

"Not an air-breather?" Colonel Cascio asked. There was awe in his voice. Colonel Cascio turned to the officer at the desk and said, "Try to get DEW Line No. 4.6 and see if they have any dope on the conformation of the UFO."

The officer repeated the order but even as he spoke his fingers were adjusting dials and levers. A line of three green lights went on.

"Two minutes to Fail-Safe."

"If it is not an air-breather," General Bogan said slowly, "it might be a commercial plane which has lost power on all four engines. It would not give off enough air turbulence for even the DEW system's new turbulence detectors to be able to pick up."

"One and a half minutes to Fail-Safe."

"If it is a commercial plane that has lost power, we'll know the answer right away," Colonel Cascio said. "A pilot can stretch a flight with dead engines only just so far and then he'll have to crash. If the blip disappears we can assume that it is a commercial plane that crashed with all engines dead."

General Bogan stared at Colonel Cascio for a moment. "Not necessarily," he said evenly. "Get those two visitors out of here."

Colonel Cascio moved toward Knapp and Raskob with an animal-like speed. He spoke to them quickly. Raskob's voice was raised in protest. At once General Bogan moved toward him.

"Now look here, God damn it, General, if we are going to go to war our lives are as involved as yours and I want to know all about it," Raskob said.

"Who said anything about going to war?" General Bogan asked. Suddenly his voice had a whiplike quality. "Colonel Cascio ordered you out of this room and that was my order he was carrying out."

"One minute to Fail-Safe."

Raskob had spread his feet. He had a pyramidal, fundamental, ferocious look about him. General Bogan realized instantly that here was a man used to fighting.

"Don't try that crap on me, General," Raskob said. "As I read the situation right now we are one minute from going to war and either I am going to get the hell out of here and back to my family in New York or I am going to stay right here and see what happens. The one thing I am not going to do is let you put me off in a toilet or one of these little cells of yours. Not without a fight. I mean that, General."

"One-half minute to Fail-Safe," the voice said. "Count down will now be by seconds. Twenty-five, twenty-four, twenty-three . . ."

General Bogan looked at Raskob and knew that he could not get the man out of the room without a fight. There were other things to do. He turned away and spoke to Colonel Cascio.

"It might not be a commercial plane on a crash angle," he said. "It might be an enemy mocked-up rocket plane which faked a flame-out on all four jet engines and then when it got below 500 feet it would be below the effective range of our radar and come in low."

A look of pain went across Colonel Cascio's face.

"You are right, General," Colonel Cascio said. "It is a possibility."

General Bogan realized suddenly that the look of pain was on Cascio's face because he had ignored a point of logic and not because of the situation.

"Fifteen, fourteen, thirteen . . ."

The teletype on the 413-L desk started to clatter. The officer in charge of the desk leaned back, away from the tape, so that the other two men could have a clear view of it. The tape came out at the normal speed but to General Bogan it seemed to emerge with deliberate slowness.

"UFO has conformation of Boeing 707 but 'grass' obscures total impression," the tape said. "Operators state that despite interference UFO had normal 707 conformation."

"Eight, seven, six, five . . ."

On the Big Board the six bomber groups were at the very edge of converging with the green crosses which marked their Fail-Safe points. Each of them was exactly the same distance from its green cross. But the distance was tiny. The blip of the UFO was now invisible although occasionally it glowed and then disappeared. In countless war games General Bogan had seen fighters and even heavy bombers come in so low and fast, jinking, weaving, taking advantage of every copse of trees and every low hill, and managing to evade the mechanical eye of the radar for hundreds of miles.

By a deliberate act of will, as deliberately as uncurling a fist into a hand, General Bogan made himself relax. Even so he felt a single drop of sweat, acid from tension, roll slowly down his spine. It did not feel like sweat. It felt like a tiny solid hot piece of shot.

He had gotten to the Fail-Safe point before but General Bogan had never had a UFO which acted in such a strange way. As he looked at the board three things happened. The mechanical voice said, "All groups at Fail-Safe point." And the six bomber blips simultaneously and beautifully merged with their green crosses.

The teletype on the 413-L desk began to clatter again. General Bogan's head turned about. As it did he saw the faces of Knapp and Raskob. Raskob's jaw was set. His eyes were unafraid. His shrewd, intelligent face understood perfectly what was happening. Knapp seemed mesmerized by the machinery. General Bogan had the impression that he did not realize what was happening. The words came, again at an excruciatingly slow pace, out of the 413-L machine. They said, "UFO is now at 1,050 feet and is clearly air-breathing vehicle. Best estimate is that it is BOAC, Commercial Boeing 707, which has regained power on two of its jets."

"It's all right, Colonel Cascio," General Bogan said. "It didn't make much sense anyway, because if they did come they surely would come with more than a single plane. Let the Vindicators orbit at their Fail-Safe point, however, until we get a positive confirmation from the Canadian fighters."

Colonel Cascio stood up and, although his face was smiling, his pink tongue licked at the corner of his mouth.

"General, they'll orbit whatever we do," he said, "it's SOP. But I'm still not sure about that UFO. Couldn't the Russians anticipate exactly the way we would interpret it and just add a couple of jet pods to the mocked-up plane and turn them on when they get within range of 413-L System?"

"It's possible," General Bogan said casually. "But not very likely. The whole picture just doesn't make sense."

The two men smiled at one another, but suddenly General Bogan had the sense that they were in conflict. Colonel Cascio lowered his eyes.

General Bogan turned to his guests. "The UFO is pretty well established as a BOAC commercial airliner which lost power on its engines and then regained them at a low altitude," General Bogan said to the visitors. "We have to stay at Condition Green until we have confirmation, but it is my best judgment that there is no danger."

"I kinda like this whole operation," Raskob said softly. "I mean it's a nice orderly thing to meet people who can tie everything up with a ribbon and foolproof. And let me tell you, General, in this world there are damn few things that are foolproof."

The teletype on the 413-L clattered.

This time General Bogan waited until the major handed him the tape. He read it to the visitors. It said, "UFO sighted visually and contacted by radio. It is BOAC Flight No. 117. It was off course due to high tail winds and loss of power on two port engines because of throttle failure which locked the throttles in OFF position. It regained power at 350 feet."

"That's it, gentlemen. I am sorry that we alarmed you," General Bogan said.

Colonel Cascio bent forward and operated a single lever. Instantly the radio-transmitted order became apparent on the Big Board. The fighters started to move in a long curve back toward their bases. The jet tankers angled away from their Vindicator group. The defensive bombers made a quick 180° turn. The big light over the Big Board went out. Men began to drift out of the room. The hum of the machines diminished.

It was Raskob who first noticed. He stared at the Big Board for a moment and turned to General Bogan with a grin.

"Now what the hell is that blip up there at No. 6 doing?" he said. "It's gone right by the Fail-Safe point and is moving toward Russia."

General Bogan spun around, his elbow lashed into the taut nervous body of Knapp and he was quite unaware of it. He stared at the board, his body suddenly felt like a terrible tortured muscle. His mind was white-hot and utterly blank. It perceived only one thing. Group 6 had flown past its Fail-Safe point. He spoke out of the side of his mouth, suddenly and comically aware of how much like a movie character he seemed.

"Colonel Cascio, get on the red telephone to the President," General Bogan said, in a firm low unnatural voice.

As he handed General Bogan the red telephone Colonel Cascio picked up the Red Phone Log. He glanced at the clock on the wall and wrote down "1030."

ch. 3

DESCENT WITH POMP AND AUTHORITY

At 10:34 Buck left his office. Out of some compulsion to orderliness he had straightened his desk, put on his jacket, and then brushed the jacket with a pig-bristle brush which he kept in one of the drawers of his desk. He thought of going to the men's room to comb his hair. The moment he stepped outside his door he realized that would be impossible.

Standing squarely in front of the door and four feet away from it, was a Marine Corps major. He was breathing hard.

"Are you Mr. Buck?" the major asked.

"Yes," Buck said and then after a pause added, "sir."

"May I please see your identification, sir?" the major asked.

Buck fumbled through his wallet looking for the card. Over the years it had become an empty formality when he passed through the White House gate. He merely lifted his entire wallet toward the Pot who nodded and he walked on in. For a moment Buck felt a sense of embarrassment. It was altogether possible that he had left the identification card at home.

He flipped through the cards in their cellophane holders. The major stared straight ahead, ignoring Buck's discomfort. The major was still breathless and the sound of air sucked in and pushed out of his nostrils was the loudest noise in the corridor. Diners Club card, law-school library card, a picture of his daughter, a picture of the Porsche just after it had been waxed, a gas-company credit card, a membership card in a professional language association, a picture of his parents. He looked in the billfold of the wallet: seven dollars. Buck looked up at the major. There was one more pocket in the wallet. The identification card was there. He almost sighed with relief.

The major took the card firmly, and glanced at the identification picture. Then he moved sideways to study Buck's profile. Buck's embarrassment deepened.

"Mr. Buck, this card says you have a small scar on your left wrist," the major said. "May I see that scar, sir?"

"Just a little thing from a high-school football game," Buck said, pulling his sleeve up.

The major stared intently at the scar. He came back to attention and extended the card to Buck.

"Follow me, sir," the major said. He started off down the corridor at a crisp walk.

"Yes," Buck said and then hesitated. If the major called him "sir," perhaps he was not supposed to call the major "sir." Buck decided not to. It gave him a sense of satisfaction as he stuffed the card back in the wallet.

By now the major was several steps ahead of Buck. Buck trotted until he had overtaken the major and then fell in stride with him. Buck, who was several inches shorter than the major, found that he was almost at a slow run.

They passed out of the White House Annex into the White House and down several corridors which Buck had never seen before. They swung around a corner and in midstride the major stopped and came to attention. Walking toward them was a tall lanky man and a woman who was taking notes on a note pad. Immedi-

ately to the left of Buck and the major was an elevator. Buck realized two things almost simultaneously:
first, the elevator was painted GI green and was operated by an Army officer, secondly, the man walking
toward them was the President and the woman was
Mrs. Johnson, his secretary.

Buck had heard of the woman before. Her nickname
was "Johnnie" and she had an aura of her own. She
walked with authority and self-assurance. She struck
a delicate balance in her attitude toward the President:
she was both a nanny and a secretary. She had started
her career as secretary to the President's famous father
over forty years before. Since that time she had become
a competent and efficient instrument of the family without becoming in the least familiar. When the President
first entered politics as a candidate for Congress he had
begged Johnnie's services from his father. Years later,
when he entered the White House, Johnnie quite automatically accompanied him. Her hair was now white,
her figure heavy, but her manner toward the President
was completely unchanged. She was not the least afraid
of him nor was she the least familiar.

When the President was five strides away the major
snapped off a salute. The President nodded at the major, moved toward the elevator with a springy walk,
the stride of an athletic person who liked physical
motion. "Tell Pete not to even hint to the newspaper
people about an emergency," the President said to the
secretary. She scribbled in her notebook. "Also call the
Vice-President and tell him exactly what has happened.
He will know what to do. Call Senator Fulbright and
ask him to call the Vice-President. Better have him
drop by the Vice-President's office."

The President came to a stop in front of the elevator. He shook hands with the major. He turned to
Buck.

"Hello, Buck," the President said. "I remember seeing you in your office a while back."

"A while back" had been several years, but even so Buck was flattered.

"Yes, sir," Buck said. "I am the Russian translator."

Without a verbal order, but more by motion of his body, the President moved all of them into the elevator, including the secretary. Despite its GI color, Buck realized that the elevator was new and efficient. Its one odd feature was in the back: a large wheel with a plaque above it which said, FOR ELEVATOR OPERATION IN CASE OF POWER FAILURE. TURN TO RIGHT TO LOWER. TURN TO LEFT TO RAISE.

The doors of the elevator snapped shut and instantly they were propelled downward. To Buck it seemed that they were dropping like a stone, in a free fall. His knees loosened slightly as the floor dropped beneath him, but he stiffened; he felt a sad and desolate heaviness in his viscera. He braced against the wall for he had the sensation that he might become sick. He had no notion of how far beneath the White House the bomb shelter was located. To vomit here, in this impeccable GI elevator with the officer-operator and the President leaning comfortably against the wall and the secretary listening to his words, and the wooden major standing at an apparently easy attention, would be too much.

They came to a cushioned stop after a few seconds. Buck's knees bent a few inches, but so did those of everyone else in the elevator. He felt relieved.

The doors snapped open. They stepped out into a large room which held half a dozen desks. On the left there was a luminous screen which covered the entire wall. It was somewhat like a movie screen, but it had thickness, a texture to it. Strange objects crawled across it, wormlike and glowing. Buck had only time to notice six green crosses, five of them standing alone, and one with a queer blob of light a few inches from the cross.

Sitting behind the desks were a number of people who were vaguely familiar to Buck. He recognized one, a special assistant to the President, and realized that the others were also special or White House assistants or staff men. All of the men in the room came to a relaxed attention. The President nodded, but did not speak. The heads of all the assistants swung back to the luminous wall. The President turned right and led his little group through a door which was swung open by a captain, his naval aide.

"That's all, Major," the President said casually. The major did not go into the other office with them.

Buck felt respect for abilities he did not possess. First, he realized that all of the assistants were at ease with the President, and, considering their credentials, degrees, books written, speeches made, reputations established, crises survived, toughness established, and the rumors of their outspokenness, he was not surprised by their poise. Secondly, he marveled at the peculiar physical ease of the President. It showed in the way he had indicated that the major should not come farther with them. It was not humiliating, it was not brusque, it was not even very obvious. It was merely a kind of easy shrug which told the major a good deal, but was not offensive.

The President led them into a small office. It held a medium-sized desk which had a number of telephones on it. There was a chair on each side of the desk. The sound of the air conditioning was like a massive pulse. The President sat down behind the desk. He motioned to Buck to sit in the other chair. The President turned to Mrs. Johnson.

"Look, Johnnie, it won't work with Pete and the

newspaper people," the President said. "Pete can handle it all right, but someone else will crack and start to call Scotty or one of the wire services or some damned thing." He paused, leaned back in the chair, held a pencil up and studied it carefully. "Tell Pete to let them all know it's urgent, but not a bonebreaker. Not yet. Off the record. No leaks. Any leaks on this and the guy and his paper are dead. Now and forever. O.K.?"

"I'll tell Pete, just like that," Mrs. Johnson said and smiled.

"What about the Pentagon group?" the President said, smiling at Mrs. Johnson, but not responding to her remark. "You're supposed to have a list or something."

"Yes, Mr. President, it's right here," Mrs. Johnson said. She shuffled through the papers she was carrying. She did it with all the expert quickness of a gambler making a fast riffle. A white card appeared in her fingers.

The precision of the riffle again reassured Buck. In the presence of people so poised and prepared he knew he would perform well.

"Give it to Mr. Buck," the President said.

Mrs. Johnson handed Buck a stiff white card. He glanced at it. At the top of the card were the words PENTAGON ALERT GROUP. It had been dated at 0800 that morning and Buck realized that the list was probably made up each day. The list contained all the Joint Chiefs of Staff, the Secretaries, and a representative from the National Security Council. Buck noticed that after the name of the Secretary for Air there was a handwritten sentence which said "In Dallas to dedicate new missile site. Back Thursday."

One of the phones on the President's desk rang and a light went on.

"That will be Bogan at Omaha," the President said.

Mrs. Johnson started to turn toward the door. "Wait just a second, Johnnie."

The President picked up the phone. He did not say "hello," but someone obviously had started talking to him at once.

By reflex Buck looked at his watch. It was 10:37.

Mrs. Johnson moved toward Buck. For the first time he noticed that her middle-aged and very smooth cheeks were flushed with excitement. She bent over Buck and spoke to him in a low urgent voice.

"At least we're better off than President Truman was in 1950 when the Korean thing started. That's one of the first things I changed around here," she said primly. "That poor man could hardly find anyone to advise him. He practically had to make the decision single-handed. He called State, the Pentagon, the Hill, here, there, everywhere. Nobody home. So he did it alone."

Did what, Buck thought to himself.

Buck looked up at Mrs. Johnson and smiled thinly. Her memory was said to be limitless, her knowledge encyclopedic, her antagonism fatal. He had heard, and he could not remember where, that when her cheeks showed small patches of pink it was the equivalent of Hitler throwing an epileptic fit.

For the first time Buck realized that this was something more than a drill, that great decisions might have to be made. His throat went dry and then, as he had trained himself to do when he was tense, his smile broadened into a wide and very good imitation of genuine amusement. He saw the President's eyes above the telephone regarding him curiously.

ch. 4

THE BLUE SKIES, THE BLACK HOLES

Five seconds after General Bogan had stopped speaking to the President the phone was back on its cradle and he and Colonel Cascio had started toward a door fifteen yards from the desk. Both were aware that they must not alarm Raskob and Knapp. They moved quickly, but without haste. It was an old drill. This was the first time their walk had intention and, even so, they walked at drill pace.

The door was labeled TACTICAL CONTROL. Colonel Cascio opened the door and the two men walked in. The room was served by a sergeant who even as he snapped to attention continued to let his eyes roam over the controls and lights and mechanisms which filled the room. The central machine in the room was a long lean console with a bank of switches running down its spine. The room hummed, a faint, rather pleasant hum, like beehives heard at a great distance on a warm day. On a table in front of the console was a desk with a single telephone on it.

"All command posts to Condition Red, Sergeant," General Bogan said.

"All command posts to Condition Red," the sergeant repeated.

With an expert practiced gesture he ran his hand down the row of thirty switches and beneath each of them a light instantly glowed red. Identical green lights above each switch went off.

"Verification?" Colonel Cascio said, looking at the sergeant.

General Bogan felt a flash of confidence as Colonel Cascio spoke. His aide knew every drill, procedure, maneuver, and manual of every room which served the War Room, and it pleased the General. Partly, he thought, because it confirmed his judgment of men, partly because Colonel Cascio's pure and simple ability was reassuring.

The sergeant wheeled and looked at the face of another machine. The machine did two things: it verified that the long central console was operating properly and it also confirmed that each of the command posts of SAC throughout the world was actually "cut in" and had received the "Condition Red." It was merely another precaution to make sure that no mechanical failure could occur.

"All command posts cut in and tactical control circuits operative," the sergeant said.

General Bogan picked up the phone on the table. When he spoke his voice would be transmitted over a network of transmitters on at least three frequencies to each of the SAC command posts.

"This is General Bogan at Omaha," General Bogan said. "I am ordering a Condition Red, not a 'go'; please confirm."

This was the "Condition Red" system. It was the step between alarm and action. It was the bringing of a massive network of men and machines to a condition of readiness. Fragments of the system would, in fact, be active, but the enormous bulk would merely come to a tense ready. Long ago the SAC researchers had learned that "color alerts" were confusing. For veterans of World War II "Red" was ominous. For others it simply meant a casual stop at a casual traffic signal.

Everyone in the widespread system knew that the ultimate alert simply meant a riding of tension, enormous preparation, an intricate series of precautionary steps. The moment that the switches were tripped and the words were spoken, a mechanism went into operation which was such a blending of the delicate and the gross, the individual and the chorus, that it was an orchestration.

As General Bogan listened to the individual duty officers confirm both the mechanical and spoken order he remembered something Colonel Cascio had said months ago about Condition Red.

It's like the start of a 100-yard dash, the colonel had said. Except that you keep coming through "on your marks" and "gets sets" and you hang there with sweat breaking out on your face and every muscle tensed to go . . . and the pistol never cracks, no one ever says "go."

General Bogan never thought of it that way. But then Colonel Cascio had been a sprint star in college, had run the hundred in 9.6. Even now there was a rumor among the enlisted men that he could run the hundred in under 10 seconds. General Bogan had never asked but the colonel looked it; he had a jaguar-lean look about him. He kept in perfect physical shape, but never made a point of it. He never talked of his workouts at the gym, never lectured anyone on obesity or physical fitness. He merely kept himself taut.

When General Bogan finished receipt of the acknowledgments, the Condition Red order was completed. It was initiated by a man, checked by a machine, counterchecked by a man, who was counter-counterchecked by another machine, and all men and machines were carefully watched by other counterpart men and machines. The immense man-machine activated itself, checked itself, coordinated itself, restrained itself, passed information to itself, carefully filtered incoming information, automatically tripped other systems that were serving it.

At Barksdale Air Force Base, Louisiana, the officer in charge of the Second Air Force put down the telephone after he had confirmed General Bogan's order. He pushed a machine which electronically checked to make sure that General Bogan's verbal order had also been fed into the responsible machine at Omaha. He then pressed a button close to the telephone. At once a scream went up from a score of klaxon horns scattered around the base. A gigantic barracks building transformed itself. An entire wall rolled away. Inside were ten station wagons, each with its exhaust plugged into a special hole in the floor, and each turning over slowly. An enlisted man sat behind each wheel. In the area behind the station wagons there were a snack bar, card tables, television sets, sofas and chairs. The space was occupied by approximately fifty men. The mood thirty seconds ago had been tranquil, an odd mixture of a fraternity house, a BOQ, and a ready room. The moment that the door swung open and the klaxons started to wail, each of the men ran for the predesignated station wagon. With a beautiful practiced precision, the station wagons tore across the vast expanse of the field. Each station wagon's journey ended beside a Vindicator bomber and the crews piled out. The supersonic bombers were already prepared by special warm-up crews. They not only warmed up the engines but they kept a constant running check on every part of the intricate bomber. The warm-up crews turned over their planes to men who were perfect strangers, keeping their eyes on the instruments until the last moment, then grinning at the strangers and relinquishing command, swinging out of the plane and into the waiting station wagons.

Two and a half minutes after the alert had sounded the first of the bombers wheeled to the head of the runway and started to whine down the long black asphalt track. Five minutes later all of the "ready" planes were in the air.

The activity at Barksdale did not cease. Instead it speeded up. As the first wave of bombers took off another series of bombers were being warmed up and another series of crews had occupied the barracks. The station wagons were back idling.

The barracks doors had slid shut. Neither the people who had gone through them a few moments ago nor the present occupants knew whether they were at war or repeating a familiar drill. The men appeared to be casual. This was also their inner reality. Anxiety had long ago been burned out.

At some bases the metabolic rate was increased so slightly by the Condition Red that it was hardly perceptible. The crews of jet tankers, for example, walked to their huge aircraft knowing there were only two alternatives: if enemy missiles were already in flight not one of the crewmen would reach his plane, but all would be crisped black somewhere along their leisurely walk. Their tankers were unprotected and in the open. The other alternative was that they were participating in a drill. The crewmen had long ago given up worrying about the two alternatives. They had learned a lesson: there was nothing they could do to alter anything in any situation.

Some parts of the system were nothing more than great offices. They were part of the "logistic pipeline." Their men and their machines performed a clerkly function, but a necessary one. They made sure that everyone in the operation had adequate supplies of everything: chewing gum, one million tons of jet fuel, tiny needles in plastic containers which had a smear of poison on the tip that could kill a man in three seconds, fresh tomatoes, black boxes in infinite variety, tubes, screws, bolts, typewriters, rubber tires, little gray cubes that, soaked in water, expanded into beef steaks, aspirin, morphine syrettes, paper and carbon paper in every size known to man, "canned" jet engines, ready to ship jet engines fresh and tuned, beans both canned and dried, life jackets, codebooks, cigarettes, leather jackets, brandy flasks, comic books, straitjackets, Geiger counters, Demarol pills, death jackets in wood or silk.

You name it, we got it, a sleepy and very proud master sergeant said as he looked over his rows of filing cabinets and calculating machines. Around the world a hundred other men like him did the same . . . in confidence, with pride, and without question.

Thousands of sleek fighter planes were being readied but only a few of them were launched. They were loaded behind revetments and in ready rooms and at the ends of runways, poised like polished needles, their wings drooping. Their time would come later.

In all of this vast system there was not a single man who knew for certain what had started the operation. Not a single man knew whether this was a genuine "go alert" or another of the hundreds of practices they had endured. The men were calm. The whole intricate mechanism functioned flawlessly.

The second system that General Bogan had activated was the Gold System. This was different from the gold telephone which connected a handful of policy-making men directly to the White House. This was the global system of missiles. These were the strange new vehicles which were launched by men, but had no living creature aboard them. Once launched, some were guided by men. But others used stars and planets to position themselves, constantly making small alterations in direction while moving at a speed of 20,000 miles an hour. They could not be launched by the men who readied them but only by the man at the very top of the pyramid. Once launched they could not be recalled. And the fact of the launching could not be concealed from the enemy.

The missiles ranged in size from the big bulky stubnosed strategic missiles weighing hundreds of tons down to the light-weight jeweled devices for tactical operations.

The work of readying the giant missiles was complex and time-consuming. Missiles like the Atlas and the Titan began to give off weird clouds as liquid oxygen filled their tanks. The Minute Man and the Polaris, which used solid fuel, began the elaborate countdown which had been done hundreds of times before.

At the Lowry Air Force Base in Colorado there was no visible sign from the air or from the ground that a huge missile operation occupied seventy square miles of Colorado prairie. This was a "hard site" base. Everything was deeply submerged below ground. Only a direct hit could incapacitate one of the three Titan missiles operated from each of the six shock-mounted complexes comprising the Lowry Missile Wing. Even if one of the complexes were put out of commission the other five would remain operational, for no one of the complexes was closer than eighteen miles to another. Inside each submerged missile complex life was completely self-contained, sealed off from the rest of the world. The missile-site base was the enemy's prime target.

The crews of the bases, depending on their literacy and background, expressed it differently: bull's-eye, homer, 4.0, knockout, prime, top priority, ten-strike, No. 1, *après vous le déluge*, horse's ass, the first goodbye. They all meant the same thing. They all knew that the enemy, any enemy, would strike first at these bases. The cities, the seaports, the ships, the planes, those could come—or go—later.

When one descended into the deeply buried command post and personnel quarters there was the sensation of entering an ingenious collective coffin. Each time might be the last. But no one really believed in either extreme—that it might be the last time, or that it was just another practice. They were emotional neuters. Long ago, under the scrutiny of hard-eyed psychologists, the claustrophobic and the easily panicked men had been weeded out. The rest had been made deliberately nerveless. They were technicians of a greater terror taught to ignore the unalterable end of their work. And, in honest fact, most of them did not believe in their work. It was a gigantic child's play, a marvelous art. It had to be done perfectly each time and it was. But it came to nothing. Hundreds of times they had run through their procedure, checked off the thousands of items, made the hundreds of thousands of reports, tabulated the millions of facts . . . and then stopped just short of climax.

As the Titan started up its massive elevator, and passed between its open 200-ton concrete doors, as its umbilical cord began to fall away in the clouds of chill swirling LOX, each man worked as if war were about to start. But each time, each of the hundreds of previous times, the order had come to stand down. The Titan had been carefully lowered back to its base.

Although an intercontinental ballistic missile requires only twenty minutes to reach a target in Eurasia, hours are required to get a missile ready for its short white-hot trajectory. Scores of men working with a network of computers, calculating, checking, double-checking, all moved at top speed but with great deliberation. The total operation was coordinated by the firemaster. Each missile also had its Fail-Safe point, but it was a point in the process of checking rather than a point in space. It was a clerical, a calm, a well-ordered Fail-Safe. But it could only proceed to a certain time. Past a precise and well-known "Positive Control" point in the countdown each missile passed into the "terminal sequence." The sequence could only be started at the order of the President of the United States.

The cavernous life, the manufactured secrecy, the incredible pitch of training, made a missile base into a strange experience. The crews lived a buried existence. The end of a tour of duty was like the end of a sentence. As the crewmen were relieved they came out into the air, blinking at the brightness, never certain that they were returning to a normal world of shopping centers and baby-tending and love-making. They had been taught that it was altogether possible that they would emerge into a black incinerated world in which their chief duties would be to avoid deep contamination and then to wage a savage fight for existence.

The details of this fight were deliberately kept ambiguous. To prepare a corps of men for defeat is almost certain to destroy their capacity for retaliation. They knew that in the ultimate situation their mood should be ferocious, but the object of the ferocity was not specified.

The men who expended their lives raising and lowering these gigantic masses of intricate and explosive material were not without intelligence or heart. They were aware of the eerie, nightmarish quality of their existence. They thought of their strange condition and they discussed it. It was a surrealistic dialogue. It was conducted by technicians with no more than an eighth-grade education and by officers with a Ph.D. The environment gave them an awesome quality. These subterraneans moved nervelessly through their artificial world, developed new outlooks and insights and oddly twisted views of themselves and of reality, evoked a new humor which was both loving and profoundly cynical, grinned a new way, were nostalgic for things like fresh air and grass, had fantasies which no man had known before because no man had lived as they lived.

Out of their subterranean places they reverted to the life aboveground without effort or strain. They seemed as normal, as uniform, as ordinary, as anyone else. But while they were below ground they were a separate breed.

In a form which would surprise a student of the classics they told the ancient myth of Sisyphus in which Sisyphus was condemned to roll a boulder laboriously up a hill only to have it tumble back again ready for another push upward. The myth trickled down from the officers to the men in strange and vulgar forms but no one mistook its import. It was always told, regardless of the language, with a strange sense of wonder and relevance.

The more speculative of the missilemen, the egg-heads among them, had also discovered an unofficial poet laureate: Albert Camus. Camus, who had understood fully the futility and the antic and the senselessness of much of modern life, had also, in a perverse way, found the principle and will which allowed him to live through the awful stresses of the French underground during World War II. Like Camus, the missilemen had learned to live seriously in a world which was absurd.

To enter a missile compound on Gold Alert was like entering a severe monastic order, utterly dedicated to the service of ununderstood mechanical totems. Quietly and systematically, without any public announcement and without any realization on the part of the public, the nation rose to a full and ominous alert.

There was also another element in the subterranean life which was pervasive, perfectly known, understood, and never discussed. There was the knowledge that the enemy was doing precisely what they were doing. Somewhere halfway around the world there was another set of silos, another pattern of hard sites, another organization of men—almost, they assumed, precisely like theirs. This is no easy knowledge to carry. It is one thing to arm the thermonuclear warhead on an immense missile. It is another to know that another person, with almost the same training, is doing the identical thing—and that he must be thinking of you—and knowing that you are thinking of him thinking of you, and on and on.

It was no life for ordinary men. One must have vision and no vision, nerve and nervelessness, absolute obedience and independent judgment. One must be outwardly friendly and inwardly cool, for life in the silos is intimate and forced and to open too much is fatal and to stay too much closed is fatal.

The subterranean men were proud men, sure of their ability. They also had developed to an almost sublime degree the capacity to forget the sum total of their task and to concentrate on their small role. They were a hard-working, magnificently trained team. They were even an enthusiastic team. But they carefully avoided any discussion of the end result of their teamwork.

ch. 5

THE FLAYED BULL

Brig. Gen. Warren A. Black came starkly awake: his eyes wide open, his toes spread and digging into the sheet beneath him, his fingers forming into fists, his stomach flat and tight. His skin was covered with a sweat that was really a slime of fear. He knew that in a few more minutes his wrist-watch alarm would go off. Aware of a thin scratchiness behind his eyeballs, he wanted to go back to sleep. But he jerked awake. Sleep was dangerous.

Sleep was where the Dream happened.

Until six months ago Black could not remember dreaming. Now his sleep was almost always broken by some variation of the Dream. It brought him awake, arched and sweating. At first he was torn between the desire to sink back in restful blackness and the fear that he might, instead, fall into the Dream. Recently he always stayed awake.

He knew there was one way that he could end the Dream: by resigning his commission. He said it to himself in a score of ways; sometimes mockingly, sometimes cruelly, sometimes in an antic mood. But the Dream did not vanish. It was also invulnerable to logical analysis. He knew, in a fleeting but dreadfully sure sense, that he could never exorcise the Dream. He could end it only by resigning. But the thought of resigning from the Air Force was torture.

The Dream always opened on a bullfight arena. Although Black had never been to a bullfight in his life, since the Dream he had checked some bullfight books. The Dream was accurate, replete with detail of picadors on padded horses, banderillas, bad music, and the background of huge ads for beer and automobiles and a milling crowd. Perhaps, Black thought, he supplied the detail from some long-forgotten book.

That bull was real enough, charging out of the gate, pawing and snorting. Its charge came to a grinding halt, its immense body reared back on its hind legs, as frozen as statuary. It came down on all fours, swung its horns around the arena, and looked, with puzzlement, for the adversary. The bull gave off a deep fundamental bellow. It was the sound of confidence. And from the people in the arena came back a deep fundamental silence.

The bull's roar ended on a tiny shattered sound of agony. A stripe of red appeared on the deep black hide of its shoulder.

The bull wheeled, spun on its hooves with magnificent speed and grace—and again gave off the thin cry of agony. Another stripe, this one white, appeared on its flank. Quickly then the bull charged and charged again and then a third time . . . endlessly, with no seeming diminution of power. But it was confused. Each time it wheeled to a stop there was another white or red stripe on its hide.

There is a matador in the arena, Black said to himself. But I cannot see him. He must be hidden by some refraction of sun on the glittering sand, some unintended camouflage of costume, perhaps by the strange assault of the colors of the arena. Black turned his head, tried vainly to see the matador, but he was never successful.

Looking around the arena, Black realized with a

pleasant feeling that everyone in the stands was familiar. They were his associates, the people he saw in
his everyday work—privates, civilian secretaries, generals, colonels, technicians, majors, scientists, professors. But he could not identify any one of them exactly. He could not attach names to faces. He only
knew they were familiar and that their faces were reassuring.

The invisible matador worked the bull closer and
closer to where Black was sitting. He could hear the
wind from its huge lungs, see the little puffs of sand
kicked up by its hooves, see the massive neck muscle
swing the horns. The bull came very close.

Then Black understood the white and red stripes.
The bull was being flayed naked. The invisible matador was not using a regular sword. He was using some
sort of instrument which neatly shaved off long narrow
slices of the bull's hide. The white stripes were cartilage and fat; the red were made by blood which ran
down the great suffering body and dripped into the
sand.

Now, directly in front of Black, the bull showed fatigue and confusion. The matador sliced and soundlessly another stripe fell away from the living flesh
beneath. There were only a few spots on the bull's
body where the hide remained. His head hung low and
his nostrils blew two tiny volcanoes of dust, no bigger
than a fist. The dust flew in its eyes and the bull, with
sadness, slowly, closed its lids.

Black looked around the arena. The familiar faces
were enjoying the scene. Their open mouths roared
approval—but no sound came out. They smiled,
pointed their fingers at the spectacle, bellowed soundlessly, beat one another on the back, danced with excitement. Tears of pleasure rolled down their faces.

Black's mood of reassurance vanished.

Then the terrible thing happened. The bull lifted its head, its agonized eyes fastened on Black. For a moment they stared at one another. And then, in some unknowing way, a pact was made. The bull's eyes showed relief.

Black felt himself becoming the bull. It was done effortlessly. It was as if his body oozed like a fog into the shape of the bull. The familiar Black dissolved, lost form and substance, slid into the body of the immense animal. Now *he* was looking up at the audience, *he* was bewildered by the strange colors and sounds, *he* was swinging his head looking for the matador.

He felt a great confusion. He also felt two kinds of dread.

The two things he dreaded had always brought him sharply awake. First, he knew that in another moment the pain of the flaying would come crashing down his nerve fiber and into his bull-brain. Secondly, he would turn and see, with his bull-eyes, the matador. Both things were so frightening that he awoke instantly.

Black tossed in his bed, looked at his watch, and saw that he had another few minutes. Idly he wondered at what point in a dream a person began to sweat. His pajamas were wet around the neck and waist and under the arms. He felt as if he had been sweating for hours. And yet, he sensed, it was probably only for a few seconds.

He forced himself to relax. Be logical, he said to himself. He sensed again that the Dream and SAC were linked. If he could resign his commission the Dream would go. But he loved the organization, he respected the people in it, it meant as much to him, almost, as his family. And its mission was so important. But a shadow lurked in his mind, a tiny burr of unrest. It vanished when held up for examination, yet an elusive doubt remained. Something was very wrong.

He felt a moment of despair. Would he continue to awaken like this, to crash from a black terror into total wakefulness? He did not like the sudden awakenings, though as an airman, some twenty-five years before, he had gotten used to them. In those days, other sounds had brought him awake abruptly, almost like shock, with an instant heightening of the metabolic rate, a gushing of adrenalin. The whine of sirens, a rough hand shaking his shoulder on a cold English morning during World War II, the thin growing frenzy of the sound of a bomb in flight . . . then, oh yes, then he had come awake instantly. But it was a different kind of wakefulness, lacking in the interior terror of his Dream.

He made a decision and sat up in bed. The Dream was forgotten. He must start the long business of getting through the day. He forced himself to smile. No sweat. Getting across midtown New York this early would be a cinch. With luck he'd be able to check out a Cessna "Blue Canoe" and run down to Andrews by himself. In any case his time was O.K. The shuttle plane could get him to the Pentagon for the ten o'clock briefing. One way or another he'd make it. No sweat.

He looked over at the sleeping figure beside him. Betty had not stirred. She needed the sleep and he wanted to shave, dress, and clear out without awakening her. He eased out of bed and fumbled in a dresser drawer for clean linen.

Black was a tall man. He had a roughly hewn, square, rugged handsomeness about him. Even his head conveyed the impression of angularity and squareness, as if it had been built up out of those sharply angular plane surfaces seen in the opening examples of "How to Draw" books. He was like an unfinished piece of sculpture, sharp edges not yet rounded off. It was not simply massiveness he conveyed, it was also a sense that he would not soften with age, his flesh would not turn to fat. He had been designed by a good draftsman, rather than by a fine artist.

His head was thickly covered with deep-brown wavy hair which he kept closely trimmed. Once in prep school he had let it grow and it had turned into a tight cap of curls. A slim and fey instructor had smiled at him across the room and said, "Our forest satyr." Black had never let his hair grow long again. His eyes were revealing and as if for protection were deep-set. They were brown eyes which fixed steadily on people. Even when he had to give a harsh reply his eyes did not waver. His perceptive subordinates could anticipate Black's mood from the narrowing of his eyes, the slow forming of laugh lines.

Black detoured into the boys' bedroom on his way to the bathroom. He had the old pilot's habit: a secret, almost subconscious, trace of permanent leave-taking with each good-bye. The boys were too big now to accept a public kiss from their father, though he would have gladly bestowed it. But early in the morning he could steal in alone and softly kiss their foreheads.

John, the twelve-year-old, was tightly balled and had orbited halfway down toward the foot of the bed, his head hidden under the covers. Black straightened him out gently, rearranging and retucking the blankets around his shoulders and neck. David, the fourteen-year-old, was spread-eagled across his bed, half uncovered and one foot out over the edge. Black recomposed the second bed and body. The two boys were opposites in this as in so many other things. He had spent his life, it seemed, re-covering David and unsuffocating John.

As he shaved, quickly and expertly with a safety razor and Aerosol lather, he regretted the time he had to spend away from the boys. Somehow, because Betty was seven years younger than he, Black felt a kind of paternalistic distance between himself and the three of them. He grinned into the mirror. That melted pretty damned fast when he was alone with Betty on what she laughingly referred to as her "responsive nights."

He had been born into the immensely wealthy Black family of San Francisco. They had been wealthy since the Forty-niner days when a young and anonymous man named Ned Black had made a strike on the small fork of the Yuba and had returned to San Francisco with a burro carrying close to 3,000 ounces of gold dust and nuggets. No one knew where he was born or if he had a family. The Blacks of San Francisco began with Ned Black. He had bought great sandy tracts of San Francisco and had sold them for huge profits.

Black had seen Ned Black's library. It was made up of books by John Locke, Fourier, Robert Owens, the great Chartists, Marx, Spencer, Ricardo. The books were worn and used. Ned Black had gone off to the Civil War and came back with an empty sleeve. He was a quiet man before he left and quieter when he returned. He lectured his children on only one thing: man was social, he had a primary obligation to his society.

The Blacks, like all rich San Franciscans, gave to the Opera and the Symphony and museums, but most of their money went into schools, hospitals, and libraries. And not a single building they gave to the city bore the name of Black. Ned's sons, grandsons, and great-grandsons all followed his quiet, intense, and private way of life. They became ministers, businessmen, educators, and a few of them, to old Ned Black's great gratification, became politicians. Ned Black thought it the most noble of professions, the most necessary of social tasks.

Whenever there was a reform movement, a commission to investigate crime, an effort to broaden education, a Black played an important role.

Warren Black had not found it easy to follow the tradition. He had no flair for politics and little interest in business. Even when he had graduated from one of the best of the Ivy League schools he felt rootless and somehow guilty. In World War II he had joined the Army Air Force and it was there first, and later in SAC, that he found his calling. He flew and fought with unspectacular success and although he loathed the destruction of life he brought himself to agree that it was necessary. He was steady, competent, and with absolutely no desire for publicity. Over the years he had developed a love for the Air Force, although he knew that it should be impossible to love such a great impersonal organization.

He had met Betty when the Air Force sent him back to his Ivy League college after World War II to study international politics and foreign policy with the famous Professor Tolliver. Betty had forced herself into one of Tolliver's seminars and commuted from Radcliffe once a week to attend. The austere old man had balked, but Betty's father was a famous professor of naval history and Tolliver had finally yielded. He pointed out bluntly that she was the first girl he had ever had in his foreign-policy seminar, that the talk often got "salty," that she would not be given grace because she was a female—female was the word he used, not "girl."

Betty nodded. When she appeared at the seminar it was more like someone coming to do battle than to discuss abstract ideas. Her face was scrubbed and without makeup. She wore severe little gray suits and she seldom smiled. She spoke with a strong even voice that

was overcontrolled. It was only midway through the
semester, when her anger emerged, that her face took
on a striking and handsome look. It surprised Black,
for he suddenly realized that she was both an attractive
and a very emotional person.

Betty had been tensed against Tolliver from the
start. She saw him as an intellectual enemy. To *see*
Tolliver as an enemy was easy. Most of the graduate
students did. To *reveal* antagonism was another thing.
Tolliver was formidable.

Tolliver was a senior professor in the field of international relations. He came from old New England
stock and his dedication to scholarship was savage, total, and complete. If his ideas led him out of the class-
room and the library and into public battle he did not
hesitate a moment.

His first public battle, when he was very young, had
been a catastrophe. Before World War I he had been
a pacifist. He had spoken and lectured and written
against involvement with the European power blocs,
he had attacked war as inhuman and obsolete, he had
led "peace parades" in New York City and Washington. He had studied ancient war, medieval war, nine-
teenth-century war, twentieth-century war. Quite un-
knowingly he became one of the foremost experts on
warfare in order to attack it.

At some point—it was never identified by anyone
precisely and Tolliver never spoke of it—Tolliver
changed. It was one of the most famous intellectual
conversions of his time. Tolliver became pro-war. He
abandoned his pacifist friends and their cause for a
position on the other side so extreme that it startled
even the interventionists: war was an ingrained part of
any society. His argument was not crude, it was stated
in the language of the scholar, it was replete with foot-

note references to history and to the psychology of aggression, allusions to Freud and the death-wish. Tolliver did not argue that war was good or desirable, merely that it would always exist as long as man organized himself into societies.

For several years in the thirties Tolliver had been intensely unpopular. He was labeled pro-English, a subversive, a turncoat. His classes dwindled in size. Liberal and radical magazines attacked him ferociously. But when America entered the war, almost overnight Tolliver became something of a prophet, a culture hero, an intellectual "with his feet on the ground." Tolliver ignored the praise just as he had ignored the criticism. He survived even the public reason which he gave for not volunteering for military duty. "Some people with brains must stay behind and develop a theory of war and peace. I'm one of those best equipped to do that. That I shall do."

He had been doing it ever since.

He was entirely a person of the mind. His age was indeterminate and no one had dared ask him. He could have been a burned-out fifty or a well-preserved seventy. His white hair was thin and seldom brushed. He had several suits; no one knew how many, for they were all the same conservative cut, the same excellent English cloth, the same hue. They all looked ruined in a few months for they were never pressed or cleaned and they were decorated with pinpoint holes where live ashes from the endless cigarettes he smoked had burned themselves out. When he stood up a small cloud of ashes fell away from him.

In a relaxed mood his face appeared weakly muscled. But it was an illusion and he was seldom relaxed anyway. Usually he seemed to be burning with fury. It showed most in his eyes—bright, blue, New England granite eyes, glittering with the hunter's excitement. In argument his face went hard-muscled; his nose seemed more beaked. At the slightest criticism of his ideas, even the suggestion of indifference, Tolliver attacked. He moved forward in his chair, his body tense. He looked somehow like a logic-chopping rat, teeth slashing into flimsy arguments, gnawing at more solid evidence with a terrible persistence. He rarely left an argument with the decision in doubt. His knowledge of war and society was so vast, his dedication so single-minded, that it seemed unlikely while listening to him that anyone could know more than he or develop a viewpoint which he had not anticipated and worked into his master view.

Tolliver paid no attention to university politics, his colleagues, campus social occasions, or other trivia. His students received his intense and narrowly focused attention, for he saw them as the carriers of ideas. Personally he knew only their names; intellectually he knew them completely. It was impossible to flatter the man; his eyes merely went icy with contempt.

The first time Betty differed with Tolliver the students in the seminar had tensed, leaned forward in their chairs and waited for the blood to flow. It did not happen quite that way. Betty had introduced some anthropological evidence that a certain Melanesian tribe waged peace rather than war. They competed at giving one another gifts, at doing small favors, at multiplying courtesies. It was clear that the example was new to Tolliver, but he attacked at once. The data were insufficient for general conclusions, he said. Let the tribes be attacked once and they would respond with conventional warlike reactions. But they had been attacked and had not so responded, Betty said. She read from the study.

When she finished Tolliver came back with a ripping

analysis. Betty countered with further evidence.

Black broke in with a neutral question and Betty glanced at him with contempt. He was in uniform and she had assumed that he would automatically support Tolliver's views on the inevitability of war.

The argument had ended in a draw. Tolliver had muttered that he would check the original study and also other anthropological evidence. From Tolliver this was close to a glowing tribute. Black congratulated Betty as they filed out of the seminar room. She cut him short. It was plain that she did not like men in uniform.

There had been other things besides his uniform she had not liked. When she learned that he was from the San Francisco clan of Blacks, she invested him automatically with all responsibility for the misdeeds of the Huntingtons, the Hopkinses, and old Grandfather Black. She knew Black was wealthy and she thought that the Air Force was Black's hobby. Once she told him, "To paraphrase Will James, you seem to have made war the moral equivalent of being a playboy."

It was during that semester that the man who was now President had started in politics, running for Congress in a nearby state. Needing all the campaign help he could get, he naturally called on his old classmates. Black was one.

Betty supported him in that initial campaign, and once chided Black and some others for their political inactivity. When Black revealed that he commuted on weekends to help in the same campaign Betty was startled. In an ornery and hilarious way, which Black later came to love, she then attacked him for being linked with the Eastern "great wealthy."

To Betty, Black seemed a perfect example of a dangerous breed: the power elite from the industrial, financial, military, and political world. It was Tolliver's seminar which gradually dissolved Betty's notions about Black. One particular afternoon Tolliver had let himself go a little further toward preemptive war than usual. A young Ph.D. candidate named Groteschele, who had just recently transferred to political science from mathematics, had been present. He argued that the war against fascism was not over: the military struggle against black fascism must now be converted into the military struggle against red fascism.

It was the first time Black had ever heard Walter Groteschele speak, and as he listened he had no notion that it would be the first of scores of times. Groteschele was the earliest of the brilliant group of mathematical political scientists that developed after World War II, a group which later included such as Henry Kissinger, Herman Kahn, Herbert Simon, and Karl Deutsch. But for a few years in the beginning, Groteschele stood alone, without peer, just as he had planned it. Now Black was only aware of a faint rasp of irritation at what Groteschele said. There was nothing on which he could put his finger, nothing he could use his intellect against—only a dim kind of restlessness, a sense that there was some obscure danger in what Groteschele said.

The professional liberals in the seminar shifted in their seats but did not speak.

Tolliver turned to Black. But instead of giving the expected reply Black outlined what he thought were the military reasons Russia, though dangerous, was a manageable threat to America.

Black spoke calmly and with authority and his eyes never wavered when Tolliver began to tense into his rigid posture of attack. When the attack came Black handled it calmly, constantly referring to expert opinions, studies, statistics, probabilities.

Betty was torn and it showed on her face. She found
it difficult to side with Black the militarist but when
finally she did it was with a fierce eloquence. The seminar did not end with the neat trimmed summation
that Tolliver liked. It ended in a sense of tension, an
odd unbalance. The students walked out gingerly.

Black moved toward Betty as the seminar ended.
She got up quickly, folded her papers, snapped them
into her briefcase, walked out without glancing at Tolliver. Her face was flushed and attractive. Black
thought: she has all the charm of a bawd unmasked at
a Sunday-school picnic.

"How about continuing this over a beer?" he said in
a low voice, leaning down just behind her ear. She
turned so quickly her nose brushed against his cheek
before he could withdraw. A blush spread over her face
and deepened as she realized it. He knew for sure then
what had remained true ever since. Betty was the
most attractive, the most interesting, and the most
quixotic girl he'd ever known. He was on the verge of
kissing her on the spot, and she knew it.

In a way, they both decided their future in having
that beer. The rest was just making all the moves and
countermoves required to carry out the decision.
There had been some difficulty about the "Black un-
earned fortune," but Betty had been reassured when
Black told her that he lived entirely on his colonel's
pay and that his share of the family income went into
a fund at Wells Fargo Bank. Black said he had no notion of what the fund amounted to, but that it was
"maybe around four million," and they both burst
into laughter.

Once, a month later, they'd taken a picnic lunch to
Walden Pond.

"But why the Air Force?" she asked. "I can understand going in at the start of the war, but I can't understand why you'd stay in afterward."

"It was simple," Black said. "What work could I do
where 'success' would be mine and not because of family background? The Air Force work was mine. The
commendations came in from majors and colonels who
couldn't have cared less about the San Francisco Blacks
even if they had known of them." He looked at her
directly and for the first time she sensed his bluntness
and honesty. "You heard I was one of 'those' Blacks
and put me into a category."

Betty nodded her head in a silent agreement that
was also an apology.

"You're my favorite militarist," she said softly.

"Don't use labels, Betty," he commanded. "Do you
think the SAC people are all anxious to have war?
Don't be a fool. We're as scared as everyone else. Look,
I was on the Strategic Bombing Survey of Germany
after the war. It's not something that's liable to make
you a warmonger."

Black paused. The survey had been a pause in his
life too. It had troubled him. For the one big conclusion that came out of the Survey was that, for all the
apparent devastation, the main thing destroyed was
people. The factories and the railways were put back
into fairly good running order in an unbelievably
short time. Indeed, bombing seemed to be an odd prod
to survival, to sharpen the impulse to strike back.

"Blacky." She took his hand and he looked down at
her, startled. She put back her head and laughed loud
enough to startle some birds into flight across the pond.
"You look as if you thought you were about to be
raped."

He could not believe his ears. He was delighted and

confused and definitely embarrassed. "Am I?"

"Are you what?"

"Am I about to be raped?"

She choked with laughter and somehow they had their arms about each other, quite clumsily. She said into his shirt, "I'm such an ass."

On this note—more or less—they were married three months later.

Black's early morning drive out Long Island to Mitchel Air Force Base was not slowed down by traffic. He arrived with plenty of time to spare for the flight to Washington. The day was clear and mild, and he checked out a Cessna 310. He had never lost his affection for a small, light plane. Even the 310 was automated, but it was still fun to fly. Someday he wanted to buy one of the quick stubby stunt biplanes that were now being reproduced, and recapture the old thrill of flying, to fly rather than to administer a plane.

As he settled on course for Washington, he felt the need suddenly of a cold drink of water, and last night's cocktail party came flooding back through his mind. He had not wanted to go at all. Betty had never taken to Groteschele. Black also knew he would be listening to Groteschele at today's briefing. So when Senator Hartmann's secretary called he'd tried to beg off.

But Hartmann was insistent. He had collared Emmett Foster, the editor of the *Liberal Magazine,* which constantly criticized nuclear testing and supported unilateral disarmament. What Hartmann wanted was a cocktail party confrontation between Foster and Groteschele. Each in his way was distinguished. They merely happened to be at opposite ends of the controversy over thermonuclear warfare. Hartmann was no fool. A Midwestern Republican with a vigorous shock of white hair, sanguine complexion, and Falstaffian girth, he orated like William Jennings Bryan and generally looked like a musical-comedy senator. But under that shock of white hair operated one of the finest minds in Washington. As a member of the Senate Foreign Relations Committee he wanted to hear the two points of view in an informal environment. He knew that Black was considered a "brainy" general and was a link between the purely tactical people in SAC and the Big Planners at the Pentagon. Groteschele had, of course, become famous after the publication of *Counter-Escalation,* which Foster had dissected and left for dead in the pages of his magazine.

Usually Betty refused to go to military-government-academic cocktail parties. To Black's surprise she insisted on going to this one.

They had arrived late. Foster was there, but Groteschele, as usual, was even later. Foster stood in a corner talking in a firm, even voice. Black realized that the man would be no pushover. To Black most "professional liberals" had shrill voices, spoke in a rush, and accused anyone who questioned their facts of favoring nuclear extermination. Facts were unimportant. Survival, common morality, humanity, damage to unborn generations—this was their chant.

Not Emmett Foster. He was a cool one and Black could tell it instantly. Even as they moved across the room, Foster, a short muscular man with hard black eyes, used words and phrases which indicated he had read the *Congressional Record* and the scientific journals and probably interviewed a number of military people. Also Foster didn't skip around. He answered questions precisely, sticking relentlessly to the point and relying on real evidence. Betty and Black listened for fifteen minutes and Betty turned to Black, her eyebrows arched.

"No fool," she said.

"No fool," Black agreed.

At that moment Groteschele arrived. He had not changed much physically since graduate-school days. A bit heavier, but not grossly so. But he was dressed better and he had the air of authority about him. He is almost silken, Black thought. He smiled easily, said something to everyone he was introduced to, patted Black on the shoulder, kissed Betty on the cheek. He smelled slightly of men's cologne.

Hartmann introduced him to Foster, but Groteschele smiled and said they had already met. Without a wasted motion Groteschele moved beside Foster, stationed himself for the debate, but with no sign of antagonism or of condescension.

Foster waited until the introductions were over and went on.

"Times have changed since Clausewitz. True, war was an institution like church or the family or private property. But institutions grow obsolete, exhaust their function," Foster argued. "Real tough-mindedness consists in recognizing that thermonuclear war is not the extension of policy by other means, it is the end of everything—people, policy, institutions.

"Groteschele," Foster said in his firm unyielding manner, "is a modern Don Quixote, dashing through the stratosphere on nuclear jaunts, talking of obliteration as if it could be made partial, hypnotized by his own words."

Foster stopped almost politely, and looked at Groteschele. Groteschele rocked on his heels, looked down at his scotch and water. He let the silence draw out. He shook his head once, a slight puzzled motion as if he were considering one argument and had abandoned it.

Betty, who seldom drank, took a long scotch from

one of the passing waiters. Black noticed that her hand trembled slightly.

Finally Groteschele spoke. His voice was extremely gentle.

"In a full-scale nuclear war between America and Russia a hundred million people, more or less, will be killed—right?" he asked Foster.

"A hundred million," Foster repeated, "or more."

The circle of people about the speakers moved restlessly. Betty finished her drink in a gulp and looked for a waiter. Black moved closer to her.

"Things would be shaken up," Groteschele went on. "Our culture and their culture would not be the same. Granted?"

"Granted," Foster said. He grinned toughly.

"Now this is a tragedy and no one here denies that," Groteschele said and his eyes swept generously over the group, lingered on Senator Hartmann. "But would you not grant that the culture which is the best armed, has the best bomb shelters, the best retaliatory capacity, the strongest defense, would have an ancient and classical advantage?"

"Which is?" Foster asked.

"It would be the victor in that it would be less damaged than its enemy," Groteschele said. "Every war, including thermonuclear war, must have a victor and a vanquished. Are you suggesting, Foster, that we should be the vanquished? Do you value American culture less than the Soviet culture?"

Betty's hand had tightened on Black's arm.

"Marvelous," Foster said and his grin was now so deep it was almost ferocious. "Simply marvelous. So neat, so logical, so well ordered."

He paused and looked at Groteschele. Groteschele did not nod for he knew this was the opening of an attack. He smiled at Foster and for the first time it was a smile of condescension.

"Groteschele, it should persuade a monkey, a high-school kid, maybe an Air Force general, maybe a Senator, but not many others," Foster said savagely. "It indicates only that you are a prisoner."

"Of what?" Groteschele said.

"Of the past, of stale ideas, of clichés," Foster said. He paused and looked around the group. "What is called for," he said, "is a complete and revolutionary breakthrough in our thinking. We are like men enclosed in a paper sack of old ideas and assumptions. The sack surrounding us appears to be complete and seamless, when in reality all we have to do is to break out of it to stand in the freedom of entirely new thoughts and approaches. What the times call for is a new Karl Marx—"

"A new Marx, Foster," Groteschele broke in, "an arresting thought. What would the new manifesto proclaim?"

"It would proclaim peace," Foster said without hesitation. "Not because peace is nice or I like my fellow humans or it is Christian or Gandhi hated violence or the sick-sick-sick kind of liberal chants it. Peace because it is the only way we can live. Get with it, Groteschele. Probability and the cobalt bomb made you old-fashioned ten years ago. Be realistic."

Foster's magazine had a circulation of only thirty thousand. The affluent and influential people he spoke before now were—one would think—more the Henry Luce type. Yet they were visibly impressed.

"Moving, very moving," Groteschele said. "But somewhat dangling, a bit suspended, no indication of how we get from war to peace. No one wants war, Foster. But the possibility of war just happens to be a reality. I want us to face realities."

"All right, Groteschele, look at it from the viewpoint of the anthropologist," Foster said. "What is war's function?"

"The resolution of conflict," Groteschele snapped.

"In primitive societies how do men resolve their conflicts?" Foster asked.

"By individual combat," Groteschele said. He had pulled his shoulders back and was somewhat more tense. This type of dialogue where his opponent turned Socrates made him restless.

"And when they become organized into tribes?" Foster said.

"Then the fighting becomes collective," Groteschele said.

"And when they become nation-states?"

"It is still violence, damn it, Foster," Groteschele said. "What is irresponsible is to suggest that as groups become bigger and the power of weapons more immense that anything is changed."

Foster cut in rudely. "Are you suggesting that a spear thrown and a nuclear bomb dropped are comparable? Just a difference in degree? Nonsense! Is it not possible, Groteschele, that war itself has become obsolete? Your superbly reasoned *Counter-Escalation* indicates that in any possible war the overwhelming majority of citizens are going to be killed. Does this suggest to you still that war is a resolution of conflicts?"

"Foster, you are hopelessly sentimental," Groteschele said. "The situation is no different than it was a thousand years ago. There were primitive wars in which populations were totally destroyed. The point is, who is going to be the victor and who the victim? It is still a question of the survival of a culture."

Foster rocked on his heels.

"A culture," he said slowly, his voice full of wonder.

"A culture with most of its people dead, the rotting smell of death in the air for years, its vegetation burned off, the germ plasm of survivors contaminated. You say I am the utopian and you are the realist. Do you really think that this world you describe is a culture?"

Groteschele was familiar with every gambit. His reply was reasonable, quietly uttered, and difficult to refute. He drew it out to great length. The spectators listened respectfully.

It was Betty who broke the spell. Before Black realized it, she had moved from his side, drunk, yet at the same time rigidly controlled.

"It is hopeless," she said, staring at the two men. "You are both romantics caught up in your fantasy world of logic and reason and that is why it is so damned hopeless. Because man himself has become obsolete. He is like the dodo and the dinosaur but for the opposite reason. His damned brain has gotten us into this mess because of its sophistication and we cannot get out of it because of his pride. Man has calculated himself into so specialized a braininess that he has gone beyond reality. And he cannot tap the truth of his viscera because that, for a specialist, is the ultimate sin."

Black had not heard her speak with such overcontrol for years. Her words fell like a pall on the group. Even Groteschele was at a loss for the right thing to say. He went through a ritual of taking a Philippine cigar from a small leather cigar case in his pocket. Since the Bay of Pigs episode he had stopped smoking Cuban cigars.

"You think I've overdone it?" As Betty spoke a new quality seemed to come over her. Black looked at her with increasing concern. An inner intensity was flow-ing from her, almost visibly. It acted like a powerful magnet on everyone present, drawing their eyes to her, holding their rapt attention.

"The world," Betty continued, her voice now edged with despair, "is no longer man's theater. Man has been made into a helpless spectator. The two evil forces he has created—science and the state—have combined into one monstrous body. We're at the mercy of our monster and the Russians are at the mercy of theirs. They toy with us as the Olympian gods toyed with the Greeks. And like the gods of Greek tragedy, they have a tragic flaw. They know only how to destroy, not how to save. That's what we're now watching in our cold war: a Greek tragedy in modern form with our godlike monsters playing out the last act of their cataclysmic tragedy."

She stopped and looked at Black quickly, as if seeking help. But before he could speak or move toward her she was speaking again.

"We all know that the big explosion is going to happen. Your concern, the two of you, is to make sure that you die intellectually correct. But my problem is more primitive. I only want to make sure that when it comes and my boys are dying that I am there to ease their last pain with morphine."

She finished in a flat voice entirely without self-pity. Her last statement seemed to give Groteschele a new assurance, a place to get back into the conversation and guide it into safe channels. His words came on gently and kindly.

"Betty," he said, "those of us who know anything about the situation feel almost exactly the same things that you have expressed. But what should we do? All go out and buy morphine? You see, Betty, I'm trying to *save* your two boys, not narcotize their death. That's the whole point of everything I've written. In spite of all our efforts, thermonuclear war may come. We must face that possibility rather than, ostrichlike, close our minds to it. And I'm trying to see that if war comes, men, our kind of men, have the maximum possible chance of surviving it."

Betty looked composed now but her fingers were digging into Black's arm.

"General Black, what do you think?" asked Senator Hartmann.

Black looked up slowly from Betty. He fixed his eyes on Foster and thought for a minute.

"I think that Betty is mostly correct," he said slowly. "Once one knows where he wants to go he can summon a magnificent array of logic and fact to support his argument. I have the awful feeling that we are reconciled, both we and the Soviets, to mutual destruction. We are now rallying our different logics to support our identical conclusions. We will probably both get the results that we want. In that case, morphine *is* more important than a bomb shelter." He stopped and for a moment he felt an excitement. It was wild and irrational: he understood the Dream. He was in a game in which the things that held him together were being stripped away. Then, quite suddenly, he could go no further.

Betty's comments had just about done it for the party. Everyone drank and chatted politely for a few minutes. Then there was the intricate ballet of social disengagement. Black knew that their host would not forget his heretical position. The Senator was a methodical man.

In the taxicab back to their apartment neither Black nor Betty had spoken. She had fallen asleep on his shoulder, her teeth grinding.

General Black snapped back to the present as the Cessna 310 approached Andrews Air Force Base outside of Washington. Looking down on the water-veined flats of the Chesapeake Bay area, he regretted that the air approach to Andrews didn't take him over Washington proper. He never ceased to be stirred by the splendor of the Washington Monument's slim white spire, the awesome majesty of the Lincoln Monument. The Pentagon, though, that was something else again. Its low, squat improbable shape was not designed to capture an airman's fancy. It was more like a great, bureaucratic land battleship pulled up alongside the Potomac. That's about what it was, mused Black, laying siege to the helpless flotilla of weaker bureaucratic ships across the Potomac.

Back to work, Blackie, boy-general, he said to himself. Life is earnest, life is real.

He brought the plane in for a skilled and effortless landing. Ten minutes later he was in a staff car and on his way to the Pentagon.

ch. 6

BOMB SHELTER, THE WHITE HOUSE

The President looked across the desk at Buck. Buck knew that the President did not see him. His eyes were slightly squinting. Buck twisted in his chair. The motion caught the President's eye. His face suddenly hardened and he seemed to come back into the room.

"What do you think of that list, Buck?" he asked, pointing at the card that Buck still held. Buck hesitated, lifted the card as if it were very delicate, glanced again at the names. He felt like licking his lips, but resisted. His mind reached for an answer, something that would make sense. It was impossible.

"I only know them as names," he said quietly. "A few I have never even heard of."

He saw approval in the President's face. Then the President was not seeing him any more, but was abstracted.

"Relax, Buck," the President said. "We're in an emergency, but we've got time, a little anyway. Time and a decision. That's what an emergency is. Now the decision is what those people on the list have to help us with. The time we can't control. It just passes."

It sounded silly, but Buck knew that the President was not thinking what he was saying. His voice and his mind were operating on different levels. Then they came together and the President was seeing Buck again.

"Buck, that group sees one another all the time, day after day," the President said. "They've probably talked over things so much that they've got a nice committee solution for everything. Right?"

"Yes, I imagine they have," Buck said.

"The only problem is that this is something they have no solution for," the President said. "Bogan told me that in Omaha they had no standard operating procedure for this kind of thing. So we've got a novel situation, something completely new."

The President swung in his chair and looked at his secretary. Quite automatically her pencil lifted, moved toward the notebook.

"Blackie's in the Pentagon group, isn't he?" the President asked.

Buck's eyes ran down the list.

"There is a General Black, Mr. President," he said. His throat felt dry.

"That's Blackie," the President said. "We went to college together." He paused. "Blackie's a bright boy, got guts and I'd trust him with almost anything. He can think on his feet, deal with a novel situation. Trouble is that either they'll make a committee solution or they'll all listen to someone like Blackie. He doesn't talk much, except when he believes in something. . . ." His voice dropped and he stared at the wall, not seeing it. Then he swung back to them, entirely in focus, speaking briskly. "Next we need someone who's not a Pentagon person, but who knows his way around. Whom do you suggest?"

He asked the question of both Buck and Mrs. Johnson. Buck stiffened. His mind went flat, incapable of memory. He could, quite literally, not recall the name of a single person. His mother? Gypsy Rose Lee? Old Mr. Carmichael in the apartment below? He must be losing his mind.

Mrs. Johnson looked at the President, then flicked over a few pages in her notebook. "They've got that Professor Groteschele out there for the briefing," she said. "He's not one of them. I mean he doesn't work at the Pentagon."

The President rocked in his chair.

"He doesn't work for the Pentagon. That's right," he said slowly. "But that book of his almost made him one of them." He paused. "O.K., Johnnie, he'll add something to a bunch of people that have been seeing one another too often. Tell the Pentagon to include Groteschele in the advisory group. Tell Swenson that Groteschele is personally cleared by me and that he can say anything he wants on any subject."

"As long as it's relevant," Mrs. Johnson said and smiled tightly.

The President grinned. "Swenson has a pretty well-developed sense of the relevant," he said.

"I know that, Mr. President," Mrs. Johnson said.

"I know that you know that, Mrs. Johnson," the President said and made a mock bow.

She smiled, turned, and left the room.

Buck sat silently with the President of the United States. He knew they were waiting but he did not know what for.

ch. 7

THE ORGANIZED MAN

Walter Groteschele awoke at precisely 5:30 A.M. He did not awake at the sound of an alarm clock and, indeed, he did not even wear a wrist watch. Despite this he was certain of the time. He was awake fully. As he swung out of bed his mind began to block out the day. It was a quick, neat process, something that occupied him only from his bed to the bathroom. By 6:10 he would be showered, shaved, dressed, nourished by one cup of instant coffee, and waiting for the train at Scarsdale. An hour to La Guardia—8:30. An hour to Washington (and his second cup of coffee, at 10,000 feet)—9:30. At the Pentagon by ten minutes to ten.

The check list was complete. The day was under control.

Groteschele stepped on the bathroom scales—185. He had weighed 165 when he was twenty-one. He knew some men who refused to weigh themselves, were afraid to get the bad news. Groteschele weighed himself every day of his life. As he stepped off the scales he even forced himself to think what the additional fat meant. Face reality, he told himself with a quiet pride. Facing reality was what had gotten him where he was.

As he showered, rubbing his body with a rough natural sponge, he ran over the physical differences between twenty-one and forty-eight. Then he had been lean and muscular. Now there was an overlay of fat about the torso. Not gross, but noticeable in a suit. Softer. Around the waist the flesh was a bulge. Where it showed most was in his neck and face. His collars were usually tight and bit into the flesh, making his face slightly pink. As he shaved he calculated whether or not it would be possible to exercise the fat off. The calculation did not take long.

He did not have time for exercise.

Only once during his five-stage (car, train, taxi, plane, taxi) trip from Scarsdale to Washington did Groteschele's mind relax and think of anything except the briefing he would present. It was in the taxicab from Grand Central to La Guardia. There was something about the luxury of a taxicab, to ride alone while others rode in buses, that made Groteschele think of his youth. Briefly he permitted himself the luxury of letting his mind wander.

Groteschele's father was a tough, brilliant, and hard-working physician, a highly skilled surgeon. He was also a Jew, unfortunately in Germany. Early in the 1930s he had seen what was coming. He had argued with other Jews in his native Hamburg that there were only two alternatives: arm and fight, or leave Germany. The great majority of his friends and relatives, anchored by their possessions and inured to the prospect of suffering, stayed in Germany. Many of them died in gas ovens.

Walter Groteschele was fifteen when his father abandoned his medical practice and moved from Hamburg, via London and New York, to Cincinnati. Before his father could practice medicine in America it was required that he take two years of residency and pass a series of examinations. He was never able to get enough money ahead to do the two years' residency. Emil Groteschele worked first as a ditchdigger for a utilities company. He could not, however, stand the calluses and the coarsening of his surgeon's hands. Eventually he wound up as a butcher in a kosher butcher shop. This was an irony, for Emil Groteschele was a Reform Jew and anything but devout. But the work did allow him to use his hands in somewhat the fashion for which they had been exquisitely trained.

Emil Groteschele was not an embittered man. He had understood clearly what his prospects were when he left Berlin. He was saving his life and the lives of his family. Nothing more. One of the few times that his son had seen him angry was when the subject of the *Diary of Anne Frank* came up. Emil Groteschele had offended the Jews of Cincinnati by arguing that Anne Frank and her family had acted like imbeciles. Rather than hiding in an attic and clutching their Jewishness to them they should have made plans to escape. Failing that, they should have been prepared to fight the Nazis when the final day came. "The steps leading up to that miserable attic should have been red with Nazi blood—and that of the Frank family," Dr. Groteschele argued bitterly.

"If each Jew in Germany had been prepared to take one SS trooper with him before he was sent to the camps and the gas ovens, precious few Jews would have been arrested," Emil Groteschele argued. "At some point Hitler and the SS would have stopped. Face it. If every Jew who was arrested had walked to the door with a pistol in his hand and started shooting at the local heroes, how long would the Nazis have kept it up? At around a few hundred they would have started to think twice. At a few thousand they would have started to shake a bit. If it got to twenty thousand, they would have called it off. But the first Jews who shuffled quietly off to death camps or hid like mice in attics were instruments of destruction of the rest."

Groteschele knew that his father considered all of life a battle. He was a complete Darwinian; so much so that he never expressed self-pity for his fall from master surgeon to journeyman butcher.

"It's a new environment. I'm not as efficient as the Americans," the muscular determined man said in a pitiless voice, as if he were talking of someone else. "The American was bred for this environment; the weak ones disappeared long ago. I was bred for a softer environment: Jewish ladies with too much fat, rabbis with ulcers, people who ate too much sour cream, lox, matzoth balls." He stared at his son. "Every group protects itself, just as the individual does. Don't waste time whining. Be good enough to get into the group you want."

His son had taken the advice seriously. He attacked knowledge as if it were an enemy. By the time he was a senior he had won every academic honor in the Cincinnati public schools.

When Groteschele went off to a small Ohio college he had three separate scholarships and not the slightest notion of what he wanted to study. His first year he took liberal-arts courses and studied his classmates. It was reassuring. They were uncertainly motivated, pleasant, anxious about dates, inattentive to lectures, obsessed with material objects—cashmere sweaters, convertibles, record players, stolen college banners. They were the new Jews, Groteschele thought, binding themselves with the invisible links of possessions, but they lacked the drive and ability to absorb punishment that the real Jew had.

Groteschele majored in mathematics. He went about

making the choice systematically. He learned nothing
from talking to his classmates. Instead he sought out
the brightest professors on the campus and questioned
them. He pushed them on what American industry
would be like in five years. Their advice was unanimous. The nation would be at war or finishing a war
and science would be going through a new surge of
progress. It would be sparked by mathematics. He was
a Phi Beta Kappa in his junior year and *summa cum
laude* at graduation; and did not, literally, know the
names of more than a dozen of his classmates.

Before Groteschele could find a job, waves of Japanese planes swept over Pearl Harbor and changed all
of our lives. By now Groteschele had developed a
prescience, a hard intuition, about what would happen
in the future. He did it by the elimination of hopes
and the substitution of the calculation of realities. He
applied his father's Darwinism in a methodical and
tough manner. He was no Cassandra but he tended
always to look carefully and cautiously at where he
would be in five years and to move with what was inevitable. His calculation led him to volunteer at once
for military duty.

He was selected for OCS and when he finished he
was assigned to a group of officers who interviewed
German prisoners as part of their processing before
being sent to POW camps throughout the country.

At first the job had a delicious undertone of vengeance to it and Groteschele did not deny this to himself. Day after day the men who had bullied Jews in
the comfortable little towns of Germany, had swag-
gered in their party uniforms, had roared and lusted
for war, now paraded in front of him. They were bit-
ter-eyed, frightened, uncertain, homesick. Groteschele

found them a disappointment and he was surprised at his own reaction.

After a few weeks the interviewing became dull. It was impossible to stay angry at lines of potato-fat men with vacuous eyes who were slack and weary from the Atlantic crossing, who always whined their ignorance of concentration camps. "Konzentration camps, ach nein, Herr Leutnant," eyes bulging with fake surprise. "Impossible. I never heard of it." And then the inevitable statement about being a little man, a man in the ranks, a man who carried out orders, a man who did his duty, a man who was secretly anti-Nazi.

After a few months Groteschele, because of his skill in German, was able to get himself transferred to the section which interviewed SS troopers. These interviews were longer, more concentrated, more meaningful. The interviewing officer could, in fact, question an SS man as long as he wished. Groteschele always guided the conversation to the Jewish question. The SS men stared back at him, unafraid and their faces expressionless, and said, "Rabbits. The Jews are like rabbits, but without the speed of a rabbit." Always it was a rabbit or an undernourished rat or a mouse to which they compared the Jews.

It was during this time that Groteschele found himself trimming off excess weight and taking daily exercises. Finally he was doing hours of bar-bell exercises, pushups, and road-work every day. He became as physically tough as the SS troopers, his belly as flat, his face as expressionless. Always, just before the interview was over, Groteschele let slip the fact that he was a Jew. Never as a direct admission, always slyly and as if the prisoner had known from the start.

It was the only thing that made the SS troopers

crack, even a little. They would stare at Groteschele's well-muscled body, his inscrutable face, his hard eyes. Then, for a moment in time, Groteschele could see fear in their eyes. It was gone instantly, the eyes shut, the expression lost. But it was enough for Groteschele. They had seen a different kind of Jew and it frightened them.

By the time the war was over Groteschele had developed a new interest. It was the study of politics. Americans had mastered technology and the scientist would continue to be a hero for some time. But the real decisions, the real power would lie with those who understood politics. Competence in politics would be the ultimate sanctuary, although partisan elective politics would be as volatile as ever. He must, he reasoned, be an expert in politics but not subject to popular opinion. He calculated that with the GI Bill and the money he had saved he would be able to get a Ph.D. at an Ivy League college and still be a few thousand dollars ahead.

His father had only one piece of advice. "If you are going to become a professor change your name to Groth," he said. "American universities have too many German Jews. They will lose their tolerance for them."

Groteschele had not changed his name. It was the first time he had rejected his father's advice, but now he was surer than his father about some things: the character of Americans, for instance, and the favorable attitude toward the Jewish intellectual in the academic world. This did not mean that he was insensitive to names. In fact he found them fascinating. He had, for example, noticed that his name was considered by most to be German and he knew that his appearance was not distinctively Jewish. He considered the possibility that he might even suffer somewhat from anti-German feeling, but he also remembered the guilty conscience which Americans had had over their anti-Germanism after World War I. All in all, when everything was added up, he calculated that he would benefit by sticking with his name and identity.

Once this decision was made the plan was simple. He knew that it would take some luck, but he was also determined to do everything possible to minimize the importance of that element.

The first thing was to become a protégé of Tolliver.

Groteschele sensed that Tolliver had an ego of formidable proportions. This was what led him to work in the area of great sweeping diplomatic moves, intricate military strategies, and it was also what led him to an instantaneous and ferocious defense of his views.

For the first year in graduate school Groteschele made no move toward Tolliver. He sat quietly in his classes and read every book and article the man had written. He watched the other graduate students as they slowly learned the pitfalls and terrors of the academic world. By the end of the first year none of them regarded it as "the ivory tower" any more. By then they had learned it was more like Kafka's *Castle:* a place of enormous tension, the scene of ununderstood conspiracies, a place of stalking and frantic flight from an unseen enemy. Groteschele watched some of the others break and remained impassive. Groteschele was certain that he would not be one of those who broke. He had been prepared for the fact that the big beautiful buildings and the book-lined studies and the quiet seminar rooms would really be scenes of battle.

At the end of the first year Groteschele's chance came. Tolliver published a book called *Models for the Future War*. The title had been a mistake. It suggested that Tolliver was, somehow, advocating war. The reviews of the book were generally negative, some of them scathing. Groteschele read the reviews carefully. Finally he found one in a liberal monthly in which it was clear that the author had not read the whole book but had skimmed the first few chapters and then used that much as a platform to expound his own theories about "the rising tide of militarism."

Groteschele wrote a 2,000-word letter to the magazine. It was a model of careful and biting analysis. The editor of the monthly, in a spasm of regret, sent Groteschele a check for $25 and published the letter as an article.

Groteschele wisely did not send Tolliver a copy of the article, but inevitably Tolliver read it. He never thanked Groteschele for the article, in fact, he never mentioned it. But in his second year of graduate work, Groteschele received a written invitation from Tolliver to be his research assistant. Groteschele never worked so hard in his life. His eyes constantly burned from reading in bad library light. He had no time for exercise and could feel his body go slack, the fat start to gather, the hard muscularity he had liked disappear.

Carefully and patiently Groteschele read all of the memos which Tolliver, as a long-time consultant to the Pentagon, received from Washington. By studying the memos and by careful questioning of Tolliver, Groteschele found what he wanted: a public gap in American military thought. Stretching over a generation, the notion had arisen that America would never start a war. Even the most hardened of the military people cautiously skirted around this question. As a result a mood had grown up which made a discussion of America striking first impossible. A few officers had mentioned it in "off-the-record" briefings and had promptly been branded warmongers and their careers carefully altered so that they disappeared from the public eye. Even among themselves the military had developed a theory and lexicon and strategy which always skirted the idea of the United States starting a war.

In his Ph.D. dissertation Groteschele attacked this taboo. He provided a respectable language and theory within which the "first strike" or "preemptive war" could be discussed. The name of the dissertation was *The Theory of Counter-Escalation Postures in a Thermonuclear World.* He gave Tolliver five copies of the first draft of the dissertation. Tolliver knew why he had received extra copies. He sent them along to Washington.

Groteschele curbed his hopes. He knew the copies of the dissertation might well disappear in the labyrinths of Washington. Or the central idea might be attacked by a powerful person, or, even more damaging, be dismissed as trivial or nutty. But his luck held. One day the phone call came.

"Dr. Groteschele, this is Colonel Stark of the Air Force in the Pentagon," a calm voice said. "We have read your dissertation with great interest and wonder when you can come to Washington to discuss it."

Technically Groteschele was not yet a Ph.D., but he sensed this was not the time to point out that fact.

"Colonel Stark, my schedule is fairly full for the next five or six days," Groteschele said cautiously. "Maybe sometime next week."

Stark cut in abruptly. There was an edge of irritation in his voice, but there was also something of respect.

"Doctor, down here we consider this rather urgent," Colonel Stark said. "After all, the security of the country is involved."

"Can you schedule the meeting for tomorrow afternoon?" Groteschele asked abruptly.

The colonel could and did. That afternoon meeting was not easy. For the first time since the captured SS troopers had made the remarks about Jews being like rabbits, Groteschele felt isolated. He was seated at the end of a long table. The other seats were occupied by six generals, five colonels, four civilians, and a secretary who was operating a Stenotype machine. Groteschele glanced at Stark. Stark's face was completely expressionless. Groteschele did not bother to look at the others. He knew that none of them were yet committed.

Quite suddenly Groteschele lost his nerve. The whole situation was preposterous. He was only a student who had once been an Army lieutenant and he was talking to professionals who had devoted their lives to the conduct and strategy of war. He sensed that he was about to make a fool of himself. Quickly, and with the telescopic capacity of the tragic moment, he saw the rest of his life. He would slide, slide, slide, always downward. He smiled woodenly down the table as he calculated where he would end, what the academic equivalent of his father's butcher-shop job would be. He would be a grade-school teacher to a bunch of idiot children.

With a terrible self-hatred he was aware of how he had physically declined, was no longer taut and trim. To them, these men of power and elegance around the table, he must look like a fattening, white-grub academic. He looked at Stark, started to ask to be excused.

"Excuse me, Colonel Stark," Groteschele said and then paused. To his astonishment his voice came out cold and steady, without a tremor. His mouth was dry, his mind a shambles, his fingers had a quiver—but his voice was rock-hard. The decision was made for him. He would read the paper just as he had written it, using the one physical attribute that was still in control: his voice. Later, reading, he realized that his paper was a wild gamble. He reviewed alternative theories of modern thermonuclear war and, with all the deliberateness of a machine gunner, shredded them to pieces. Inevitably he must be damaging some of the men in the room. The knowledge made his fingers tremble even more. His mouth went cottony, but somehow the words continued to pour out with even more control. When he finished his review of "obsolete alternatives" he sensed that he had probably bruised every man in the room. There was nothing to do but go on.

When he came to his own theory his voice became sharper, more incisive, although the words were more ambiguous. Without smiling, using his new vocabulary, he presented the alternative of the United States striking first. However, he never quite used those words. He took the people around the table to the edge of the abyss, forced them to look over the edge. Then, his language still cold, he described a situation in which the abyss was not threatening, but was in fact a magnificent and glowing opportunity. The whole presentation took one hour and ten minutes. He was not interrupted once.

When he had finished and had squared his papers in front of him on the table Groteschele stared straight ahead.

The first person to speak was an elderly, white-haired man in uniform at the far end of the table. He had a deep and authoritative voice that emanated from a face made of leather, and four stars decorated each shoulder. Groteschele had not noticed him before, but sensed at once that he was the senior officer in the room. He was, in fact, in charge of strategic plans for the Air Force and had deliberately not identified himself with any single point of view. Ruthless on weak logic and thin evidence, he had the reputation of listening with an open mind to any proposal that was sensibly presented.

"Dr. Groteschele, speaking for myself only, I congratulate you on an extremely clear and lucid presentation of a complex problem," the general said. The general looked at his hands, smiled, and went on. "Your alternative is a difficult one. I believe it might be the right one. At the least it should be thoroughly discussed."

Groteschele relaxed. He was safe. He hardly heard the other voices as they murmured various reasons for approving Groteschele's paper.

When the briefing broke up, Stark invited him to dinner. Groteschele smiled, aware that the invitation had come *after* the briefing rather than before. He accepted. The dinner was small, but Groteschele knew that the men there were powerful. And he was the prize, the sought-after expert. Eyes turned to see him when he spoke. Others broke off their conversations to listen.

"My God, did you hear the Old Man say that Dr. Groteschele might have 'the right one'?" Colonel Stark said. "That's the closest he has ever come to a commitment."

They stared at Groteschele. He did not smile. Calmly he went on to describe some of the implications of his position.

That had been the start.

Soon he was practically commuting to Washington. Conference followed conference. Discussion papers appeared at regular intervals. Each trip, each conference, gave Groteschele access to new and valuable information. He was cleared for access to top-secret material. He had free communications with the experts working on the fantastic frontiers of defense developments.

His doctoral dissertation was published under the title *Counter-Escalation*. It was instantly reviewed by Hanson Baldwin in *The New York Times* Sunday book-review section, and was the lead. Walter Millis reviewed it for the *Herald Tribune*. For a book of its type it sold very well, over 35,000 copies. Its reputation spread everywhere. Liberal journals attacked the book. A pacifist group burned it in Marin County, California, and then had second thoughts about book-burning and apologized to a nonlistening public. The book was discussed on two national television panel shows. People who had never read it had violent opinions about it.

With a speed that startled him he now became a public personage outside the defense and academic communities. He analyzed the reasons for his success and finally satisfied himself. There was a morbidity about his subject matter which somehow flowed over onto Groteschele and gave him an aura. He was extremely careful never to discuss classified information in public, but even so he could draw a picture of how the United States would look after a thermonuclear first strike, the awful seductions of surrender, the number of children who would suffer malignant genetic defects from radioactivity. Looking coolly at a room full of people he would tell them how many decades it would take the survivors of a thermonuclear war to regain the standard of living of medieval days. He could see the audience stiffen, tongues licking at the corners of their mouths, the signs of nervousness and fascination multiply.

Groteschele knew that he was regarded as a magician.

The awesome powers on which he was expert, the facts of life and death and survival, the new cabalistic language of the nuclear philosophers and high scientists of physics, were merely matters of fact. But the layman, the rich socialite, the industrialist, the politician, endowed Groteschele with *control* of the things he described.

The attention and the flattery were deeply pleasing to Groteschele. He did not disguise the fact from himself. He handled the incidental aspects of fame easily. There was more money, lots more money, and Groteschele turned it over to an expert business manager. He learned to dictate into portable dictating machines while riding taxicabs or airplanes. He learned that it was dangerous to get drunk the night before an important meeting. He became a consultant to various foundations and business firms, but selected them with great care. He wanted nothing to impair his relationship to the Federal government, for he knew full well that his status in Washington and the information which he obtained there were the sources of his power. Groteschele went through three different administrations without threat. Many of the high military officers and policy-makers did not agree with him, but he was a valuable commodity. He was an innovator, a barb, an egghead with a steel-trap mind, and even those who disagreed with him violently knew they were duty-bound to consider the alternatives which his thinking produced.

Groteschele had been, after the success of his book, besieged by academic offers. He evaluated them very carefully. He finally chose a distinguished university close to Washington which agreed to give him half-time duties for a single semester, but to pay him a full salary. The university also had bought a commodity, a name, a reputation, and knew it.

So much had changed for Groteschele so quickly.
He thought briefly of his relationship with women. He
was not handsome or attractive sexually, and he never
had been. He had always explained it to himself by
saying that women who were otherwise attracted to
him were repelled by his mind. But this, too, had
changed. When he walked down the long corridors of
the Pentagon, groups of secretaries stared at him with
tight little fascinated smiles. He nodded but did not
speak. To his surprise, brilliant and beautiful women
sought him out. If he wanted, so it seemed, he had only
to stand still at a cocktail party, scan the women speculatively, settle on one . . . and then let the situation
develop at the woman's initiative. The course often led
him to her bed.

Groteschele was married and had a fifteen-year-old
daughter. Wife and daughter were strangely identical:
slight, nervous, possessed of a thin prettiness. His
daughter was a brilliant student and it was her academic record which Groteschele found most attractive
about her. Like the wives of many busy and successful
men, his wife had faded away into a cool domestic
haze. He had married her in Cincinnati years ago and
at the time she had had the freshness of youth and it
had seemed an appropriate union. Groteschele never
took her on trips and when he was home their conversations were brief and perfunctory. She sensed that his
sexual life was extramarital, but the knowledge gave
her relief. She had never really enjoyed sex, and after
Counter-Escalation there had been something about
her husband's sexual behavior which disturbed her.
She felt ravished and quite impersonal even when
locked together with him—as if she were nameless to

him, an anonymous figure upon whom he exploded a deep rage. She tried to convince herself it was passion, but knew it was not.

Passion had recently led Groteschele to an experience that shocked him profoundly in that it revealed so starkly the wellsprings of his power. It had started at one of those frequent off-the-record discussions with a group of high-level businessmen and political leaders. This one had been in Washington, the Metropolitan Club. Only a highly selected group was present that evening, about twenty-five men and women altogether. During drinks, one woman had stood out. Elegant, slim and lithe, she was a woman from a world he did not know. He sensed that she had a competence with men that had become almost arrogance. He had seen a few others like her. They gave off the subtle signs of wealth, family background, education and boredom. It was like a number of elegant odors in the air. It also had something to do with the smile: such women smiled infrequently and never at women. When they smiled at a man it was like a congratulatory handshake; it had nothing of the simper or of the coquette in it. Men for such women were not a diversion, they were a necessity. Groteschele sensed this and felt somehow threatened. He avoided such women.

The speech went well. It was a variation of the same one he gave them all. They never wanted to hear anything new, they just wanted to hear it from him. Afterward, over more drinks, little groups came up to present pet arguments. He looked around the room, wondering when they would start to break up. No sign yet. He could not leave too early. Part of his $750 fee involved just this sort of boredom. There was a slight tug at his elbow. He turned around. It was his hostess and just to the side the woman, the elegant one.

"Evelyn, this is Walter Groteschele, our famous guest; Evelyn Wolfe. Evelyn has been dying to meet you. She's made me promise to take a small group to a bar so she can hear you at closer range," the hostess said, and fled.

"She overdid it a bit, but I would like to talk to you," Evelyn Wolfe said.

Eight of them wound up in one of those countless chic hotel bars of Washington. Evelyn Wolfe sat next to Groteschele and in a few moments he had the bewildering sensation that they had somehow been cut off from the others at the corner table, almost as if some barrier to sound had been drawn around him and Evelyn Wolfe. Groteschele slowly began to realize that this was an extraordinarily attractive woman. She was intelligent, she was poised, mannered, informed, and intense, but he had met at least a score of women that possessed these qualities. What she possessed in addition was a kind of burning intensity, a hard focusing of all her emotions on some undefined objective. She did not converse. She aimed at a target. By the time they had had four scotch and waters Groteschele realized that the target was himself. Normally he would have been flattered. But this time he felt a slight shiver of apprehension. This woman had an almost cobra-like manner of following what he said. Her beautifully coifed head, her face marred only by a mouth that was too small, actually wove back and forth with slight undulations as Groteschele talked about war games, the strategy of surrender, megatons, and Doomsday systems.

Most people, especially women, listened to Groteschele's description of American and Soviet tactics with a kind of unconcealed look of either bafflement or horror. Groteschele could not make out the look on

Evelyn Wolfe's face. He only knew that her concentration was enormous. She spoke very little. When he described the Doomsday system, hinting that it was semiclassified, she closed her eyes for a moment and a slight smile started at the corners of her mouth.

"Beautiful," she said.

Just that single word unaccompanied by an expression of horror or astonishment or dismay. For a moment Groteschele's careful poise was broken. He went on automatically talking about the likeliest survivors of an all-out thermonuclear war, his way of giving a droll ending to his macabre description, of letting people down easily. They would be the most hardened of convicts, those in solitary confinement. Another group likely to survive would be the file clerks for large insurance companies, because they would be housed in fireproofed rooms and insulated by tons of the best insulator in the world, paper.

"Then, my dear Miss Wolfe, imagine what will happen," Groteschele said, feeling himself regaining his poise. "The small group of hardened criminals and the army of file clerks will war with one another for the remaining means of life. The convicts will have a monopoly of violence, but the file clerks will have a monopoly of organization. Who do you think will win?"

Evelyn Wolfe looked straight at Groteschele. Then she shook her head. Groteschele was confused.

"I would like you to take me home now," Evelyn Wolfe said, and she was up on her feet and into her mink coat before he responded. She did not say goodbye to the rest of the group, but they all looked up as she and Groteschele left.

They were in Groteschele's car and three blocks from the bar before Evelyn Wolfe spoke.

"You were being mischievous about the war between the convicts and the file clerks," she said, leaning her head back against the seat. "In fact, you know that no one will survive the Doomsday system. That is the beauty of the whole thing."

"No one, Miss Wolfe, has ever called it beautiful before," Groteschele said with a laugh.

"They have been afraid to," she said. "But that is what they feel."

"You mean that everyone is possessed by the death-wish?" Groteschele asked in his best professorial manner.

"No, damn it, don't be so deliberately stupid," she said sharply. "Everyone knows they are going to die. What makes you fascinating and what makes your subject fascinating is that it involves the death of so many people. Quite literally everyone on earth." She paused a moment and then spoke savagely. "Damn it, I wish I were a man and a man who could push the button. I would not push it, you understand that. But the knowledge that I could." She shivered in her mink coat.

As Groteschele turned off of Massachusetts Avenue and threaded through Rock Creek Park, he felt a sudden hard understanding cross his mind. It was not he, Groteschele, the physical man, who was attractive to women. It was Groteschele, the magic man, the man who understood the universe, the man who knew how and when the button would be pushed. He was a master of death and somehow that gave him potency.

"Why wouldn't you push it?" Groteschele asked softly. "There it sits. More power in that button than anyone in all time has ever possessed. But it's never used until you push the button. Why not push it?"

"Because I would die along with everyone else," Evelyn Wolfe said.

Her voice came to a queer faltering halt. Groteschele felt a very deep excitement.

"That is one statement you do not really believe," he said with authority. "Do you think that life is the most important thing to a person? You don't think it for a moment. You know I don't. I can name a dozen ways of living to which you would prefer death."

She was leaning back against the seat, her eyes closed, the lacquer of sophistication dissolved from her face. She looked curiously young. Like a hungry young girl.

"Go on," she said. It was the first time that night she had implored him.

"Knowing you have to die, imagine how fantastic and magical it would be to have the power to take everyone else with you," Groteschele said, spinning out what he had never said to himself. "The swarms of them out there, the untold billions of them, the ignorant masses of them, the beautiful ones, the artful ones, the friends, the enemies . . . all of them and their plans and hopes. And they are murderees: born to be murdered and don't know it. And the person with his finger on the button is the one who knows and who can do it."

The sound Evelyn Wolfe made was not a moan. It was the sound of wonderment that a child makes . . . even if the child sees cruelty.

"Stop in one of those little side roads," Evelyn Wolfe ordered.

Groteschele obeyed.

The moment that he turned off the motor her neat trim head struck at him. It was like nothing he had ever experienced before. She kissed him violently and then whispered words in his ear at the same time that her hands moved over his body. In one way he felt raped, attacked by someone stronger than himself. At the same time her words were words of the most extreme submission, bringing out every bullish impulse in his body.

He never recalled perfectly his feelings. It was too quick a mixture of self-revelation, of shame, of wonderful obscenity, of feeling a child under his hands and knowing she was a woman, of her words ending and her hoarse breathing beginning, of a savage pride that his softening body was capable of so much, of all this happening in the little universe ringed round by gearshift and leather seats and instrument panel, of soft little hands that arched into claws, of the sound of cloth ripping, of expensive perfumes mixed with the smell of her, and, chiefly, that this was a complete surrender.

When finally he placed her small body in the corner of the car he knew she was satisfied. But he was wrong. Her eyes still glittered and she came back across the seat at him. She took his hand and raised it to her lips. She kissed the palm of his hand and then taking his little finger in her mouth she softly sucked it and then bit it so sharply that he jerked.

Suddenly, in a way from which he had always protected himself, Groteschele realized that in his own person, convoluted and intertwined, were two knowledges of death. In one way, the public way, he was a respectable high priest of civic death. This dialogue he had raised from a secretive conversation to a respectable art. It was a game at which he was exquisite. Almost by his own single-mindedness and wit he had introduced to a whole society the idea that a calm and dispassionate and logical discussion of collective death was an entertainment. By refinements and logical innovation he had made municipal death a form of style and a way of life.

But now, with his body aching and sweat soiling his

shirt, he realized that in him there was also a personal beast of death. He realized that he had always feared women because in each of them there was the buried but inextinguishable desire to love a man to death. Evelyn Wolfe was simply more obvious and direct about it than the others. She would, without mercy and as if it were her due, draw the energy and juices and fluids and substance from his body through the inexhaustible demands of pure sex.

Groteschele realized that he had never in his life distinguished between sex and love. And now it was too late.

He pulled his hand away from Evelyn Wolfe's mouth, started the car, and, accelerating wildly, shot through Rock Creek Park. He roared a single great peal of laughter as the car left the park. The black internal beast of death he would never recognize again. And he would not have to, for he had the other great and public death as his amulet. It was enough for any man. And it was more than most had ever had.

When they got to Evelyn Wolfe's house, she leaned toward him and invited him in. He reached over and gave her a short savage slap across her open mouth. She did not recoil, she did not cry, she did not even move. She simply sat silently for a moment, her eyes crystalline with a sense of loss. She waited a full fifteen seconds and then opened the door and walked firmly up to her house.

At ten minutes to ten, Groteschele entered the Pentagon without haste or any sign either that he had exerted himself to get there or that he worried about what lay ahead. In the four hours and twenty minutes that he had been awake, he had organized the briefing he would give that day, anticipated the reactions of certain secretaries and generals, and decided upon the arguments he would hold in reserve to counter their possible challenges.

It was going to be a more than usually satisfying day.

ch. 8

THE PRESIDENT AND THE TRANSLATOR

The President was looking at his pencil intently. He held it up to the light, seemed to be studying the lettering on its side, to wonder at its six sides, to admire the point.

Buck looked at his watch and felt a dull shock: it was only 10:38.

As the time spun out, a long second after a long second, like half-frozen drops unable to separate themselves from a nameless mass, Buck became calmer. The pencil is like a totem to the President, he thought. He looks at it and thinks of other things.

He quickly calculated the difference in age between himself and the President. It was only twelve years. For the first time he realized the maturity of the man facing him. Somehow it made Buck sad, gave him a sense of loss. There was no way, and he knew it deeply, that he could ever overtake this other man in experience, in toughness, in drive, in durability, in span. It gave Buck no great sense of regret and surely not of envy; it was merely that until that moment he had thought everything was possible. Not that he wanted to *do* everything, but he wanted it to be theoretically possible. But he knew that in ten times twelve years he could not become like this man across the desk.

"Buck, this may all be over in the next few minutes," the President said, turning the pencil slowly, looking away to see Buck. "It probably will be. The bombers will find out their mistake and turn around and head back or we will make radio contact and recall them. Right now we don't know why they flew past their Fail-Safe point and we can't raise them by radio. By itself neither event is catastrophic. But this particular situation has never occurred before. The entire positive control system depends on our ability to maintain verbal contact by radio. That's why we are here. Possibly it will get very sticky."

The President paused. Buck knew he did not have to respond, but he found himself speaking.

"I don't know about the details, Mr. President," Buck said, surprised at his own words, "but if the military people were sure it was something they could solve themselves they wouldn't have called you. You're down here because they know it is a serious problem."

The President stopped turning the pencil. "You interested in politics?" he asked.

Buck paused. "No, sir, not particularly."

"I remember. You're studying law."

"Yes, sir." Again Buck was amazed by the man's memory, and profoundly flattered.

"You've got a nice political feel," the President said. "Bogan in Omaha has instructions to get through to me in a number of very specific and detailed situations. He also has one general instruction just in case something happens that the specific instructions don't cover. You stated the general instruction just now: whenever anything occurs that looks serious get on the red phone."

The President paused again. He looked back at the pencil.

"Look, Buck, if things get really serious we might have to use the 'hot wire' which connects me with the Kremlin," the President said and paused. "For the first time."

Buck knew that late in 1962 Washington and Moscow had agreed to maintain a constant telephone connection between the American President and the Premier of Russia. It had promptly been labeled the "hot wire." Buck also knew that it had never been used. For the first time since his phone rang that morning, a chill went through Peter Buck.

"Most situations I can handle myself," the President went on, "but I don't speak Russian. You do. You might have to translate for me and the translation has to be not only literally perfect, but it should catch every emphasis I intend and the tones I use to convey meaning. So from now on you listen to every conversation I have on the phone. As soon as the conversation is over I will tell you what I think of it. Don't argue with me, but just make sure you understand what I feel. All right?"

"Yes, sir," Buck said. "It's new to me, but I'll try."

The President leaned back in his chair and closed his eyes. "That's all you can do. That's all any of us can do." When he spoke again it was in an intimate and completely unguarded manner, a kind of verbal free-association.

"I've talked to Bogan in Omaha twice since 10:30," he said. "Good man. Old type flier. Not afraid of all the new equipment. If he's worried, I'm worried. O.K. Then I talked to Wilcox. New Secretary of the Army. He's tough, but too tough for a new man. Too sure. We listen to him, but we take his advice slow. Very, very slow. Now the switchboard is trying to get Swenson. You know Swenson?"

The President did not open his eyes. Buck realized that he was both relaxing and giving instructions at the same time.

"No, sir," Buck said. "I know he is Secretary of Defense, but that is all."

"To Swenson we listen and if he gives advice we take it all," the President said. "Unless I tell you otherwise, whatever Swenson says is what I think."

The phone rang and the President opened his eyes and nodded at Buck to pick up his phone also.

"Mr. President, it's Swenson at the Pentagon," a dry small voice said. "I am in my own office, but have an urgent call to come to the Big Board room. There was also the word to call you." The voice stopped. There was no apology or hesitation, merely that Swenson had conveyed all the information he felt pertinent.

"It might be nothing, Swenson," the President said. "It might be big trouble. One of our groups of Vindicators flew through its Fail-Safe point and is headed toward Russia. Positive Control has broken down. Omaha doesn't know how it happened. I talked to Wilcox in your Big Board room and he doesn't either, but he is talking tough. I'd like you to get down there and be ready for anything. Keep that college professor Groteschele there and don't let the military boys drown him out. Also Blackie, General Black, is there. Keep him there whatever happens."

"Any particular reason, Mr. President?" the Secretary of Defense asked.

"No. He is an old friend and a classmate. I know him and trust him in any situation," the President said with no apology.

"Yes, sir, I understand," Swenson said. "Anything else?"

"That's all," the President said.

The phone clicked dead instantly and without a farewell salutation.

The President grinned at Buck.

"Wastes no time," the President said. "I wish I liked the sonofabitch a little better. All I can do is respect him. But that's enough."

Buck had seen Swenson from a distance, but had never heard him talk. Even so he knew a good deal about the man. He was something of a legend, a fable, in a capital which was accustomed to unusual men. Swenson looked like a clerk who had come to power by mistake. He was thin, shy, easily embarrassed, and at the same time abrupt, incisive, and cold. Socially he seemed to be a man who wanted to blend into the gray background, who shrank from contact. He dressed with an unmistakable flair for the totally inconspicuous, almost as if his clothes were camouflage. A *Time* cover story had stated, "He is the only self-made millionaire in the United States who looks as if his clothes were bought by his wife off the racks at a discount house." In high school and college class photographs Swenson was the person no one could remember. Meeting him face to face it was impossible to conceive of Swenson as a bold administrator, a courageous innovator.

It took powerful and sensitive men only a few minutes, however, to realize that when they faced Swenson they faced an equal. If they were especially perceptive they sensed that in a peculiar, understated and almost eerie way Swenson was their superior. He had a calm, steely mind that would, if Swenson had allowed it full swing, have been dazzling. But he went to great pains to conceal his extraordinary intelligence. Swenson listened carefully to everyone in whom he had confidence, his head tilted to one side carefully evaluating what was said. The moment there was a flaw in logic or a missing piece of evidence he asked a quiet question.

Talking to Swenson was not a task that the average man liked. It was too much like a quiet and merciless interrogation. In his months in the Pentagon Swenson had quietly shifted dozens of admirals and generals out of important positions on the basis of a five-minute conversation with them. Men of the first quality, men who possessed the capacity for real power and a deep intuition, responded quickly to Swenson. Lesser men never quite understood Swenson. They were not around him long enough. Quietly and without injury to their reputations, they were disposed of. Swenson could not tolerate incompetence.

The President picked up the red phone. He nodded to Buck to pick up his phone.

"Get Omaha again," he said.

The big clock on the wall showed 10:40.

ch. 9

THE VINDICATORS

Early that morning, while it was still dark, Lieutenant Colonel Grady, the commander of Group 6, had stood beside his Vindicator bomber and examined it in the cold, harsh, unblinking floodlights of the airstrip.

It is a dream bomber, Grady thought. On the ground it looks ungainly. Its wings droop. Its landing gear is very high to allow a great sleek pod to be slung under the regular fuselage. The pod contains extra bombs, or fuel, or air-to-air missiles, or deception apparatus. The pod is beautifully streamlined and makes the Vindicator look somewhat more muscular. On the ground, however, motionless and quiet, the Vindicator has the flamingo look of long improbable legs attached to a powerful body.

Once aloft, however, the Vindicator is sheer beauty. The wings rise, the landing gear retracts, and the Vindicator has a graceful jeweled lapidary look. Inside it is even more sophisticated and elegant. Although it is an enormously intricate piece of machinery, it is flown by only three men. Everything has been miniaturized, transistorized, servo-reinforced, and automated. It is flown by a pilot, a bombardier, and a weapons operator. In fact, the plane has been so mechanized that it could fly, fight, and drop bombs served by only a single man.

There was more than an esthetic and mechanical reason why older men like Grady who flew the Vindicator loved the plane. They realized, some of them, with all the agony of a doomed love affair, that it was probably the last of its type. Maybe the RS-70 would be something like the Vindicator, but the old-timers knew they would not fly them. For them the Vindicator was the last plane. The Vindicator had pushed the cooperation between men and machinery to its uppermost limit. The next plane would surely be so fast, complicated, and intricate that it would be flown without humans aboard. The plane would, in fact, be a guided missile.

But the Vindicator crew, Grady thought proudly, still exercises judgment, the plane still responds to our hands. Our eyes scan the countless instruments. We must bring her screaming and protesting in for taut landings.

The bombardier and weapons operator walked by Grady and climbed into the plane. Like most of the younger airmen they did not glance at the Vindicator. They squeezed into the plane, map cases in their hands, eager to get into their burrows, fasten on their helmets and set about their tasks.

Grady looked up once more at the molded perfection of the Vindicator's shape, ignoring her ungainly landing gear, and climbed aboard. Two minutes later he had her screaming down the runway. Behind him five other Vindicators leaned into the takeoff. Three hours later they were 60,000 feet in the chill air over Alaska. It was just turning daylight.

Once seated and strapped into the Vindicator, the three-man crew cannot move about. The plane is so full of machinery that the three tiny places which the men occupy hold them as tightly as individual burrows. They can talk on the intercoms and they can, if they wish, also talk normally to one another by removing the lower part of their face plates. But the crew almost never talk except over the intercom; in fact, the crew members make very little small talk with one another, partly because their training has discouraged it, and partly because they are seldom close friends.

It had recently become SAC policy to circulate crew members at random among planes. The objective was to get identical performance from all men so that they acted as identical units of a class rather than as individual personalities. Given the cost and the speed and the importance of a Vindicator, no one wanted to count on camaraderie or crew morale for a mission to be successful.

There were no brothers-in-arms aboard a Vindicator, Grady thought. He had met his two crewmen before, but had never talked with them at any length. He would not, he knew, talk much to them while aloft. Each man's burrow was also his duty. Within eyesight were hundreds of dials to watch, gauges to check, knobs to turn.

In case of a fatal emergency each man's burrow would be automatically catapulted out from the plane at an enormous speed and, containing its own oxygen and control system, would bring the crew member safely to earth, or sea. At least that was the theory, but no one had yet been catapulted at maximum speed from a Vindicator without sustaining grave injuries. At maximum speed the ejection capsules were traveling faster than bullets, and the air, so soft and gentle when still, was suddenly hard and brutal. When ejected a man was whacked around unmercifully in the tumbling, spinning capsule. It was something Vindicator crews tried not to think about.

For all these reasons the crewmen of the Vindicator

were a proud and highly qualified lot. Even in their loneliness they took a pride, for the great glistening smooth-packed machinery they flew also gave them a sense of self. The fact that they were locked into the mechanism, embraced by it, yet in control while at their positions gave them a feeling both of individuality and of being bound tightly to an organization.

At 0530 the flight of Vindicators was topped off with jet fuel from two huge jet tankers. They performed the operation flawlessly, sucking thousands of gallons of fuel from the tankers in a matter of minutes. They continued their orderly flight plan, each plane locked into the V-shape of the group, not varying position by more than a few feet although they were flying at over a thousand miles an hour. Beneath them the darkness of the land began to break, immense chains of mountains shouldered up into the faint light, a glacier glittered icily.

They received the radio order to fly toward their Fail-Safe point without comment. They had all done it before. Grady led the group in a great sweeping arc through the sky. They picked up speed and still maintained flawless position. Grady felt the pride of a perfect performance as they completed the change of course. They flew in a nonevasive arrow-straight line. Evasive action was useless at this point and merely expended fuel.

Captain Thomas, the bombardier, handed Grady a form which said "Fuel range past Fail-Safe estimated 3,020 miles."

Grady came up on the intercom and acknowledged the written form.

"Thomas seems all right!" Grady thought to himself. He looked over at the captain. All he could see was a pair of fine brown eyes, dark eyebrows, and a few square inches of white skin. The rest of Captain Thomas' face was covered by a helmet, oxygen mask, and microphone. Grady looked back at Lieutenant Sullivan, the weapons operator. Seeing only the eyes, he realized with a shock that their acquaintance was so slight he could not even reconstruct in his mind what Sullivan looked like. But he was impressed with Sullivan's hands: they had long sensitive fingers and when they moved, to touch a knob or control, they moved with an absolute precision and a definite and utter mood of assurance.

Grady, Thomas, and Sullivan, Grady thought to himself. No good war novel here. The whole damn crew is Anglo-Saxon. What we should have is a Jew in it and an Italian to give color. He almost came up on the intercom to mention this, but stopped himself short. Because of his seniority, Grady had missed the intensive indoctrination which the younger crew members had gone through at various training centers around the United States. He had noticed that they seemed to have almost no sense of humor about their work, and besides, these boys hadn't read the war novels. For a moment, a quick piercing slice of time, Grady felt like an old man, part of an older generation.

In the next moment he forgot everything, for Thomas handed him the clipboard with the information that they were a hundred miles from the Fail-Safe point. At once, with a sense of exquisite control which was very deep in his muscles and his brain, he began a long sweeping curve which would bring him just to the edge of the Fail-Safe point. He knew without having Thomas check that the other five Vindicators had begun to turn with him. This, for Grady, was why he had joined the Air Force. It was an act of pure artistry and it filled him with a thrill of pleasure. He felt the

Vindicator tilt, saw the wings move, felt a slight change
in pressure against his harness and knew that they had
probably lost 125 miles an hour by their long skidding
maneuver movement across the sky. Grady hoped that
they would stay at the Fail-Safe point for a few minutes this morning. It was the one time when he could
still fly the plane with a sense of independence and
autonomy. For at the Fail-Safe point the group commander could fly random patterns at random speeds
as long as he did not go beyond the Fail-Safe point,
and did not vary his altitude by more than 1,000 feet.

The sun shone jaggedly on the western horizon. It
shot out long rays of bright light which illuminated
the high darkness, but left the land black. The outline
of distant mountains was etched sharp. Once, by some
miracle of refraction, a whole glacier flamed blue-
white for a moment and then died. The flash of the
glacier reminded Grady that the people on the land
were still in darkness and it gave him pleasure. In a
few more minutes they would be in first light, but now
the great altitude of the Vindicators gave them sole
possession of the light. The knowledge of dark and
lightness allowed Grady a sense of satisfaction. He
knew it was a childlike sense of superiority. It meant
nothing. But it was precisely for these seemingly childlike reasons that Grady had wanted to fly. This time
his pleasure was short. At once he was thinking of the
day when planes would fly themselves; when flying
would become a combination of engineering and science and men would be merely spectators.

Quite reflexively, as if to demonstrate his control, he
put the Vindicator into a sharp turn. The enjoyment
of it, Grady thought, can be only man's. Machines
could probably do it just as well, but they would have
no sense of excitement, no pleasure at the beauty of

the six planes holding their positions while traveling at high speeds. The outboard planes, with longer sweep to cover, would put on just enough speed to maintain the V-shape.

"Sullivan, how is the group holding formation?" Grady asked over the intercom.

"Perfectly, sir," Sullivan said instantly. "Even No. 6 is not out of position by more than five yards."

Grady smiled behind his oxygen mask. He must remember to compliment Flynn, the pilot of No. 6, when they landed. The No. 6 plane labored under a special disadvantage. Although she carried no thermonuclear weapons, the No. 6 plane was, paradoxically, the most heavily laden of any plane in the group.

In every group this was the plane that carried a maximum load of defensive apparatus and devices. It was this plane which could jam the enemy radar gear, receive and analyze and attempt to foil enemy attack, spread decoys throughout the skies, and act, as Grady had always figured in his mind, as a wise but tuskless elephant might do in leading a group of muscular young bulls into action. The No. 6 plane was always flown by specialists who thoroughly understood the incredible intricacy of its weird perceptions, methods of analysis, and means of defense.

Grady moved the yoke and the Vindicator leveled off. The slight strain on his harness relaxed. He glanced around his limited arc of sky and saw it turning from a crystal gray to a deep endless blue. Then he received two signals which made his body go rigid even before his mind understood fully what had happened. In his earphones there was a sudden beeping noise repeated in short staccato bursts. Automatically he looked down at the Fail-Safe box which was installed between him and the bombardier. For the first time in his flying career the bulb on top of the box was glowing red. Then his intellect caught up with his reflexes: this was the real thing. Both he and Thomas looked up from the Fail-Safe box simultaneously. Thomas' eyes seemed nonchalant. Grady's response was unhesitating. He reached for the S.S.B. radio switch. This would put him in direct contact with Omaha. It was the Positive Control double-check. Immediately, Grady knew, he would hear from Omaha the reassuring "No go." Something had gone wrong with the Fail-Safe box. It would all be corrected. He flipped on the S.S.B. switch. A loud, pulsating drone filled his ears. No voice signal was possible.

"Request permission, sir, to verify," Thomas said crisply.

"Permission granted," Grady said automatically.

To his own ears Grady's voice sounded small and chilled. He was stunned at the tonelessness in Thomas' voice, the expressionless look in his eyes.

Grady reached into the map case beside his seat and took out a pure red envelope which bore in black letters the words "Fail-Safe—Procedure March 13." Thomas was taking out an identical envelope from his map case. As Grady's fingers tore open the envelope he looked at the face of the Fail-Safe box. There were six apertures, each of them about an inch square. Always, until this moment, the apertures had been blank. Now in bold white figures there were three letters and three numbers: CAP–811. The Fail-Safe box was an intricate machine made up of a radio receiving device, plus six wheels, each of which contained either all the letters of the alphabet or the numbers from 1 through 9. When the radio receiver within the box was activated by a direct signal put into the machine by the Intelligence officer on each base and unknown to any crew member, letters and numbers would appear in the aperture.

Grady got his envelope open and took out a thick white 3- by 3-inch card. On the top line was the date and below it were the words and letters CAP–811. He held the card directly over the machine to make sure that he was not mistaken. Thomas, in the meanwhile, had taken out an identical card which he held next to Grady's. They both confirmed that the machine was showing the correct code sequence for the day.

"Request permission to authenticate on the secondary channel, sir," Thomas said.

"Permission granted," Grady said.

Thomas removed a red plastic cover from a dial which was labeled FAIL-SAFE ALTERNATE CHANNEL. Without a moment's hesitation he turned the dial to the right. Instantly the red light and the beeping stopped. The letters and numbers disappeared from the apertures in the Fail-Safe box. Grady scanned the sky again, felt his muscles bulging against the tight harness. His mind was utterly blank. In three seconds the beeping started and the light went on again. The Fail-Safe box was now receiving its signal on a different channel. When Grady looked at the six apertures they again said "CAP–811." Again Grady held his card directly over the apertures and Thomas held his card next to Grady's. They checked.

Grady felt a spasm of doubt, a kind of upwelling of disbelief. It had never happened before, it could not be happening now. He thought of alternatives: he could not radio General Bogan at Omaha. He could keep circling at Fail-Safe, hoping for some other form of verification. And then he looked at Sullivan and Thomas. They were looking at him casually, their eyes unblinking and unquestioning. They were innocently implacable.

Grady felt as if his vertebrae had suddenly fused together. His hands did not shake but he felt all bone and muscle and cartilage. He was aware that Thomas was looking at him with something like puzzlement in his exposed eyes.

Grady felt that something had happened to the vital living parts of his body—the heart, brain, eyes, ears, and tongue had died. He felt for a moment that he would not be able to speak. He ordered his tongue to move, to speak the words he knew he must say.

"I read it as CAP–811," Grady heard his voice say. This was the procedure in which they had been drilled thousands of times, but the voice did not sound like that of Grady. It seemed to come from somewhere in the intercom system, to be a mechanical and inhuman voice.

"I verify your reading as CAP–811," Thomas said.

"We will now both open our operational orders," Grady said, and again the voice did not seem to belong to him.

Grady reached down for the envelope in the map case. For a brief second he saw Sullivan looking at him. Again he had the impression of blankness, the eyes without the mouth and with the exposed flesh squeezed tight by mouthpiece and helmet, told nothing. If the masks and helmets were off, Grady thought, would Sullivan's face be filled with terror? Somehow he doubted it. Sullivan looked back at his tubes and analyzers. Grady began to open the operational plan.

Squarely on the middle of the envelope containing the plan and in small red block letters were the words TOP SECRET. In smaller black letters in the lower left-hand corner was a sentence which said TO BE OPENED ONLY AT SPECIFIC ORDERS AND UNDER CURRENT OPERATING INSTRUCTIONS. In the lower right-hand corner

were the words DESTROY BEFORE CAPTURE OR ABAN-
DONMENT OF AIRCRAFT. The flap closing the envelope
was sealed at three places. The envelope was well designed to accomplish two purposes: it could not be
opened without detection, but it could be opened
easily.

Grady broke the seals and looked at the familiar
format of the operational plan. It was all contained on
a single stiff piece of paper. The rest of the enclosures
were alternative plans, escape routes, survival techniques, a cellophane-wrapped card which Grady knew
gave the names of possible American agents within
Russia and which would dissolve into a shapeless piece
of cellulose the moment it touched water, even the
amount of moisture that one had in his mouth.

The top line of the plan said: "Target: Moscow."
The second line said "Approach and penetration," and
described the altitude and speeds at which they were
to fly. No. 6 plane was to take the lead. There were
detailed instructions on what to do under varying conditions of fighter plane, missile, and antiaircraft
attack.

On another line there were instructions as to bomb
placement and settings. Under optimum conditions
twelve bombs would be laid symmetrically over Moscow to explode at an altitude of 5,000 feet, Vindicators
to bomb from an altitude of 60,000 feet.

In some unguarded and unclassified part of Grady's
mind there was a stunning montage of old motion pictures of bombs exploding at Eniwetok and Los Alamos
and Bikini. The twelve great fireballs would gently
touch and then feeding upon one another would gradually mold into a huge shuddering second-long unbearable white and heloid shimmer of pure heat. Deliberately, and aware that this vision was part sensual,

Grady snapped off the picture. Thomas' large cool blue eyes were looking at him.

"Do you want to come up on the TBS, sir?" Thomas said.

The TBS was a very low-powered radio which would carry only a few miles and was designed for communication between the planes in the group. Its signals were deliberately designed so that they could not be heard beyond a short radius.

"Just a minute, Thomas," Grady said. He felt a strong necessity to do something more but was not clear what. A dread sense of lonely helplessness engulfed him. He knew there was only one explanation for his jammed radio and the "go" order on his Fail-Safe box: the Russians had started an attack. Further hesitation might play into Russian hands. He must follow his orders. This was what all his years of training had been about. No time now for doubts. He shook his head clear.

Grady looked into the eyes of the two strangers—the two magnificent technicians who might have been hundreds of other anonymous experts. Behind his mask he licked his lips. The four eyes rested lightly on him. They were without accusation. He imagined them to be burning with certitude, glowing with an innocent assurance. Indeed, why shouldn't they be? The machines were with them. Somehow, in a way he could not understand, the four cool eyes soothed the nerve in Grady's mind. He felt the surety of command flow back into him. When he spoke, his voice was for the first time his own and it was confident.

"Switch on the TBS, Thomas," Grady said. With utter confidence he picked up the microphone and began to give penetration orders to the group.

ch. 10

THE BRIEFING

1000 HOURS

There was a sergeant standing at the door of the conference room. He saluted Black as he approached.

"General, they have moved the conference to the Big Board room," the sergeant said. He shrugged before Black asked the question. "I don't know why, General. Scuttlebutt is that the Secretary of Defense is going to be there. That draws the flies, so they needed more room."

Black smiled at the ramrod-straight sergeant's jazzy lingo (probably a college boy "doing his time"), turned and almost bumped into General Stark. Stark had heard the sergeant. The two men started off for the elevator which would drop them down into the suspended concrete cube hundreds of feet below the Pentagon.

"I think Swenson wants to see Wilcox in action," Stark said. "I hear that he doesn't think Wilcox was the best choice for SecArmy, so he may be along to roast him a bit."

"Maybe," Black said, but he doubted it. Swenson would size up a new man but not roast him.

The briefing was for Wilcox, the new Secretary of the Army, but beyond that Black did not try to follow Stark's logic. Stark was a contemporary of Black's, they were both young generals on the way up, but they were very different. Stark had made his way politically.

He was quick, but he relied on the brilliance of others to form his career. Black had concluded that Stark would have made general on his own talents, but he enjoyed the Machiavellian role. He traded in gossip, inside dope, and a prescience for what would happen in the future. Stark's being political was not because of laziness or doubts of his own ability. Indeed he worked with great energy and had ability, but he loved the intricacy of personality conflict, was fascinated with the struggle between powerful men. Had he been dull, he would have been a superb manager of prize fighters. Being brilliant, he was a manager of men with ideas. Stark had discovered Groteschele and had managed his career beautifully. As Groteschele became famous Stark became a general officer.

"I read your memo on counterforce credibility the other day," Stark said to Black. He paused. "I don't think Groteschele is going to discuss that today."

Black nodded. It was Stark's way of requesting that a subject be ruled off-limits. He was meticulous in mentioning these informal limitations. Stark played a hard and very tough game, but he played by the rules. Once when he was a chicken colonel a classmate had leaked an item to Drew Pearson. Stark, Black realized, was really morally outraged. He had systematically and with the certitude of a Torquemada broken the colonel's career.

"O.K., but what I said in the memo about credibility still holds," Black said. "It's damned nonsense to spend billions of dollars to develop a 'military posture' which might or might not be credible to the Russians. Who needs more muscle now? Neither side. It gets down to a guess in a psychological game, Stark. This thing of piling bombs on bombs and missiles on missiles when we both have a capacity to overkill *after* surviving a first strike is just silly."

"All right already, O.K., O.K.," Stark said and laughed. "But let's don't argue it today."

"Not in front of the Big Brass," Black said bluntly.

"Oh, my God, Blackie, you're so damned hard-nosed," Stark said.

They smiled at one another. The ground rules for the day had been laid down.

The Big Board room was dominated by the huge illuminated board which occupied an entire wall. The room had the same information-receiving capacity as the War Room at Omaha, but it lacked the array of desk-consoles. This was a room where the Joint Chiefs of Staff and the Secretary of Defense would gather in case of war. They would make decisions which would be implemented by other centers around the world. This was a room for strategy. Omaha, and all its counterparts, was a place for tactics. This was the room where the decisions were made. They were carried out elsewhere.

The Big Board room showed its character. It was a mixture of the executive suite and a military headquarters. Stark and Black were early and the technicians were testing the Big Board. In a random casual way they ran over various systems, cut in on streams of information, threw various projections onto the screen. At the moment, it was tuned in only to the SPADATS system, a shorthand phrase for "space data analysis." The headquarters for SPADATS was located in Colorado Springs, but the information was projected onto the Pentagon screen with a clarity that was uncanny. As General Black watched, SPADATS switched to a Samos III satellite orbiting high in the stratosphere. Words began to crawl across the bottom of the board.

"SAMOS III #15 is moving 20,000 miles an hour,

300 miles above the earth, and has just been instructed to commence photographing the transmitting pictures," the words said. "It is making a routine scan of a part of Russia which includes a Soviet ICBM site. Selective discrimination follows."

The screen dissolved and then hardened up. The picture was different from the ordinary Mercator projection. This was an actual picture of a vast reach of land and lacked the hard lines of longitude and latitude. There was a range of mountains, black on one side, for it was dusk and the eastern side of the range was in shadow. There was the great twisting course of a river and the countless smaller tributaries that flowed into it. The rest of the landscape, seen from so high up, was brown and featureless, bathed in the soft magenta of sunset. In some parts of the screen there were great white clouds and Black estimated that the largest of them was actually a storm front over two hundred miles long.

"The picture will now come to maximum close-up," the words on the bottom of the screen said.

General Black always enjoyed this particular process. It was marvelous, intricate, and it was dizzying. He always had to remind himself that the Samos pictures were being transmitted instantly. What he saw was happening halfway around the world a split second previously. By a combination of processes done at Colorado Springs and in the Samos III itself the picture grew as if the Samos III had turned and were rushing toward the earth.

The picture took on definition with a speed that was terrifying. Water suddenly showed in the great river and the next second it glinted in the tributaries. Villages popped into view as small rectangles and an instant later individual houses could be identified. Huge forests came into focus and then copses and then single trees. The picture centered on a cleared area pocked with the unmistakable circles of rocket silos. Scattered behind revetments were trucks. Casually, for this was only a drill, the picture bore down on one of the trucks. The rest of the ICBM reservation was squeezed out of the picture.

The technician operating Samos #15 was pushing the equipment to its limit. It was a marvel to observe, an almost unbelievable scientific spectacle. It sent Black's mind spinning ahead into the future. He had heard scientists discussing the ultimate possibilities of such long-range technical espionage. One day there would be more than a vague outline of a truck, its details would be clear and sharp. Black's thoughts, captivated by the prospect, filled in the fuzzy picture now on the screen before him. . . . Two men were leaning against the truck. They wore leather boots, Red Army uniforms, and their caps were pushed back on their heads. One of them held out something to the other. The definition became sharper, zoomed in closer, focused on the exchange. Gradually the huge screen was filled by four enormous hands, hair on the back of them, the fingernails dirty. Two fingers of one of the hands held a picture of a girl. The details were contrasty, not clear, but she had a round Slavic face, was smiling, and had her head twisted to one side in a coquettish manner. . . . At this point the picture on the Big Board dissolved and with it Black's fanciful enlargement.

The truck he had just seen on the Big Board was real, though, Black reminded himself. Its driver was completely unaware that his mission had been caught by a camera 300 miles in the sky, transmitted 8,000 miles to an information center, and then projected another 2,500 miles and viewed on this screen with an interval of no more than one second between the action and its depiction on the screen. For the first time the Samos III, its marvelous camera and its future portent, made Black restless. It seemed somehow an invasion of privacy, this subtle and soundless observation of anything on the surface of the world. Blackie, he said to himself, for a man who supported the U-2 flights, all versions of the Samos and a dozen other ventures, you are getting soft. He turned to Stark, determined to make small talk.

"What do you hear about Wilcox?" Black asked.

"The usual stuff, but he pulled a smartie two days ago," Stark said and laughed. "Someone sent him a two-page memo for circulation to the entire staff. Wilcox stuffed a sixty-page essay by Emerson between the two pages and approved it for circulation. It came back all duly initialed, but not one damn comment or question about contents. Wilcox called everyone in for a chewing-out session. They say the blood was ankle deep before he finished."

Black laughed. The story fitted well with his mood. Wilcox sounded like he might liven things up a little. No wonder Stark was a little on edge over today's briefing session.

Black glanced idly around the room. It was filling up now. One group had gathered at the opposite side of the room around the red telephone which connected directly to the President at all times. It was like a fire-insurance policy. Your main hope was that it never would be used.

Black walked toward the long conference table in the center of the room. It was an impressive slab, as if the designers had tried to combine a large board of directors' table with a university graduate-seminar table.

Around the long table, neatly placed, were high-backed leather armchairs. In front of each chair was a precise blotter layout, a fat, large new scratch pad, and two pencils, precisely arranged and guarding either side of the scratch pad. At intervals, in the center of the table, were sterling thermos jugs and official tumblers. Beyond the table on the other side along the wall was "the reservation." There were two rows of slightly less impressive armchairs, carefully designed to show that their occupants, while significant, were the less important staff assistants. The barrier was invisible. Someone could, if he wanted and there was a vacancy, sit at the big table. But no "reservation Indian" ever made that mistake. He might hunger to sit at that table, but he would know precisely when he was qualified.

By now the room contained about twenty men, over half of them in uniform. They had a sameness of look: graying, middle-aged, ruddy, powerful-looking men. Did men look this way because they were the power types, Black wondered, or were they chosen for power because they looked this way? Black watched Stark making his way from group to group. Stark was obviously pleased today, pleased with himself. He was assured that Black would not bring up disturbing doubts about credibility. It would be a Groteschele-Stark day.

These briefings, necessary and valuable, were becoming increasingly unpleasant to Black. The disagreements were difficult to state, but once stated they had to be pursued and they were impossible to resolve. Much as Black loved SAC and the men he worked with in and out of the Air Force, for five years he had had the growing sensation that "things" were slipping out of control.

The calculations of Soviet intention and capability

had started as a straightforward and direct exercise in logic. But at some point the logic had become so intricate, so many elements were involved, so many novelties flowed into the system, that for Black it had blurred into a surrealistic world.

We matched and surpassed their capability and then guessed at their intentions. They then ran a series of tests and surpassed our capability and guessed at our intentions. And then we guessed what they guessed we were guessing. Meanwhile years ago each side had developed the capacity to destroy the other even after suffering a massive surprise first strike.

Black often had the sensation in a meeting that they had all lost contact with reality, were free-floating in some exotic world of their own. It was not just SAC or the Pentagon, Black thought. It was the White House, the Kremlin, 10 Downing Street, De Gaulle, Red China, pacifists, wild-eyed right-wingers, smug left-wingers, NATO, UN, bland television commentators, marchers for peace, demonstrators for war . . . everyone. They were caught in a fantastic web of logic and illogic, fact and emotion. No one seemed completely whole. No one could talk complete sense. And everyone was quite sincere.

Black remembered when the sense of unreality had started. It was a few years before when Groteschele had brought up the Kahn example of what would happen if an American Polaris submarine accidentally discharged a missile at us. The submarine commander would have time to make radio contact and explain what had happened so that SAC would know the missile was an accident. Everyone at the briefing had nodded, thinking that ended the discussion. But Groteschele had persisted. The Soviet would detect the missile in flight, would know it was *our* accident and would detect the explosion. But they would worry about our reaction. How could they be sure that we knew it was our own missile? Might they not fear our "retaliation" and, prompted by this fear, attack us in the confusion? So might not the best Soviet tactic be to strike at once? Indeed, might not the best strategy of each side, even if both knew it was an accident and both knew whose accident, be to strike at once?

They had, Black thought, slipped by that one cheaply. They had decided that all possible steps should be taken to assure against accidental discharge of a missile.

Maybe he should resign his commission. It hit him again. It had been coming to a head within him for a long time. Curious, he thought: he could live with his conscience and with his beliefs in almost any other arm of the service but the one he loved. But SAC and especially his own role in SAC (the link he furnished between operations and the Strategy Analysis and Evaluation Section) made his private thoughts seem like rank heresy. But why did it torment him so much more than it did the others? From the outside they looked happy in their jobs, but who could tell? He supposed he looked as untroubled as they.

A stir on the other side of the room caught his eye. There he was. Groteschele. It was as if he had opened a door from last night's party and walked right into the Pentagon: the same confident, aggressive, jutting thrust. The same stride. In company with Groteschele came Wilcox, Carruthers, the Navy Chief of Staff, and Allen, of the National Security Council.

Everyone in the room had observed the entry of the big brass at the same time. The room "knew" it. An instant before it had been a room with one personality, relaxed and informal. Now it had become a room which had snapped to attention in all sorts of little ways hard to detect. It was the effort everyone was making to seem to behave as if the brass were not there that made the difference.

Groteschele proceeded to the head end of the long conference table. As he did so everyone else began finding seats around the table. It was clear that the Secretary of Defense was either not coming or would arrive late and had sent word for the briefing to start.

Stark handled the opening remarks easily and deftly. Then Groteschele began talking in his positive, slightly patronizing way. He announced the subject: accidental war. The subject had been cropping up in the news lately. There had been a few articles in magazines. The military people had, of course, been working on the problem for years and in detail.

"In the old days, six months ago," Groteschele said with a chuckle, "most of the talk about accidental war was what we now call the madman theory." He went on about the possibility of SAC squadron commanders going berserk and trying to save the world from the Communists.

It hadn't been a joke, as Black knew well. Groteschele's reference was to the special psychological screening system which the Air Force had inaugurated in 1962 to assure that no "mentally unfit persons" would have contact with the preparation or discharge of atomic weapons. Black had been among the first within the Air Force to propose and support the program. He was not sure even now that the problem could be disposed of summarily. The men in SAC were trained for destruction. They were "preprogrammed" to attack Russia.

"What frightened us was not so much the madman problem," Groteschele was saying, "but its opposite: at the last moment someone might refuse to drop the bombs. A single act of revulsion could foil the whole policy of graduated deterrents. Say, for example, that some PFC at a transmitter simply decided not to carry out the order for an attack. That could ruin us right there."

It was behavior in a showdown that the whole SAC training program was designed to prepare for. The tests, the indoctrinations, the training—all were designed to convert normal American boys into automatons.

"Automatons. That's what some of our critics call them," Groteschele said evenly. "But they are also patriots and they are courageous. And haven't we always honored the Marines simply because they did exactly what they were ordered to do?"

To hell with Stark, Black thought.

"Professor Groteschele, one moment," he said. "Isn't it true that the 'go' reflex, the will to attack, is so deeply indoctrinated in our SAC people that even those who pass our psychological screening are more likely to err on the side of 'go,' rather than on withdrawal?"

"At one point, General Black, maybe," Groteschele said. He controlled his impatience with the interruption. "But we analyzed the possibility and built in some protections. Even if you had a madman in command of a wing—even, General, if he had several colleagues who shared his madness, they could not carry out their will."

Groteschele glanced at SecArmy. Wilcox was bent forward attentively. Groteschele then launched into a description of the elaborate checks, decoding systems, and other devices designed to assure that war could not happen through human error.

"It is impossible, quite impossible," Groteschele concluded. "The statistical odds are so remote that it is impossible. Or as impossible as anything can be. The 'go' process will not operate until the President orders it. Even then the Positive Control routine requires a double check."

Black hesitated. He knew Groteschele wanted to move on. But he also knew that Groteschele was skirting a real problem.

"What if the President went mad?" Black asked abruptly. "He is a man under considerable pressure."

Black, as some in the room knew, was the single person there who could, because of his friendship with the President, raise such a question. But Groteschele, with a pang of envy, also knew that Black would have said it even if he had never seen the President.

The shock in the room was palpable. The SecArmy frowned at Black. Groteschele glanced quickly at the SecArmy, then around the table. He knew he did not have to answer Black directly.

"Then we would have trouble," Groteschele said with a laugh. He shrugged, held his hands up as if imploring for common sense. "But it is not likely."

The room relaxed. Black was still unsatisfied, but he knew when to stop. Still, he thought, it was possible. Woodrow Wilson had been President for two years after a stroke. High officials have cracked under the strain. Forrestal had jumped out a window. It was possible for the President to come down with paranoid schizophrenia, Black thought. Not likely, for American politics ruthlessly screened out the unstable personalities, but a possibility.

Maybe, Black thought, the whole damned game is taking me apart. He felt the diminutive terror start somewhere in his guts. It was something to do with the

Dream. At sessions like this the individual stripes of
hide were sliced off his skin, each one leaving him less
intact, more pained. And yet, he thought desperately,
this is where I belong, where I am needed, where I can
contribute. He allowed his mind to wander, searching
for the moment when the real face of the matador
would be revealed, for the instant when the real sword
would slice in between his shoulders and end his inde-
cision.

Groteschele was now proceeding to the possibilities
of machine error. This was new stuff. Nobody really
knew anything about it. Groteschele was always the
statistical type. It was odd how flesh-and-blood human
events disappeared into numbers. Groteschele was ex-
plaining that of course there was a remote mathematical possibility of machine error. He had calculated the
error. In any year the odds were 50 to 1 against accidental war. This, Black remembered, had already been
made public in the Hershon Report. But the report
was several years old and the people at Ohio State who
put it together made it clear that they did not have
access to confidential information. The situation was
much worse than they had reported because everything
had gotten more complicated.

"Putting it another way," said Groteschele, "and
with the present rate of alerts and the present computerized equipment, the odds are such that one accidental war might occur in fifty years."

"Does not the increasing intricacy of the electronic
systems and the greater speed of missiles make that
figure worse each year?" Black asked. He had in mind
the public warning, several years previously, by Admiral L. D. Coates, the Chief of Naval Research, which
admitted what all insiders knew: electronic gear was
becoming so complex that it was outstripping the

ability of men to control it; complexity of new generations of machines was increasing the danger of accidents faster than safeguards could be devised. The
statement had never been countered but simply ignored.

Groteschele paused, smiled tolerantly at Black. The
SecArmy leaned toward one of his aides and asked a
question. The aide looked at Black, smiled as he talked
quickly in SecArmy's ear. Black knew what he was saying: General Black is the professional heretic.

"In theory, yes," Groteschele said. "But we completely pre-test every component and every system is
checked by another. The chance of war by mechanical
failure is next to zero."

This was not true, but Black did not choose to con-
test it. He forced his anger down and deliberately
looked at the Big Board. It was like a vast moving
mosaic, decorative rather than functional. Blips appeared, grew bright, traveled short distances, then vanished. The Big Board was not taken seriously until the
light over it indicated that someone had decided to
come to some degree of alert.

In how many places in the world, Black mused, were
there just such strategy boards run by just such computer systems, picking up, identifying, and discarding
just such radar signals? Our big operation at Omaha,
of course. Probably at least one other standby
"Omaha" at some other part of the country. Then
there was the President's bomb shelter: probably another computerized strategy board layout there. Maybe
there was more than one Presidential bomb shelter.
Maybe one at Camp David, or the summer White
House, or who knows where else.

Then, in addition, he knew there was always, every
minute of every day, a converted KC-135 aloft: a minia-

ture, emergency "Omaha," in case everything else should blow. Probably another one on some super aircraft carrier somewhere. Still another on one of the nuclear submarines. How many others? Several in England, certainly, France, perhaps, and West Germany. Russia? Yes, surely there would be almost as many as there are in the United States.

Black knew that four KC-135s were reserved exclusively for Presidential use as a flying command post in case of emergency. Since 1962 they had been scattered about the country so that the President was never far from one. Whenever the President flew overseas one of these planes was quietly and unobtrusively included in his escort.

Surely each one of them in every country was similar. And the men in them, too. Today, throughout the world in each one of the Big Board rooms, staffed by busy, competent, dedicated men, probably the same signals were being received, analyzed, and projected. The big brass everywhere was watching similar strategy boards, studying the same blips, thinking out, or talking out, the same strategic puzzles Groteschele was now discussing.

Black plugged back into the discussion. Groteschele was now classifying various types of possible machine errors. Accidental war caused by some machine failure. Miscalculation by the computers, misinterpretation by the staff of human interpreters (the "overriders" as the computer boys call them). And then the big one, electronic failure.

Big, Black thought, because no one knows anything about it. We just know that in any system so complex and so dependent upon intricate electronic equipment, the possibility of electronic failure or error must always be borne in mind.

"But the Positive Control Fail-Safe system is the ultimate protection against mechanical failure," Groteschele was saying, his voice heavily persuasive. This was the ultimate safety factor in the whole system. This was where it all rested. So, we were all reassured. And indeed, Groteschele was very reassuring today, except that his nervous chuckle kept getting in the way. Black understood why. Groteschele knew more than he was saying.

It just was not that simple. Everyone knew it who had anything to do with the black boxes of the Positive Control system. Their components were 100 per cent double-checked on regular rotation schedules. Every possible condition to which the equipment might be subjected in operation was simulated. It was simulated in actual duplication systems and it was also simulated on computers with meticulously devised mathematical formulas expressing every possible way the equipment might fail. On computers the bombers were "flown" and the "go" signals were "given."

Variable atmospheric conditions could be predicted, operational deterioration of the equipment could be estimated, vibration characteristics of the Vindicator bombers could be factored in. Stress variables could be translated into mathematical formulas, and with these formulas the computers could test out the black boxes.

But the whole system had one big flaw in it. Nobody could ever be certain that the black boxes would actually work properly in a showdown. The reason was simple. There had never been a showdown, and there could never be a sure test showdown.

A showdown meant war. The whole Positive Control system really depended on equipment that could never really be tested until the time came for its first use, and because of this nobody could ever really know in advance whether or not it would work right. The Fail-Safe machines could be truly tested only once: the single time they were used.

There was ample evidence from the experience of the Electra planes and the now obsolete DC-6s that a serious flaw in an elaborate machine could survive every experimental situation—and then in real practice come completely unstuck.

This was material for the grim inside humor which went the rounds of SAC gossip. The DC-6 had been a beautiful drawing-board plane, except that the first ones to go into service caught fire in flight. Then it was discovered that the one thing they hadn't calculated was what flight wind currents would do to fuel overflow spillage. The fuel was deflected by an invisible band of air to a point directly behind the engines where the air-intake vents sucked in the gas spillage, converting the plane's storage compartment into a quite unplanned fire chamber.

Great corporations can also be injured when their computerized positive control systems break down. Black remembered the consternation a few years back when *Fortune* had demonstrated this point about General Dynamics. The Convair 990 was a 200 million-dollar demonstration of the fallibility of computerized simulation. Convair designed a drawing-board airplane that checked out to be the fastest commercial jet in the computer "flight tests," so they decided to save money, skip the costly prototype stage, and go directly into production. Only the 990 didn't perform as designed. Nobody knew why, and the enigmatic computers that had been so reassuring could not be charged with malfeasance.

General Black also knew that Groteschele was sliding past another important factor. Each machine had to be adjusted and installed by men. And men, regardless of their training, suffered from fatigue and boredom. Many was the time that General Black had seen a tired and irritated mechanic turn a screwdriver a half turn too far, fail to make one last check, ignore a negative reading on a testing instrument. On a plane, such errors would mean only that an expensive piece of machinery and a few men would be lost. On a Fail-Safe black box—and the men who adjusted and installed them had not the remotest notion of what they were—the slightest accident could trigger the final disaster.

Black glanced around the table. Stark was watching the strategy board. New blips had just appeared and Stark was toying nervously with his pencil as he followed their progress. Black looked at Wilcox. He sensed that Wilcox was mentally rejecting the possibility of accidental war. It depressed Black, and he felt that he should do more, but he knew he could not.

Groteschele's patronizing voice reached back into Black's consciousness. Now the voice was talking about what if there should be an accident. An "interesting" problem, it was saying.

"Suppose the Russians caused an accident," suggested Groteschele. "Suppose it were a true accident. Suppose it was a 50-megaton missile aimed for New York or Washington, what could be done? How could we really know it was an accident? How could they prove it? Would it make any difference if they could? Even if we believed it to be an accident, should we not retaliate with everything we had?"

Good questions, Black agreed, but no answers were offered. It didn't seem to be a real discussion about real problems. Black remembered the flurry of excitement a few years before when some scholar had published a paper on the strategy of surrender. The argument

had been simple. If either side strikes first, is not surrender the only possible strategy for the other side?
What is to be gained by retaliation? There had been
a series of Congressional hearings, and then no one
heard any more about the strategy of surrender.

Black's thoughts were interrupted. Groteschele had
stopped talking. Everyone was looking at the Big
Board.

The large alert signal at the top of the board had
flashed on. The board still showed the blips Black had
just seen Stark watching. The six blips were six bomber
groups in the air almost at their Fail-Safe points. There
was also an unidentified blip somewhere between
Greenland and Canada. Black noted that the clock
above the Big Board showed 10:28. Groteschele paused
to look around at the Big Board. He turned back to
his audience, saying, "Well, we're in luck. A nicely
arranged alert for our discussion. You can't count on
these for a Pentagon lecture any more. The equipment
has become so much more accurate that they only occur about six times a month now."

Groteschele tried to recapture the attention of his
audience by delving into an explanation of the need
for maximum reaction times in evaluating an alert.
Even though more and more ICBMs were becoming
operational every day, he explained, they would not be
used immediately in a crisis. They had the defects of
their virtues. They were too quick. They allowed too
little time for thought and the detection of error. This
had led to a return to manned bombers for a first-strike
retaliation rather than immediate reliance on the
newer long-range rockets. The bombers provided hours
of revaluation and analysis, the rockets only thirty
minutes. Besides, regardless of the outcome, even if the
entire country were devastated the rockets could al-

ways be thrown in at the end.

The Big Board was proving more seductive than Groteschele. His voice rose slightly.

"Now if the Soviets really have a high-level satellite which carries a rocket, then we are in danger," he said and paused, his voice heavy. "Real danger. For then the reaction time would be down to fifty or sixty seconds. Not even enough time to call the President."

But Groteschele had lost his audience. All eyes remained glued on the Big Board. Soon the foreign unidentified blip would get identified, and fade off the board . . . a Canadian airliner off course, a heavily compacted flight of birds, and so on. Then the SAC groups would veer off their lines of flight and disappear from the board. Yes, Black could see, it was happening now.

The foreign unidentified blip was fading out. The room, which had grown quietly tense, now relaxed. Cigarettes were lit and pencils returned to doodling exercises as men tried to shed their nervousness in their private ways. Soon a messenger would come in with SPADATS' explanation of what the blip had been. Then Groteschele could resume, happily monopolizing the attention of his audience again.

One by one, five SAC groups began in turn to veer off. Only one group was left on the board. Then as Black watched unbelievingly it flew past its Fail-Safe point. He glanced at Stark. Stark was erect in his chair. Wilcox was oblivious of what had happened. Most of the other officers had turned back to Groteschele. Stark stared at Black. He raised his eyebrows.

Black looked at Groteschele. What happened to Groteschele came and went so quickly that Black was not certain he had seen correctly: Groteschele's eyes glittered and he shuddered. To Black it seemed an expression composed of apprehension, excitement, delight, and opportunity. Then it was gone. Groteschele stood absolutely still, staring at the board. Black realized that only three men in the room fully understood what had just happened.

Then the whole board went black. Apparently the operator did not think the action of Group 6 to be important. Maybe he had just not noticed it. Stark scribbled a note to Black. It said, "Ever see a group go past Fail-Safe before?" Black shook his head. Stark started to get up from his chair. Black knew he was going to check with the tactical officers in another office. Stark froze halfway up.

A phone had rung. It did not ring loud, but it did ring distinctively. A steady persistent unbroken ring. It was the red phone. None of the men in the room had heard it before. Wilcox was not aware of the import of the ring, but he sensed the tension around him. He came to rigid attention. An Army general ran across the room to the red phone. It did not look at all unseemly for a general to be dashing to answer a phone. In fact it seemed to be done in nightmarish slow motion.

The general listened for a moment. He turned back to the room woodenly. Looking at Wilcox he said with excessive clarity: "Mr. Secretary, the President is calling from the White House bomb shelter. He wants to speak to the senior person present. That is you. I am directed to see that the Joint Chiefs and the Secretaries convene here immediately." He laid the receiver beside the phone and dashed from the room.

Wilcox stumbled around out of his chair and virtually fell toward the phone, stealing a look at the Big Board as he did so.

The Big Board had lit up again. And now it projected just two things; the Fail-Safe point of Group 6 and the blip of Group 6. They were already inches apart. Group 6 was headed toward Russia.

ch. 11

THE URGENT MINUTES

1039 HOURS

"There is nothing further to report, Mr. President," General Bogan said. Colonel Cascio was staring straight at the Big Board. "Group 6 is about two hundred and sixty miles past Fail-Safe and continuing on what is apparently an attack course."

"Do you know what happened to them?" the President's voice asked.

"No, sir, we do not," General Bogan said. "There is a chance, an outside chance, that they made a navigational error and will swing back."

"Have they ever made a navigational error that big before?" the President asked crisply.

"No, sir," General Bogan said. "But when you're traveling over 1,500 miles an hour, a little error can throw you a long distance off."

"Let's rule that one out," the President said. "Why haven't you been able to raise them yet by radio?"

"We don't know for sure, Mr. President," General Bogan said. "We have tried them on all frequencies and can't make contact."

"Why?" the President broke in, his voice impatient.

"First, there might be natural meteorological disturbances, and our weather people say there is a big electrical storm just behind the Vindicators," General Bogan said. "Secondly, the Russians might be jamming our radio reception—"

"Why the hell would they do that?" the President asked.

"I don't know," General Bogan said, paused, and then went on. He spoke slowly, his voice unconvincing. "There is a remote possibility that their Fail-Safe black boxes might be giving them a 'go' signal *and* that Russian jamming is preventing our verbal Positive Control system from operating."

"Is that possible?" the President said sharply.

General Bogan paused. Then his voice gained confidence. "No, Mr. President, the odds against both systems failing at the same time are so high I think that is impossible," General Bogan said. He was aware that Colonel Cascio was watching him. He felt an undefined and nagging discomfort. "Almost impossible."

"All right," the President said. "Now if we do regain radio contact will they respond to a direct order from me to return?"

"They will answer, sir," General Bogan said, "providing we can reach them by radio within the next five minutes." Then he paused. "However, if after that time their black boxes still tell them to 'go' they are under orders not to turn back even if someone who sounds like you orders them back. You can see the reason for that. The enemy could easily abort a real attack just by having someone around who could make a good imitation of your voice. Those people in the Vindicators have to obey the Fail-Safe mechanism. They can't rely on voice transmissions."

Something like a sigh came over the speaker.

"All right, let me sum up," the President said. "For reasons which are unknown to us Group 6 has flown past its Fail-Safe point and right now seems to be on an attack course toward Russia. We can't raise them by radio, but there's an outside chance that we may later. What is their target?"

"Moscow," General Bogan said bluntly.

"Holy Mary, Mother of God," the President said in a low and very slow voice. He said it again, as if to shake off a terrible reality. There was for a fleeting moment something of the acolyte, the altar boy, in his voice. When he spoke again, however, his tone was strong. "What is the next step?"

"If we follow standard operating procedure the next step would be to order the Skyscraper fighter planes which are standing by at Vindicators Fail-Safe to attack them," General Bogan said. Colonel Cascio's head jerked sideways and he stared at General Bogan. "The fighters would first try to raise the bombers visually and divert them. Failing that, they would press home an attack with air-to-air missiles and cannon fire."

There was a long pause on the line. Then the President spoke.

"Who gives that order, General?" the President asked.

"You do, sir," General Bogan said.

"General, order the fighters to start their pursuit of Group 6," the President said without a moment's hesitation. "I assume that will take a few minutes at least. Tell them to hold fire until they get the direct order from me. I would like to delay the actual firing on the group until the last possible moment."

Bogan and Cascio heard the click of the President putting down the phone without waiting for an acknowledgment.

1041 HOURS
THE PENTAGON

Swenson had come into the Big Board room. He was accompanied by two of his aides. They were both tall men and they emphasized his slightness.

Swenson stood at the door for a moment and looked at the people in the room. They had all come to attention, had torn their eyes away from the Big Board. Swenson made his count, nodded, and they all sat down. He walked to the chair at the head of the table, and as he reached it the red phone, which had been moved directly in front of him, rang. As he leaned forward to pick up the phone Swenson looked casually at the Big Board. He seemed little in the chair—little and very confident and orderly. His presence eased the tension in the room.

"Yes, Mr. President," Swenson said.

It was possible to link the red phone to a loudspeaker so that everyone in the room could hear it. Swenson chose not to do that.

"Mr. Secretary, General Bogan at Omaha has told me that he recommends that we order our fighter planes accompanying Group 6 to shoot them down," the President said. This was not precisely the truth and the President knew it. However, he wanted Swenson to face the decision most abruptly and nakedly. "The decision is mine, but I would like the advice of you and your people."

"Mr. President, do you want me to discuss this with them right now or shall we call you back?" Swenson said. He was glad he had not put the conversation on the loudspeaker. In Swenson's methodical mind was stored the fact that shooting down the bombers was standard operating procedure. By phrasing the problem this way the President was forcing them to make an evaluation rather than follow a set procedure.

"I will hold the line for your opinion," the President said.

"General Bogan at Omaha has recommended to the President that our fighters be ordered to shoot down Group 6," Swenson said in a calm voice. "The President is awaiting our advice before giving that order. Gentlemen, what do you have to say?"

Of the men at the table only Swenson and Black knew that this was standard operating procedure. Of the rest of the group Wilcox was the most shocked. His face flushed.

"Jesus Christ, order Americans to shoot down other Americans?" Wilcox asked. "It would . . . it is indecent. I'm against it."

Swenson's eyes were veiled. He looked around the table. Groteschele's hand went up.

"Mr. Secretary, I oppose it on the grounds that it is premature," Groteschele said levelly. He wanted to overcome Wilcox's apparent hysteria. "After all, sir, our planes have not yet reached Soviet air space. In fact, they are hundreds of miles away from it."

Swenson's face was still impassive; he might have been the presiding officer at a small Midwestern corporation's board of management meeting.

"We must do it and at once," Black said flatly. "First, if we do not give the order now the fighters may not be able to overtake the Vindicators. Secondly, if we delay the order we lose any bargaining position that we might need later with the Russians. They are watching Group 6 and our fighters right now and are trying to guess what we are doing. And keep in mind that there are other steps after this and they involve much more than the crews of six bombers. A lot may hinge on the Russians believing what we tell them. You can be damned sure that the moment those planes penetrate Soviet air space the President is going to be in a tough spot talking with the Russians and will need everything he can get to bargain with them."

Another point occurred to Black: if only one fighter made it and brought down one bomber perhaps the others would turn back—but he did not really believe it. He knew that the Vindicators would bore in even if they had to do it singly. They had been too well trained to panic at the sight of a single bomber exploding. They had also been steeled to the possibility that enemy planes, simulated to look like American planes, might make an attack.

Swenson's eyes opened fully; they were bright and attentive. He glanced quickly around the rest of the men at the table. There appeared to be nothing left to say. Black was the one who had summed it up. Swenson knew that some of the others didn't agree, but sensed that Black had the logic and the facts. He admired Black's cool presentation and sensed that the President would be thinking in much the same way.

"Mr. President, it is our belief that it is a tactical decision, but it is our unanimous view that the fighters should be ordered in," Swenson said, looking directly at Wilcox.

Swenson put the phone back in its cradle. Wilcox's face was a mottled pink.

1042 HOURS
THE WHITE HOUSE

Buck had heard all of the conversations. He stared at the President. The President had one leg thrown over the arm of his chair and occasionally he puffed at a long thin cigar. His posture was reassuring to Buck. Everything that Buck had heard on the telephone had tightened his stomach muscles and only the President's physical ease kept Buck from trembling.

"Get Omaha again," the President said into the phone.

Almost instantly they were through.

"Yes, sir, Mr. President," General Bogan's voice said.

"General, order the fighters in," the President said.

"Let me confirm that," a strange voice said on the circuit. "This is Colonel Cascio, General Bogan's assistant. Do you want the fighters to press home the attack even if they have to go to afterburners? That will nearly triple their consumption of fuel and almost certainly mean that none of them will be able to make it back." The voice paused, then spoke with more firmness, almost a tough arrogance. "Mr. President, those fighters are America's first line of defense against a Russian attack. In putting them on afterburners to chase our own bombers we will be sacrificing our fighters' defensive capability at the very time we may need it most—the Russians may attack at any moment now."

The President paused. Buck watched him scribble some words on his pad. They said, "Sacrifice fighters convince Russians an accident? Give up defensive capacity of fighters . . . will they believe?"

"General Bogan, I repeat the order," the President said, coldly.

"Mr. President, the fighters swung away from the Vindicators when they got the all clear," General Bogan said. "In effect, the Vindicators and the Skyscrappers have been flying in opposite directions for some minutes. The Skyscrappers have only a slight edge of speed over the Vindicators. There is some doubt that they can overtake the Vindicators."

"I repeat, General Bogan, that the fighters are to overtake and shoot down the Vindicators even if it means going to afterburners," the President said.

1044 HOURS
OMAHA

"Colonel Cascio, order the fighters to attack Group 6," General Bogan said as he put the phone down.

Colonel Cascio came halfway out of the chair in a spasm of protest.

"That means that you have decided our bombers are making an accidental strike on Moscow?" Colonel Cascio asked. His voice was shocked, but there was also a hard underlay of rebellion.

"I have and the whole damn system has," General Bogan said savagely. "The machines, the men, the diplomats, the President, all of us. Why the hell do you think we have fighter planes following the Vindicators? Just to protect them if they 'go'? Don't be silly. We always knew that one of their tasks was to shoot down the Vindicators if there was a mistake. All right, there has been a mistake. Get on the horn to the fighters, Colonel."

Colonel Cascio lifted his hand. It was a peculiar gesture. It was partly a plea for time, partly as if he were warding off some grotesque thing, partly the gesture a child makes when threatened.

"General, the fighters—"

"Colonel, get on that horn and give the order," General Bogan said. "Every second you delay takes them further away from the Vindicators."

Colonel Cascio began to move the levers and buttons that would put him in direct voice communication with the fighters. But even as he did this he kept talking.

"Even if they catch the bombers, General, which isn't likely, they won't have enough fuel to get back," Colonel Cascio said. "They'll go down in the ocean or on enemy territory."

A voice came up on the War Room intercom. It was the officer in charge of Fighter Direction.

"General Bogan, we are in voice communication with Tangle-Able-1," the voice said. "You can talk to them on Channel 7, Single Side Band."

General Bogan nodded and Colonel Cascio lifted a lever. Instantly there was the blurred static-heavy sound of long-distance radio transmission.

"Do I tell them in code or clear language?" Colonel Cascio asked.

"Clear language," General Bogan said. "That is standard."

Colonel Cascio knew this. It had been hammered out after months of discussion that if a situation arose in which our own fighters must shoot down our own planes there would be no disadvantage and, possibly, some advantage in having the enemy hear the transmission.

"This is Tangle-Able-1," a young strong voice said through the static. "I read you five by five at last transmission."

Colonel Cascio bent forward and spoke into a microphone, his voice only slightly thin and weak. "Tangle-Able-1, this is Colonel Cascio on the Omaha staff." Sweat now stood out on his forehead. "Group 6 has flown through the Fail-Safe point and is on an attack course towards Moscow. It is a mistake. I repeat: it is a mistake. Go to afterburners and overtake and attack Group 6."

There was a moment's silence. Then the young voice came back loud and clear.

"Roger. Go to afterburners and overtake and attack Group 6," the voice said.

Colonel Cascio leaned forward and switched the lever off. To General Bogan, watching, Colonel Cascio's posture was that of a child crying soundlessly.

1044 HOURS
THE SKYSCRAPPERS

The lead plane of the six Skyscrappers made a long sweeping turn. The voice of the captain in charge of the flight came up on the TBS radio. He knew he could be heard only by the six planes in the flight.

"I don't know what those mother-grabbers back in Omaha are doing, but you all heard the order," the captain said. "We overtake and shoot down the Vindicators."

"That will be the day," a twenty-one-year-old pilot of one of the fighters said. "Us with a 50-mile-an-hour edge on the Vindicators and those bastards halfway to Moscow already."

"By SOP they will divert a KC-135 to refuel us," another voice said sweetly. "It does 560 an hour, we do 1,600. By the time we run out of fuel they'll be about a thousand miles away. Everything is beautifully organized."

"Don't knock the staff people," a voice said mockingly. "After you run out of fuel you make a thousand-mile glide back to the tankers. Any flier worth his salt should be able to do that in a Skyscrapper."

Someone laughed briefly. They knew that the elegant little plane with its short wings would start to drop like a stone as soon as it lost power.

None of the six pilots thought they would overtake the Vindicators. They knew they would not be able to fly their fighters back to their bases. If they thought of anything they thought of two things. First, would the ejection capsule and parachute really operate at 1,600 miles an hour? Second, how long could a man live in arctic waters?

"Cut the chatter," the captain in command said. "On the mark, go to afterburners."

The captain counted from five down to one and then said quietly, "Mark." Six fingers shifted six levers. Against the six young and doomed bodies the seatbacks slammed relentlessly. From a hundred tubes toward the end of the jet engines raw fuel poured into the hot flames of the exhaust. The planes trembled under the instantaneous acceleration and then steadied down to the chase.

1044 HOURS
THE VINDICATORS

Lieutenant Colonel Grady looked out and down. In front of the Vindicators the surface of the Pacific was black, so black it was purple. It looked not at all like water, but like thickened darkness.

Grady felt motelike, tiny, pushed by the great expanding aura of light behind him. He wished, in a quick irrational flash, that the sun would hold. To fly in darkness seemed protective.

Grady glanced quickly at the other two men in the Vindicator. They were intent on their instruments.

Suddenly Grady envied them their innocence with a remorse so great that it was close to hatred.

1045 HOURS
THE WHITE HOUSE

"Get the Pentagon back again," the President said.

The President's leg was still tossed over the arm of the chair, his cigar had developed only a small ash.

Swenson came up on the telephone.

"Mr. Secretary, if our fighters shoot down the Vindicators it will be tragic, but the big problem will be over," the President said. "I would like your people to be thinking about what we do if the fighters cannot shoot down the bombers."

ch. 12

WORDS, STATISTICS, AND OPINIONS

Swenson looked around the room. For a moment he debated whether or not to turn the Big Board off, but decided to leave it on as a reminder of the urgency of the situation. The problem was to get the fullest possible answers to the questions in the least amount of time.

"Gentlemen, Omaha is plugged in with us and General Bogan and Colonel Cascio are listening in at that end," Swenson said. "Mr. Knapp, the president of Universal Electronics, and Congressman Raskob are also at Omaha on a visit. I have given them permission to listen to our discussion and to comment if they have something to say."

Swenson's voice had been almost excessively calm. Now when he spoke again, there was in his voice the sharp metallic ring of urgency.

"In a very short time the President will be back to us and he will want answers to some questions," Swenson said. "First, what happened? Secondly, what to do if the fighters cannot overtake the Vindicators? Thirdly, what are the Russians going to think of all this? Fourth, what will they do about it? The discussion will be only on these points."

Swenson glanced around the table. His eyes stopped when they came to Black. Black's unblinking eyes, deep-sunken, almost invisible, looked steadily at him.

"General Black, will you very quickly bring us up to date on what has happened," Swenson said.

"Mr. Secretary, the first thing to face is the fact that we are flying blind," Black said. "No one knows exactly what has happened. All we know for sure is that SAC Group No. 6 flew through its Fail-Safe point and, unless stopped, will attempt to make an attack on Moscow. Basically only two things could have happened: a compound mechanical failure or someone in Group 6 has gone berserk."

"Statistically a double mechanical failure is almost impossible," Groteschele growled.

"But it is conceivable, is it not?" Swenson asked the question so sharply that Black wondered if somehow he had been briefed on the earlier discussion.

Groteschele hesitated. "Of course it is possible, but . . ." Groteschele said, but stopped when Swenson swung his head away.

Bogan's voice boomed over the loudspeaker. Somewhere a technician adjusted the volume and it seemed almost as if Bogan were in the room.

"I agree with General Black, but Colonel Cascio has a doubt," General Bogan said. "Very briefly his argument is that the Russians have devised a way to mask the real position of Group 6, which is probably flying back toward the States. What we read as Group 6 on the radar is actually a group of Soviet bombers up there for precisely one reason—to lead us to believe that we have accidentally launched a bomber group at Russia. I disagree with this analysis. But it should be considered."

Around the table there were multiple signs of restlessness. Groteschele scratched on a pad of paper. Others reached for cigarettes. Stark looked down the table at Black. Black remained impassive, but he tensed for Swenson's reply. A lot would depend on Swenson's reaction to Cascio.

"Thank you, General Bogan," Swenson said, without taking his eyes from Black's face. "I agree with your evaluation of Colonel Cascio's argument. Now, General Black, will you continue?"

"Every surveillance device we have has been thrown on the Russians," Black said. "They have seven bomber groups in the air at this moment. None of these can reach America without refueling. None of them is flying an attack course. All are following hold patterns inside Soviet control borders. An abnormally large number of Russian fighters are in the air, in fact approximately half of their fighters are air-borne. However, a simultaneous computer analysis of their flight patterns does not reveal a definite aggressive pattern. The Russians have launched no rockets as yet. Our devices which pick up sudden discharges of energy are probably our most reliable surveillance instruments. I am confident that the Soviets have not used their ICBMs as yet."

"What do you make of it?" Swenson invited anyone's comment but his tone said "keep it short."

"They have the same problem with our Group 6 as we had earlier with the UFO," Allen of the National Security Council said. It was the first time he had spoken. "They don't know what it is, why it is there, or even if it is ours."

"The best answer happens also to be the simplest," Black said calmly. "The Russians probably picked up the same unidentified object we did. They understood why our planes started to fly toward their Fail-Safe points. This thing has happened scores of times and they have gotten familiar with the pattern. So far no sweat. But when one of our groups did not turn back they knew it as soon as we did. That accounts for their launching an abnormal number of fighter planes. My guess is that right now they do not consider our Group 6 to be hostile or aggressive although the behavior of our fighter planes will probably begin to worry them in a few minutes. If they see the fighters actually try to shoot down the Vindicators, they will know there has been some big and dangerous mistake."

"Or they will think we are sending them in as a ruse," Groteschele said sharply.

"That is correct," Black said. "Whichever of these interpretations they make will be alarming to them. Even so, I would not expect them to take any kind of retaliatory or offensive action that could not be recalled unless Group 6 actually invades their air space or we start to take what appears to be broader hostile action in support of Group 6."

Allen of the NSC walked back to his chair at the table. He had been speaking on a phone at the far end of the room.

"Mr. Secretary, I have been talking to the National Security Agency people," Allen said. "As you know they keep a 24-hour a day surveillance on Soviet communications, making tape recordings of everything that is said." (Black looked at Stark. They had both heard that when the U-2 went down with Powers the NSA people had listened to the Soviet antiaircraft crews talking on the radio and knew that Powers had lost power and dropped to 36,000 feet.) Allen went on, "They tell me that there is no significant increase in Soviet military communications and they estimate that right now the Soviet military apparatus is not on a full alert or in aggressive position."

"Professor Groteschele, would you care to comment

on what the Russians might be thinking?" Swenson said.

General Bogan's voice cut in flatly and without apology from Omaha.

"Who is this Groteschele, Mr. Secretary?" General Bogan asked. "Why is he sitting in?"

Swenson's reply was polite but edged with ice. "Professor Groteschele is a recognized authority on many of the matters before us and was invited here at the express wish of the President."

Groteschele smiled. Quite unconsciously, he stood up, the posture of the professor addressing students. He chuckled and then abruptly broke it off. He had seen Swenson's face, stony hard, eyes a flat commanding blue. The look Swenson gave Groteschele was as explicit as a command.

Then Groteschele, to Black's astonishment, spoke crisply, without ambiguous words and without evasiveness. The Russian leaders are Marxist ideologues, he said, not normal people. They believe history is determined by nonhuman events which will assure the victory of Communism. Nuclear war would interrupt the process of this historical determinism. Russians have more to lose by war than we. Therefore, an American first attack would bring Russian surrender rather than nuclear retaliation.

Black felt a reluctant admiration for Groteschele. He disagreed with most of what Groteschele said, but when the chips were down and the crisis came, the man had stated his position without reservations.

"Just why would they surrender if we hit them?" Swenson asked.

"They are human calculating machines, Marxist fanatics, not motivated by rage or hate," Groteschele said evenly. "If they are hit first, even by one or two bombs, they know that if they retaliate they can destroy us or a substantial part of our people and resources. But they also know that we would have a second strike capacity which would devastate them. The important thing, for the Marxist, is to keep at least part of the Soviet Union intact. They would not be particularly worried about the survival of a capitalist country. In fact, many of them believe that capitalism must play itself out to its inevitable historical defeat before Communism can really succeed. To put it crudely: they want to be around for a while, and if the price they have to pay is that some free countries are also around they will pay it. They will not allow the world to be destroyed. They aim to dominate it eventually and they want it reasonably intact. So they would surrender."

Swenson looked back at the Big Board. The fighter blips were very close to Group 6. He swung around abruptly.

"In short you believe they are utterly in the grip of an ideology," Swenson said. "Their logic and their fanaticism will make them act in a perfectly determined manner. Is that correct?"

Groteschele hesitated. He could not tell how Swenson evaluated this argument. He took a deep breath.

"Yes, sir, that is what I think," Groteschele said slowly.

Again Black felt a flash of admiration. Groteschele was putting a whole career, a reputation, a school of thought, nakedly on the line. There was a good chance that before the day was out it would face judgment.

Swenson looked around the table, his silence inviting comments.

Groteschele could not afford the silence.

"What I am arguing, Mr. Secretary, is that although

my interpretation seems unusual and novel it is simplicity itself," Groteschele said. "We should do nothing. If I am correct the Russians will surrender, and if our leaders are sufficiently resourceful the threat of Communism is over forever."

"Do nothing," Swenson said quietly.

Groteschele *was* tough. Swenson was an amateur historian and a student of modern leadership. He had learned that all of the powerful leaders had known when to wait. The capacity to do nothing at the right time was part of great statesmanship. Swenson did not for a moment accept Groteschele's analysis or his evidence. But his conclusion might be right.

"Mr. Secretary, I think all of that is a lot of crap," General Bogan's voice cut in harshly from Omaha. "Look, I am under the gun more than any of you. I have to take all of this stuff from the computers and translate it into action. Don't kid yourself. There are going to be three or four Russian generals at crucial spots who will react exactly the way I do: the best defense is a good offense. They will attack without giving a damn about what Marx or anyone else said."

"Any other comments?" Swenson asked.

Groteschele had seated himself, but he was bent forward in his chair, tense with excitement. By his own act of will, he was almost at the point of committing the total energies of one hundred and ninety million people in an enormous military decision.

Swenson glanced at Black.

"Everything in Groteschele's argument depends upon the extent to which Russian leaders are dominated by Marxist ideology," Black said. "He believes that domination is complete. I think he is wrong. The CIA did a long study on this and it came to the conclusion that Soviet leaders made their decisions as

Russians and later justified them as Marxists. Forget they are Communists and judge their acts objectively and they behave much like leaders in any other country."

On the Big Board the fighter blips were seemingly only inches away from the Vindicators. Everyone listened to Black, but they were watching the Big Board. The lead blip suddenly ejected two tiny phosphorescent dots that sped out ahead of it. Then the blip began a long lazy downward curving arc. Black knew that the plane had flamed out because of a lack of fuel, had fired its missiles, and was now falling toward the icy waters. He sensed the pilot's first sensation of terror, the awful feeling of a dead plane under one's hands. The suspense of waiting for the capsule to eject, the slow swinging parachute's descent into the icy arctic waters, and the last few numbing moments before death.

Swenson's voice cut in with authority.

"The lead fighter has gone in," he said. "We can assume that none of the others will be successful. Now where do we stand?"

Groteschele made an oblique approach to pin down his position.

"Mr. Secretary, let me remind you about the Doomsday tapes. Both the Soviet Union and we have the ability to launch a first strike, to have most of the missile sites survive an enemy strike, and to launch a second strike," Groteschele said. "Assume that every person in America were killed by Russia's second strike. The Russians know that the Doomsday tapes would then go into operation. This means that weeks or even months after all of us were dead the silos scattered in hard and locked-up sites around the United States would go into action and destroy what is left of the Soviet Union. What is more important is that the Russians know we have those tapes. And that we would use them. Group 6, however its accident happened, has provided a God-given opportunity. One of our groups is well launched toward Russia with a reasonable chance of success. I am convinced that the moment the Russians realize that, they will surrender. They know they cannot escape our second strike or ultimately our Doomsday tapes. Group 6 has given us a fantastic historic advantage. By accident they have forced us into making the first move, the move we would never have made deliberately. By making that first move, by cracking the gigantic tension, we will get a premature surrender from our enemy. We should advise the President that no efforts be made to recall them. At the same time we should tell the Soviet leaders that they have been launched by accident."

The second and third fighters launched their futile missiles and went into the long spiral which ended in icy death.

Swenson waited a moment, as if allowing the subtleties of Groteschele's argument to sink in.

"We must still tell the President how this happened," Swenson said. "We have heard Colonel Cascio's theory that it might be a Russian subterfuge or trick. Any other ideas?"

"I do not think that Colonel Cascio is correct, but one part of his argument is helpful," Black said. "If the Russians did think that Group 6 was part of a planned attack, they would at once try to jam its radio signals so that we could not give it guidance or instructions."

"But why would they not leave the channels open so that we could recall the group if it was a mistake?" Swenson asked.

"Because they are as suspicious as we are," Black said. "Our standard operating procedure is to try at once to isolate any Russian bomber group which launches what looks like an offensive against us or our allies. Here we are both victims of our suspicions. Though we both know that there is a possibility of bombers 'getting loose' by accident, we assume the other side would do it deliberately. Hence we try to frustrate their efforts to contact their bombers or to control the flight of their ICBMs."

There was a murmur of voices from Omaha. Swenson cocked his head to one side. Then General Bogan's voice came out loud and clear. "Knapp probably knows as much about the electronic gear as anyone else," General Bogan said. "He is a little reluctant to talk but I have asked him to. Is that agreeable, Mr. Secretary?"

"Yes," Swenson uttered the single word. It underlined the sense of urgency.

The new voice came on, weak and reedy at first, then gaining in confidence. "The more complex an electronics system gets, the more accident-prone it is," Knapp said. "Take our missiles. Each of them is, in the design stage, checked, double-checked and thoroughly pretested. All of their characteristics have been put through simulated conditions long before the missile is even built. All along the line everything checks out perfectly. Each of the missiles should fire and fly beautifully. But it never happens that way in practice. The Atlas is the most reliable missile we possess. But what happens: we make our first moon shot and it misses by 25,000 miles. Take the old X-15. It was a very small piece of equipment. It was perfect on computers, flew like a dream. It was a beautiful little computerized space needle launched from a mother plane. But there were very few X-15 flights in which something entirely unforeseen did not go wrong."

"How does this apply to our situation, Mr. Knapp?" Swenson asked abruptly.

"In this very direct way, Mr. Secretary," Mr. Knapp said, his voice rising. "Pile all those electronic systems on top of one another and sooner or later there will be a deteriorated transistor or a faulty rectifier, and the thing breaks down. Sometimes even those marvelous computers suffer from fatigue. They start to get erratic just like overworked humans."

"Mr. Secretary, what Mr. Knapp is saying is wrong because it overlooks one factor," Groteschele cut in angrily. "Even if the machines fail they are supervised by humans. The human could always reverse or correct the decision of the machine."

Knapp laughed and it was a thin, abrupt, and pitiless laugh. "I wish, sir, you were right," Knapp said. "The fact of the matter is that the machines move so fast, are capable of such subtle mistakes, are so intricate, that in a real war situation a man might not have the time to know whether a machine was in error or was telling him the truth."

Black felt a sharp sense of relief. If Knapp had not said this he would have had to. Coming from the "outside" it carried more weight.

"Mr. Secretary, I don't know if you want a politician's guess," Congressman Raskob's voice said from Omaha, "but you're going to get it. No politician, and I don't give a damn whether he is a dictator or a democrat, could survive if he allowed one of his largest cities to be destroyed without taking some kind of action against the enemy. People can be awfully damned vengeful. I don't know how Khrushchev thinks, but one thing is sure: if he lets Moscow get blown up without taking action against us, he won't live to write about it in his memoirs."

The red phone rang. Swenson picked it up smoothly, with no more emotion than if it were a social call at home. No one in the room knew precisely what he would say. But what he said would be the official opinion of an institution made up of millions of men and billions of dollars of equipment and a staggering amount of information. Black looked at Groteschele. Groteschele had, now that the decision was close, relaxed in his chair.

"Mr. President, it is our opinion that Group 6 did actually fly through their Fail-Safe point," Swenson said. "This was probably due to a compound mechanical error. There is an outside chance that the Soviets might have triggered or contributed to the mistake by making some experiment or jamming procedure of their own. We doubt that there has been a human error or that the Commander of Group 6 has gone berserk."

He stared at the pad in front of him. He began to make some notes. There was an almost visible rise in tension in the room. They had given an opinion. There was, as yet, no decision.

Swenson looked up and spoke to the table at large, the phone held loosely in his hand, his voice calm.

"The President wants to know what the chances are of those six planes getting through to Moscow," he asked. He looked at Black.

"One or two of the six will probably get through," Black answered promptly. "Maybe more."

"Two," Swenson said into the phone. He listened, looked up again.

"Even with the entire Soviet defensive apparatus concentrating on them?" Swenson repeated the President's question.

"Our Vindicators fly so fast that they won't be able to use all of their defensive apparatus," Black said. "They just can't get it in front of the Vindicators in time. They will have to shoot down the Vindicators with what is already there plus maybe a few additional fighters. It's an intricate calculation, but we have made it scores of times and it is based on a consideration of what the Soviets have in the way of defense and what our Vindicators have in the way of evasive capacity."

"They will be unable to concentrate effectively against the Vindicators because of their speed," Swenson said into the phone.

Swenson put the phone down.

"The President is assuming that two of the planes will get through," he said slowly. "We have moved into a genuine crisis. He is going to talk to Khrushchev on the phone."

ch. 13

THE CONFERENCE LINE

"I think we are ready to talk to Premier Khrushchev, Buck," the President said. "The operator is prepared for the call. Just tell her to complete the Moscow connection."

Buck picked up the phone. Instantly the operator said, "Yes, sir?"

He gave her the instructions. At once there were the sounds of a long-distance call being completed, but there was a strange lack of static on the line. As the operator worked, Buck looked at the President.

The President seemed almost asleep. Buck had heard of his capacity to take quick short naps. Buck realized that the President had also developed a capacity to live with crisis. If he allowed each crisis to take its toll he would have died long ago of anxiety. Now, his eyes half-closed, his face relaxed, the President looked younger, closer to his real age. No one, Buck thought, ever makes the complete adjustment to constant tension. Responsibility had laid pouches under the President's eyes, etched lines around his mouth, given his powerful hands the slightest tremor.

"Hello," a voice said suddenly in Russian. "Khrushchev is here."

"Premier Khrushchev, the President of the United States is calling," Buck said quickly.

The President came quickly forward in his seat, picking up his phone.

"Who else?" Khrushchev said. Incredibly, his tone sounded almost jovial to Buck. "That is what the line was set up for."

Buck translated for the President.

"Premier Khrushchev, I am using the telephone line which your government and mine agreed should always be kept open. This is the first time it has been used. I am calling you on a matter of great urgency."

This time another voice on the Moscow end of the line began to translate what the American President had said. At once the President nodded to Buck and then began to speak. Buck translated quickly, speaking over the voice of the Moscow translator.

"Premier Khrushchev, because of the urgency of the matter I hope that you will agree to the use of a single translator," the President said. "Of course, I have no objection to your translator listening to make sure that my translator is giving you a faithful rendition of what I say, but time is very short and the problem is urgent. Two translators would only complicate it."

There was a long moment of tension after Buck had translated. Buck felt squeezed buglike between the wills of two men. Although they were separated by thousands of miles it was almost as if their strength poured through the line. Buck, for the first time in his career, felt uncomfortable while translating. He sensed that this first clash of wills was important. He wanted to be out of the room, to remove himself physically, yet, at the same time, he was fascinated by what was happening.

Khrushchev yielded, but without giving much. "It is a little thing," he said. "I agree to using your translator."

"Premier Khrushchev, I am calling you on what may turn out to be a small matter," the President said. "But it is the first time it has happened and it could be tragic if it is misunderstood."

"Does it have to do with the aircraft we have detected flying toward Russia from the Bering Sea?" Khrushchev asked bluntly.

The President's eyes widened a bit. He recovered and then incredibly, he winked at Buck.

"Yes, Premier, that is why I am calling," the President said. "I am sure that your radar and tracking devices are as competent as ours and that they detected a somewhat unusual pattern."

"They reported it to me fifteen minutes ago," Khrushchev said. His voice was flat. It revealed nothing. Buck felt a game of word-poker was being played through him. Khrushchev continued speaking levelly. "We have not yet made a positive identification. I presume you are calling to inform me that it is another of those allegedly off-course reconnaissance flights. Mr. President, I have warned you in speeches, in diplomatic notes, through military channels, that your constant flying of armed planes around the periphery of the Soviet Union was a menace to peace. The scandalous U-2 incident was only the most dramatic example of your constant provocation. Have you ever wondered how long the patience of—"

"This is a mistake and it is a serious mistake," the President cut in coldly. He nodded for Buck to translate. Buck talked over the voice of Khrushchev, his voice somewhat shaky. Khrushchev came to a halt. Buck repeated what the President had said.

Khrushchev grunted. "All right, tell me," he said, in a tough peasantlike voice. "Tell me the secret."

"It is not a secret," the President said. "A group of

bombers has flown past its Fail-Safe point. I assume that you understand our Fail-Safe system?"

"Yes, I understand what you call your Fail-Safe system," Khrushchev said. "You have talked enough about it in the papers. Has it turned out not always fail-safe?" What sounded like a laugh came through the phone.

The President turned white at the corners of his mouth. Then he also laughed.

"That is correct," he said. Buck sensed that the laugh came hard, but was somehow necessary. "A group of our bombers with a speed of over 1,500 miles per hour and each loaded with two 20-megaton bombs is flying toward Russia."

Khrushchev spoke in a musing, tolerant, shrewd voice, the voice which an older man uses when rebuking a boy.

"We shall watch with great interest while you recall them. Only two weeks ago in a speech you gave to the young soldiers of your Air Academy in Colorado you said that the Air Force could never be a threat to peace, only a deterrent to war," Khrushchev said softly. "I hope this little incident will change your mind."

The President moved a pencil in his fingers, drew a hard circle on the yellow pad in front of him.

"Premier Khrushchev, this is not the time for moralizing. It is much more serious than you think. So far we have been unable to recall them," the President said, and his voice also was soft and tolerant. "Accidents can occur anywhere and be made by anyone. If the captain of your submarine the *Kalinin* were alive he could tell you that."

The President was referring to a secret incident in which a Soviet submarine had ventured inside the three-mile limit off San Francisco eight months previously and had immediately been tracked and sunk by U.S. Navy destroyers and helicopters. Neither Russia nor the United States had ever mentioned the incident in public.

The silence which spread through the vacant seconds was ominous; when Khrushchev spoke his words came slowly, each one edged with bitterness. "Are the planes from the Bering Sea being flown by madmen?"

"We are not sure, Premier Khrushchev," the President said. "It may have been a mechanical failure. Your radio-jamming devices may have made it impossible for us to establish contact with the planes. Right now they are, apparently, flying on orders which are normally received by mechanical transmissions. But we are not sure. All I can tell you is that it is an accident. This is not an attempt to provoke war, it is not a part of a general attack."

"And how is an ignorant Russian like me supposed to know that?" Khrushchev asked. His voice was harsh, but still somehow condescending, rebuking. "How do I know that you do not have hundreds of planes coming in so low that our radar cannot pick them up? How do I know—"

Again the President nodded at Buck and interrupted Khrushchev.

"Because, Premier Khrushchev, you have detection devices that give you almost the same information that I have," the President said. "Also if you will give me the time to explain I hope to prove to you that we regard it as a serious accident, take responsibility for it, and are trying to correct it."

The President stopped. The silence drew out, went past what was a polite break in conversation, became a test of will. Buck shifted in his chair. Again he had the sensation of being caught, buglike and about to be squashed, between two powerful forces. It was physically unpleasant.

"Go on, Mr. President," Khrushchev said.

"As your people have told you, there is a flight of high-speed fighters which accompany each group of our bombers as they fly toward the Fail-Safe point," the President said. "Your detection apparatus will soon tell you that those fighter planes have been flying at full speed, using afterburners, to try and overtake and shoot down our bombers. They are doing that at my direct order. Three of them have already run out of fuel and have, presumably, gone into the sea."

There was a short silence, but it possessed a new quality. When Khrushchev spoke Buck could tell he was startled.

"You mean you are ordering American fighter planes to shoot down American bombers?"

"That is precisely what I mean," the President said. "I have already given that order. If you have access to a plotting board you should have been able to see the fighters reverse their course and try to overtake the bombers."

"Mr. President, I am sitting in front of a plotting board," Khrushchev said. "My experts have already detected the change in number of your fighters." He paused. "We were not sure that they really launched air-to-air missiles at your bombers. We are still not sure that they have run out of fuel. Perhaps they are diving at a low altitude to escape our radar and are flying back to their bases—or into Russia."

"Then sir, your radar apparatus is defective," the President said. "We clearly saw three of the planes shoot their rockets and then fall into the ocean. At 20,000 feet the pilots were automatically ejected and their capsules were clearly visible on our radar."

Khrushchev grunted softly. "They were clear on our radar also, Mr. President," he said. "I really did not doubt that they were making an effort. I wanted only to hear your explanation. I also wanted to know if they had made the pursuit at your specific order." He paused and when he spoke his voice was oddly neutral. "It is a hard thing to order men to certain death, is it not?"

"It is," the President said simply.

Again there was the sound of background conversation on the Moscow end of the conference line. Buck could pick up only a few of the words. He quickly wrote a sentence on a pad and turned it to the President. It said, "Someone is trying to persuade him that it is a trick, arguing for 'strike-back in full power' or something close to that."

Suddenly Khrushchev's voice came distinctly over the line. "*Nyet,*" he said savagely. "I will make my own decisions."

Then his voice went level and was under control.

"Mr. President, some of my advisers are convinced that this 'accidental attack' and your phone call are a ruse," Khrushchev said. "They want to strike back at once. I have forbidden it. After all, Soviet air space has not yet been invaded. I must tell you, however, that if your fighters are not successful in shooting down your attacking planes we will be forced to shoot down the bombers ourselves. Then we will come to an alert and will prepare our ICBMs and other retaliatory devices. We must do this to make sure that the 'accidental attack' is not a mask for something more serious. Your single group of bombers does not disturb me in the least. We can handle them. Your real intention I do not yet know. I will protect myself."

"Premier Khrushchev, I understand that you must take these steps. I hope you will be able to shoot them down. But let me urge you to take no steps which are irrevocable. I give you my word that this is a mistake. But you are also aware that if you start to launch missiles I cannot forbid our forces to do the same. If that happens there will be very little left of the world."

"I think we will be able to take care of our interests, Mr. President," Khrushchev said and his voice was tougher.

"I want to make sure that you understand that this is an accident and to ask you to do nothing which is irrevocable," the President said evenly.

"I understand," Khrushchev said grimly. "Is there anything more you wish to say?"

"Yes, Premier," the President said. "I have made arrangements for a second conference line to be established between our tactical Air Force headquarters in Omaha and your counterpart officials in the Soviet Union. If you will give permission, that conference line can be established at once." The voice hesitated. Buck looked up. The President took a deep breath, like a tired pitcher before he winds up and throws again. "Our people in Omaha will give every assistance to your forces in shooting down our bombers should our fighters fail."

Khrushchev was silent for a few seconds. When he spoke, the words snapped out with what Buck considered genuine rage.

"Mr. President, the forces of the USSR are perfectly capable of defending our country. We do not need or welcome your technical assistance."

"The choice is yours," the President said evenly. Then his voice went low, so low that Buck had to ask him to repeat the words. Looking at the President, he realized that the President was doing this deliberately. "Premier Khrushchev, I must, with regret, tell you that regardless of what you do, two of those six planes will, in all probability, be able to fight through to their target. We have new evasive devices and masking techniques which I don't think you know anything about. My experts tell me that two of the planes will probably hit the target."

Instantly Khrushchev's voice changed. "What is their target?"

"Moscow."

The silence that ensued lasted almost twenty seconds. It was broken by Khrushchev.

"I will call you back, Mr. President, when we have seen how the fighters do. Keep that second conference line you mentioned ready for use." His voice was opaque, seamless, pitiless, completely unrevealing of emotion.

The President put down the phone and looked at Buck. Then he stood up.

"Let's go out and look at the board," he said.

He led Buck into the next room, where his special assistants were gathered before a miniature version of the Big Board in the War Room at the Pentagon. None of the assistants turned to look at the President. They stood up, but they kept their eyes on the board. They knew he was there to watch the consequences of his own acts.

In the five minutes that followed not a word was spoken in the room. Two things happened. The last of the fighter planes shot its rockets in futile pursuit of the Vindicators and went off the screen. The Vindicators came up to and then passed over the light green line which marked the Siberian border of the Soviet Union.

The President waited another minute. He nodded at Buck and they went back into the smaller office.

Buck knew what had happened. The technical conditions of war now existed. An invasion had been made.

ch. 14

THE CALCULATION AND THE WAIT

Now the world was living on two levels. There was an overt public level and a covert secret level. On the overt level the world's business proceeded serenely, innocently, and in its normal fashion: men worked, died, loved, and rested in their accustomed ways. But alongside this normal world, and ignored by it, the covert world went about its huge task of bringing two war plans to readiness. At that moment the covert, counterpoised world of war was in a waiting stage; its war dance had come to a high level of preparation and then stood arrested, held in a miraculous balance, a marvelous intricate suspension brought about by suspicions, intentions, information, and lack of information.

They waited. They waited in conference rooms, in war rooms, at rocket silos, in combat information centers on aircraft carriers, on submarines lying in muck at the bottom of the ocean, in fighter planes, in ready rooms, at computing consoles. Even men in motion were waiting. Over Russia fighter planes rose in waves, flew toward the edge of Soviet air space . . . and waited. Rockets came up from deep pits . . . and waited. Missiles were trained toward the east . . . and waited. Radar sets were warmed up . . . and their operators waited. Conventional antiaircraft weapons were readied and manned . . . and waited. On two continents whole armies of men, fleets of planes, scores of bizarre weapons were brought to a hair trigger of preparation and carefully restrained.

Everywhere the military muscles and nerves tightened, came to a hard attention. For some it was an ignorant attention: thousands of men did a task they had practiced hundreds of times before without the slightest notion of whether this performance was urgent or casual. Most of the men worked with only a tiny fragment of knowledge. But in a few places there were men who could see the full picture of what was happening, or, worse, what might happen. For these men the waiting was exquisitely painful; the quiet screamed; the peace was agonizing.

One such place was the War Room at Omaha. Every man and instrument in the War Room was at readiness. The place glowed. The lights from thousands of little dials, the merged loom from scores of scopes, and the light from the big world map on the wall had wiped out the pools of shadow.

General Bogan sat at the desk directly in front of the map. He was aware of the many men who were sitting quietly, but tensely, at desks or in front of consoles or watching the faces of various machines. Now the entire operation was working at capacity. Every machine whirred, every man was attentive, there was a beautiful symmetry to the operation. Only one thing was different. That was the sure knowledge that this was reality, the end of practice, the ultimate point.

General Bogan sat quietly at his desk, his eyes watching the motion of various dots across the world map.

"Let's get a close-up on Group 6," General Bogan said.

The projection on the map began to change at a dizzy speed, as if a camera were swooping down from some great height. General Bogan marveled at the ingenuity of the machine's design. Using radar which was housed in one of the satellites launched a few years before, they were able to pick up a radar image of any locality in the world simply by tuning in on different satellites in different locations. This radar picture was then linked to an actual map of the Soviet Union and the progress of runaway Group 6 could be traced.

Group 6 had spread out before the actual penetration of Soviet Russia. To fly too close to one another would increase the chance of two planes being destroyed by an enemy missile. Now Group 6 was a few miles inside the Soviet border, which was drawn in a heavy red line on the projection.

The few men in the War Room who were talking fell silent.

"Put the Soviet fighter planes on the projection," General Bogan said.

A flock of small white blips appeared, all of them meticulously grouped on the Soviet side of the red line.

"This is Enemy Defense Performance Desk, General Bogan," a mechanical voice said. The desk was keyed to come on with an interpretation when its information was projected onto the Big Board. "The No. 6 plane, which carries only defensive equipment and devices has moved into the lead. Apparently it has already launched some masking devices for, as you can see, the Soviet fighters are not grouping at the point where Group 6 crossed the border. On their radars the targets probably appear spread over several hundred miles and they are starting to get blips on a good number of objects without being able to determine which are real and which are decoys."

"Have they launched missiles of any kind?" General Bogan asked.

"Not yet," the Enemy Defense Desk said.

At that moment the Soviet fighter command ordered its planes into action. Instantly the Big Board began to blossom. Blips raced up the board, homed on decoys, raced relentlessly down their electronic tracks and then detonated themselves in little mushrooming blips which quickly disappeared.

"The little dots that appear suddenly and then disappear are missiles," the Enemy Defense expert said. "The largest blips are fighter-bombers which are probably equipped with their own radar and air-to-air missiles. So far none of the antiaircraft shots have been nuclear. They are the conventional warhead. As you can see, our diversion and evasive devices are working well. The No. 6 plane which is now angling away will probably drop a new set of window."

Each of the planes was equipped with radar-jamming and obscuring devices which were called "window" and were advanced developments from the older strips of foil designed to produce false images on enemy radar screens. The Vindicators also carried other decoys, some of which could be launched by small rockets, and antimissile missiles and automatic devices to detect and identify approaching enemy missiles and compute the precise time for firing the antimissile missiles.

"Right now the Soviet radar is probably picking up some hundreds of blips and they are running each of them down systematically," the voice went on. "On the scope that you see the decoys had not been projected. Our equipment is programmed to ignore signals from our own window. On the Soviet projection the only thing they are sure of is the location of their own missiles and fighter planes. For the Soviets it is a pretty difficult task, General, trying to follow a couple of hundred blips and vector their own planes in on them over air space of several million cubic miles."

General Bogan felt an odd mixture of pride and helplessness. For years every man in the room, every piece of machinery, had worked and drilled and practiced for the first terrible moment of action. Now it had begun. But there was a bewildering difference. When this magnificently balanced mechanism was being perfected, no one had ever contemplated that it would be used to counter some terrible mistake. Even so, General Bogan could not restrain a sense of admiration for the efficiency with which the Vindicator bombers were feinting, fighting back, and pushing on the attack.

He could not put down a sense of guilt. If the attack had been legitimately ordered the Vindicators would be receiving help. A B-52 especially equipped with jamming equipment and more elaborate decoys than the Vindicators could carry would be accompanying them. Jamming and masking devices located around the borders of the Soviet Union would have gone into action. But these parts of the mechanism had been ordered to stand down. The Vindicators were fighting through entirely on their own. General Bogan also felt a deeper uneasiness. If he were able to give the Soviets the information he had, their chances of shooting down the Vindicators would be greatly increased. But he forced the idea down into some black recess of his mind.

"How much of their defensive armament have the Vindicators had to fire so far?" General Bogan asked.

"So far they have been following standard operating procedure with No. 6 plane firing air-to-air missiles at any missile or plane that is closing a real target," the mechanical voice said. "No. 6 has run through 55 per cent of her armament. The other planes each have a full load of air-to-air missiles."

On the screen one of the Soviet fighters suddenly altered direction and started to fly directly at the lead plane in the Vindicator formation. The two planes were closing on one another at a combined speed of over 3,000 miles per hour. General Bogan felt his chest go tight. His viscera warred with his mind. His mind willed that the Soviet fighter would be successful. His viscera, conditioned by years of training, was knotted in a desperate sympathy with the Vindicator.

Suddenly the decision was made. A small blip fell away from the No. 6 plane, hung suspended for a moment, and then, like a meteorite trailing a miniature phosphorescent tail, it began to speed toward the Soviet fighter. It was a Bloodhound and General Bogan estimated that its speed was over 1,500 miles an hour. The Soviet fighter suddenly began to zigzag in the air as some mechanism aboard the plane sensed the rush of the missile. Finally, when the Bloodhound was only a few miles from the Soviet bomber, the Soviet fighter itself dropped an air-to-air missile which turned in the direction of the Bloodhound. It was too late. In the next second there was a great mushrooming blotch on the screen. The warhead of the Bloodhound had gone off. The Soviet air-to-air missile and fighter and Bloodhound all disappeared in the blotch. The American bomber veered away from the blotch, which spread out like a green, dangerous fungus growth. Then abruptly it dimmed and the blotch disappeared.

"Jesus, I'll bet the crew on that Vindicator got a shaking up," a voice said in the rear of the room.

North of the Vindicators another Soviet fighter suddenly altered course and was joined by a second. They both ran down their electronic tracks, stalking the invisible targets. No. 6 plane veered toward them, but at that moment each of the Soviet fighters released two air-to-air missiles. They streaked, amoebalike but at great speed, toward the closest Vindicator. The attacked Vindicator and No. 6 simultaneously loosed a total of six air-to-air missiles toward the two fighters. The four Soviet missiles came at a much slower speed. The Vindicator missiles sped toward the Soviet missiles, wavered a moment, and then went on toward the larger targets.

"Oh, Christ," Colonel Cascio whispered. "They went right by the missiles."

Two seconds later the two Soviet fighters went up in a rolling green blip. But their four missiles continued to bore in. The attacked Vindicator began to jink in the air, rapidly altering course and altitude. It also shot off four more missiles. But the Soviet missiles were too close. They closed on the Vindicator, seemed to converge and then the Vindicator disappeared in the explosion.

There was utter silence in the War Room. It was the first time that most of the men had "seen" a plane destroyed. For General Bogan it was not. In World War II he had seen planes destroyed on radar and with his own eyes. Now, he knew, was the time to establish the mood of the War Room. He turned on the intercom so that everyone in the room could hear him.

"Apparently the Soviets have a very slow missile which compensates by a long range," he said distinctly. "That is a longer range than we had calculated their missiles possessed. The computing systems built into our air-to-air missiles detected the four Soviet air-to-air missiles, but 'calculated' that they were moving so slowly that they must be drones or reconnaissance planes, and so they ignored them and continued toward the Soviet fighters. You can't win 'em all."

Instantly he was aware of the unintended irony. The

Vindicators must lose, must all be destroyed, or God knew what might happen. But all his deepest reflexes were with the Vindicators. They were *his*. He felt slightly sick, torn by cross-currents of loyalty and of logic.

"General, it's going to get worse before it gets better," someone said to him.

He turned and it was Raskob standing with his legs apart, a dead cigar in his mouth, staring at the board. Even in the dim light, General Bogan could see that Raskob was very pale.

"You're right, sir, it's going to get much worse," General Bogan said.

"Will all our men hold firm?" Raskob asked. "Not just the ones here, but the ones in the air? After all, those are our men getting killed out there and it's tough just to stand by and watch it. Is anyone likely to crack?"

"Not likely, Congressman Raskob," General Bogan said. "They've been screened, tested, rehearsed, and drilled until they can't be sure what's a drill and what's for real."

"I hope you're right, General Bogan," Raskob said. "I don't know what the President is doing, but whatever it is he'd better be right. Khrushchev isn't going to sit around forever and watch those planes move in on Moscow. The whole thing rests on the President's ability to persuade Khrushchev it was an accident. If he doesn't, then we're going to have all-out, 100 per cent, slam-bang, hell-bent war. That's right, isn't it, General?"

"Yes, sir, that is right," General Bogan said.

He felt a sudden sympathy with Raskob. He was a tough man, quick at making calculations and then at facing up to them. It was the first time that General

Bogan had faced the fact that everything now rested with the President. Barring some miracle, one or two of the bombers would get through. And if the Soviets did not believe the attack was innocent or made in error they would be forced to respond.

"No notion of how it happened, eh, General?" Raskob asked.

General Bogan felt an odd fuzziness, a thin coating of confusion, slide over his mind.

"No, sir, not the slightest," he said. "They told us that the system was foolproof. Oh, some parts might break down from time to time, but the whole system would check itself out, they told us."

"They told you," Knapp said and there was wonderment in his voice. "Always that unknown *they*. Those of us who manufactured the gear, who had some notion of what it was being used for—we never told anyone that it was infallible. But somewhere in Washington *they* had to say it was perfect, that it couldn't make a mistake. General, there is no such thing as a perfect system and *they* should have told you that."

"Look, friend, in Washington you don't get appropriations and bigger staff and more personnel by saying that what you're doing is not perfect," Raskob said roughly. "You stand up in front of the Appropriations Committee and you convince yourself that the system is perfect and then you tell the Committee it is perfect. And there isn't a mother's son on that Committee who can say you nay. Because we just ain't boy geniuses at electronics and all this stuff. So we give them the dough. What the hell else can we do?"

"Nothing, not a thing," Knapp said. "Except listen to the right people. Look, for years there has been a fellow named Fred Iklé, who has been working with the Rand Corporation and the Air Force on how to reduce war by accident. He has found flaw after flaw in the system, at just the same time that the newspapers were saying it was perfect. Kendrew over in England has talked about accidental war for years—loud and clear. So have dozens of others. Most of us, the best of us on the civilian side," and he spoke without pride, "we knew that a perfect system is impossible. The mistake was that no one told the public and the Congress."

"What should we have done?" Colonel Cascio said suddenly, and his voice held a kind of baffled anger. "Just sit on our duffs while our enemy goes ahead and arms to the teeth and finally gets to a position where he can *tell* us to surrender and we know we have to do it?"

"No, son, we had to do what we did," Raskob said wearily. "In politics if you sit still you are dead. I guess it's the same in the military game. But maybe we should have recognized that past a certain point the whole damned thing was silly."

General Bogan sensed that Knapp was in a terrible agony. His hunched and hard-driven body, his burning eyes, his ravished face, looked like a statue of anxiety. General Bogan could guess the reason: much of the machinery in that room had been developed and manufactured by Knapp and he had carried the burden of knowledge within him that it was far from foolproof. Right now he was wondering why he had not spoken out.

Only Raskob, the politically toughened man, could see the other side. His eyes remained glued on the board and when he spoke his voice was a mixture of pity and hard-bitten reality.

"Well—that's one bomber gone. If those Soviet fighters start shaping up a bit maybe we can avoid the worst."

The small group felt rather than saw Colonel Cascio turn in his chair. His eyes burned up at Raskob. He was oddly bent as if his body were undergoing an invisible physical torture. He did not speak, he only stared with hatred at Raskob.

Raskob looked down at him without emotion.

"There can be much worse things than the loss of six bombers, son," Raskob said. "It's a pity that those eighteen men have to fight their way in and probably get killed in the process. But think a minute about all of the people, millions and billions of them, all around the world, walking around in total ignorance that they might be killed in the next few hours. Do you ever think about them? Well, that's what politics is all about and that poor guy in the White House who has to make the big decision knows that."

Colonel Cascio's eyes did not change. He blinked once and then turned back to his controls.

The remaining five Vindicators were now widely scattered, but in a carefully calculated dispersion. Each was at the maximum range at which they could protect one another and be protected by the No. 6 plane. Still they were so dispersed that no single Soviet shot could down two of them.

"How are the Soviet fighters doing?" General Bogan asked, still on the intercom.

The Enemy Defense Desk responded at once.

"Apparently, General, they are badly confused by our masking and window," the voice said. "They have not yet started to concentrate on Group 6. They are still scattered, chasing decoys."

Somewhere in the War Room a voice cheered and instantly was joined by a score of others. General Bogan felt a kind of exultation start in his own throat, but quickly repressed it. There was a strange perversion about his feelings, a heightened sense of paradox. Again the thought flicked in and out of his mind that he, standing before the board in the War Room, could help the Russians distinguish between plane and decoy. When he spoke there was a hard lash in his voice.

"Let's knock that off," he said. "This is no God-damned football game." There was instant silence. "Remember that. It might get hard in the next few hours."

He looked around and saw the glint of resentment in a dozen eyes, shoulders hunched with anger. They were well trained, but not for this sort of incredible game.

"How much of her defensive gear does No. 6 still have?" General Bogan asked.

"Twenty-five per cent," the voice said. "She is slowing down the rate of defensive fire, apparently to conserve missiles for the run on Moscow."

On the southern flank of the Vindicators a Soviet fighter began to firm up on an intercepting course toward the closest Vindicator. The Vindicator turned away, but the Soviet blip also altered course. They would still make an intercept.

"Fire, fire," a voice said very close to General Bogan. He looked over and saw it was Colonel Cascio. He was half out of his chair, his teeth wet and prominent, his lips drawn back. "Fire before the bastard gets one of those long slow ones off at you."

"Colonel, if you say one more word like that I will throw you out of this room and have you court-martialed," General Bogan said in a low voice.

No one else in the War Room had heard the exchange.

Colonel Cascio whirled in his half-bent posture, like a boxer badly hurt and covering. He stared at General

Bogan and then his eyes cleared. He sat down.

The Soviet fighter was joined by three other fighters and they formed a long box formation as they ran down their intercept. The Vindicator jinked once more. So did the Soviet fighters. Instantly the Vindicator fired four missiles. The Soviet planes each fired a single missile and continued to speed toward the Vindicator. At the same moment their detection gear told them they were fired upon and the Soviet fighters turned sharply away. It was too late. Five seconds later all of them were destroyed. But their four missiles ran with an agonizing slowness toward the Vindicator. It turned and ran, but was not fast enough. The missiles came in remorselessly. Again there was the merging, again the slow, exploding, engulfing blip.

General Bogan felt his fingertips shaking against his trousers. He felt for a moment as if he were being exposed to some strange torture; some spikelike split of his allegiance; some rupturing of his life. He yearned for the bottle of whisky in a faraway office.

As if by order, the breaths of two-score men were released from their lungs. It made a weird contrapuntal chorus of sighs. Congressman Raskob muttered something to himself. It sounded like "Four more to go."

ch. 15

THE CONFERENCE LINE

The phone on the President's desk rang. It was a strong unbroken ring. The President looked at Buck, arched his eyebrows, and Buck picked up his phone.

It was Moscow.

The first voice that spoke was that of Khrushchev.

The moment he heard the voice something in Buck's mind went alert. He heard perfectly and literally what Khrushchev said, but he also sensed something else. It was the same person speaking but in a different voice. The voice ended each sentence with an odd lifting sound.

As Buck translated the literal words he searched back over his experience. Something was there, elusive and subtle, but heavy with meaning.

"We have only a few hours left, Mr. President," Khrushchev said. "How should we use them? You have launched an offensive attack against our country. Without provocation or cause. You state it is an accident. But meanwhile we lie defenseless before you."

"Not quite defenseless, Premier Khrushchev," the President said. "You have hundreds of fighter planes, countless ICBMs, missiles for defense. In fact in your recent Warsaw speech you boasted of the invulnerability of the Soviet forces."

Krushchev grunted. Then oddly and out of character, he sighed.

Instantly things fell into place in Buck's mind. He recalled listening to a record at the Monterey Language School made by a Russian peasant in which the ultimate in resignation and despair was precisely this sequence of petulance, a grunt, and a sigh. Even when joined to the most ordinary words their meaning was one of great sorrow—a sorrow so great that no words could convey it. It was not a matter even of inflection. It was a matter of sound and wind and something deep in the chest.

Buck reached for a pad of paper in front of him and in quick bold letters he wrote "Khrushchev's mood is sorrow." The President read it upside down as quickly as Buck wrote it. When he had finished the President drew a large circle around the statement to indicate he understood.

The silence on the line went past the point of tension. The tiny, and usually inaudible, screech of static now seemed to be a scream in their ears. The President started to doodle on the pad in front of him. He traced the head of an arrow, started to draw the shaft and then, very deliberately, lifted his pencil from the pad and held it between his forefingers, the eraser touching the forefinger of his left hand, the sharp point of lead pushed into the flesh of his right forefinger. His hands were steady.

When Khrushchev spoke, it was to Buck like a bell fractured, a flash that ripped darkness, a pinprick through the eardrum. And yet, oddly, his voice was gentle.

"It is ironic, gentlemen, but now, at this moment when we still have time left, the time that is left is empty and without use," Khrushchev said. Buck's confidence was strengthened. He was certain that Khrushchev was in a sorrow so deep that it was close to agony. "There is a period during which we can do nothing. After that? I do not know. If the bombs fall on Moscow I know. We will strike back."

Buck translated quickly, but the President seemed to be listening abstractedly, his head cocked to one side as if he were making a difficult calculation. He nodded at Buck, the calculation made.

"What luck have you had in your attacks on our bombers?" the President asked.

"Luck? No luck at all," Khrushchev said. "But earned results, yes. By earned results we have gotten 860 of our supersonic fighters vectored in on the hundreds of targets which suddenly appeared on our radarscope. That, Mr. President, was a tender moment. One group of our experts was convinced that your scientists had developed a method of camouflaging the approach of bombers until they were actually in our territory. They argued that what appeared as decoys were actually real bombers. They urged that we retaliate instantly with all of our ICBMs and our bombers."

"Why did you not do that?" the President asked. Buck looked at him sharply. The President nodded for him to translate the question. To Buck it seemed brusque and antagonistic.

"Ah, that is a nice question," Khrushchev said. Buck was bewildered by some inflection, some subtle inclination, some fugitive meaning. Khrushchev's words were as ironic and heavy as before, but his delivery was evasive.

"Why did you not launch an offensive?" the President said again.

Buck hesitated. The word "offensive" in Russian can take several different meanings. In one sense it means to question a man's virility. In another to be crudely egotistical. In another to be a challenge. Buck looked at the President. With the gnawing tension growing within, he knew he must not give the wrong word to Khrushchev. It might be enough to trigger the peasant temper, to bring the powerful fingers stabbing down on the buttons.

Buck made up his mind.

"Why did you not defend yourself by counterattacking?" he translated the President's words.

Khrushchev said in a quiet voice, "I held back the retaliation because I still had time to take the gamble that you were sincere. Also I knew that it would be the end for both of us. A peasant who becomes a politician, Mr. President, is not without insight. The generals are not happy. Just as I can guess your generals are not happy with you. But there is a time for common sense . . . which occurs as often among the low as among the mighty."

The President started to speak and to his own surprise Buck found himself lifting his hand, restraining the President. The Russian was thinking aloud and Buck sensed some gain in not interrupting him. The President nodded.

"Of the 860 planes we sent up 70 were, by great valor and ingenuity, able to attack one or another of your Vindicators," Khrushchev went on. He paused. "We have been able to destroy only two of your planes."

"What were your casualties?" the President asked.

"Very high," Khrushchev said. "Out of the 70 planes which launched attacks somewhere around 65 were destroyed. And by means of which we have no understanding. Most of them simply exploded in midair. And for that we got two of your bombers."

"What of the other four?" the President asked.

"There is little to be optimistic about," Khrushchev said.

Incredibly, doubting his senses, Buck heard Khrushchev yawn. He looked up sharply at the President. The President had heard it also and his lips went white. Then, again from some buried part of his mind, Buck remembered a Russian at Monterey who had yawned all during a seminar—and committed suicide the next morning.

"Maybe yes, maybe no," Khrushchev said.

Now his voice had something of the old toughness in it. "Only time will tell."

"Time must not be allowed to tell," the President said, and his voice was so cold that Buck was startled. "I offered to give you our help in shooting down those Vindicators. You refused it. What is your attitude now?"

Khrushchev hesitated. The President had put it as nakedly, as bluntly, as one could put it. Buck licked his lips. Instantly he wondered if Khrushchev was doing the same.

"Mr. President, I agree to setting up the conference line between your tactical people in Omaha and my people in Ziev," Khrushchev said. His tone was still quiet. "If there is a chance, we must try and kill the Vindicators. Wait—while I make arrangements."

The President pressed a button on his desk and an aide appeared. Briefly the President instructed him about the line between Omaha and Ziev. Buck surmised that Khrushchev was doing the same thing.

When Khrushchev came back on the line, the President picked up the conversation in an entirely different tone—calmly, almost idly, it seemed to Buck.

"Premier Khrushchev, we know now that Soviet and

United States bombers, and indeed our whole offensive and defensive apparatus, are almost mirror images of one another. But let me ask you a question. What sort of experimental work have your military and scientific people been directing at our planes as they orbit at the Fail-Safe point?"

"Ah, ah, ah, that is a good one," Khrushchev said. "That is something that I have just found out about in the last hour."

Buck's tongue translated, but his mind and his intuition were frozen. First, the President had come to a hard attention; his eyes glittered like those of a mongoose before it closes in under the venomous muscular curve of a cobra's body. But at the same time Buck realized that the President had already won some dim and obscure, but terribly critical, point. Khrushchev's expressions were those of a man in a deep and fundamental turmoil. The words were still intact, the syntax irreproachable, but like an animal in its final cul-de-sac that wheels and faces its enemy, there was a note of ultimate calamity.

"Yes, but what is the answer?" the President said.

When Khrushchev spoke, his voice had steadied. He had made a decision.

"Mr. President, in the last hour I learned of a piece of research which we have been undertaking but which was unknown to me," Khrushchev said. "I am certain, Mr. President, that such things could take place in your country."

"Of course, Mr. Khrushchev," the President said. "I am aware that I am unaware of a great deal."

Khrushchev laughed softly.

"This particular experiment was undertaken by a joint research team of mathematicians, radar experts, computing-machine specialists and weapons-systems experts," Khrushchev said. "We were aware of your general strategic approach, the system of planes aloft, planes on standby, and the rest of the procedure including the Fail-Safe point. This did not take much intelligence. But this particular team had orders from our general staff in Moscow to see if it would be possible to discriminate an actual attack from a routine Fail-Safe flight. Our observations told us where your Fail-Safe lines must be. We then established mathematically another line which, if penetrated by your planes, would indicate a true attack."

"What are you getting at?" the President asked. Buck could tell from his face that he already knew the answer. The President had gained some of the offensive.

"Today, Mr. President, our analyzers calculated that a true attack might be imminent. They may have been wrong. But we figured our only chance to prevent it was to try jamming all radio frequencies so that your bombers would be unable to receive the 'go' signal ordering them through their Fail-Safe line. We had to prevent you from changing the standard Fail-Safe control into an ordered attack. Mr. President, we may have succeeded. But who knows?"

"Holy Jesus," the words slipped from the President's mouth. "What an irony. The whole operation was calculated on the basis of a trust in the infallibility of our Fail-Safe controls. We've both put too damn much trust in the system."

"Yes, Mr. President, and it is even more ironic than that. We don't know whether our jamming efforts succeeded and were a contributing cause, and neither do you. But we do know that these are your bombers and they are attacking Moscow. All right, maybe accidents on both sides. But right now, what do we do? Now, quickly, Mr. President, how can you convince me that your planes are on an innocent mission?"

"Just a moment, Mr. Khrushchev," the President said. "From what you have just said it must be obvious that our planes do not bear all the guilt. Your own scientists have told you that they were trying to jam our radios. The guilt, if there be any, surely must be shared."

"Mr. President, there was no reason in the world why I needed to tell you that we had conducted, perhaps mistakenly, that jamming operation this morning," Khrushchev said. "The fact that an obscure team of scientists may have miscalculated is of absolutely no relevance. In the eyes of the world you have wantonly and without provocation attacked the Soviet Union and may, in fact, destroy Moscow. What Indian or Thai or Japanese or African or European will believe that so monstrous a thing was really tripped by our jamming your radios? No one. More importantly, no Russian would tolerate for a moment the destruction of Moscow without retaliation. Forget the mechanical mistakes and traps and countermeasures. The mistake, you agree, started on your side. But we may suffer the consequences."

"What do you intend to do, Mr. Khrushchev?" the President asked.

"I am trapped, Mr. President," Mr. Khrushchev said. His voice was riddled with despair. "I am perfectly prepared, Mr. President, to order our whole offensive apparatus to take action. In fact, I intend to do precisely that unless you can persuade me that your intentions were not hostile and that there is some chance for peace."

"Your experts should be able to tell you that I have ordered all American bombers to fly toward their bases and land," the President said. "Not a single American plane, aside from those in Group 6, is making a hostile gesture toward you. Does that sound like the preparation for an all-out war?"

"The military people have already told me that," Khrushchev said and his voice was tired. "On the face of it you look innocent, but how do we know what else is happening? What other plots do you have up your sleeve? Where else will your electronic systems break down?"

"We have no plots of any kind," the President said. "Your people will be able to verify that in plain voice and with top priority I am sending a personal message to all Polaris submarines not to fire, not even to prepare to fire, their missiles, unless they receive a direct order from me." His voice was not pleading, but he spoke with an urgency which even Khrushchev must detect. "I cannot give a guarantee against further mechanical failure. Neither can you."

Khrushchev sighed. From a long distance came the single word "No."

Buck almost groaned. He waved to the President, a sign that no more could be asked. Khrushchev had given everything.

"Premier Khrushchev, I think it would be wise for you to remove yourself from Moscow so that you will be out of danger," the President said. "That will allow us to continue to negotiate even if the worst happens and the bombers get through. I pray that it will not happen, but it may."

"I have already made arrangements to remove myself and some of my staff from Moscow by helicopter," Khrushchev said at once, in a firm voice that suddenly toughened. "Moscow will not be evacuated. There is no time. It lies here innocent and open, defenseless. If it is destroyed there will be little time to talk, Mr. President."

"I am aware of that," the President said. "But I will do anything in my power to demonstrate our good will. I only ask that you not take any irrevocable step. Once you launch bombers and ICBMs everything is finished. I will not be able to hold back our retaliatory forces and then it would be utter devastation for both of us."

"I know, Mr. President," Khrushchev said. "We have been over that before; each of us has made the calculations endlessly in his own mind, has heard them from his advisers. But if Moscow is obliterated" —a kind of helpless rage shook his voice—"am I supposed to sit still, watch our biggest city destroyed, and then come hat in hand to you and ask that we reopen peace talks in Geneva? It would be absurd. I am not a man, we are not a people, that likes to look absurd."

"I agree with much of what you say," the President said. For the first time Buck saw great physical tension, even pain, in the President's face.

There was a long hesitation. Then Khrushchev spoke again.

"I will come back on the line when I am a safe distance from Moscow," Khrushchev said. His voice was toneless, flat, empty.

The line clicked dead.

"Mr. President," Buck said, "may I say that you handled him beautifully. He acknowledged the possibility that they might be wrong and—"

Buck stopped. The President was not listening. His face was slack, softened by despair. He was staring at his scratch pad, searching the firm black cabalistic signs for some meaning.

Again Buck had the sense that something had

slipped by him, that in the literal meaning of the words he had missed some larger import.

"You have broken him, Mr. President," Buck said. "He is shaken."

The President looked up. His eyes were dark, but the pupils glittered like small pools of agony.

"He is not broken, Mr. Buck," the President said. "He has his back to the wall and he is suffering, but he is not broken. Unless we can show him that this is an accident, that we are not doing it deliberately, he will launch an all-out attack on us."

Buck felt his stomach knot. In the rush of translation, in the thrill of the negotiation, he had forgotten the stakes. He stared at the President.

"What do we do now?" Buck whispered.

The President looked across the table at Buck. He shook his head slowly as if to clear it.

"We do what we must," he said slowly. "Get General Black at the Pentagon."

While Buck put the call through the President leaned back in his chair. He put his hands over his eyes, his teeth clenched together, the muscles at the back of his jaw tightened into hard knots. Then he relaxed.

"General Black, Mr. President," Buck said.

The President held out his hand. He took the phone without opening his eyes.

"Blackie," the President said, his voice quiet and firm. "Do you remember the story of Abraham in the Old Testament? Old Bridges at Groton used to use it at least six times a year for chapel."

Oh my God, he's cracking, Buck thought, cracking wide open, and the whole world with him. He found himself actually looking around for means to escape, for a door to run through. But the general's voice came back calm and reassuring.

"I remember, sir," Black said. He stood awkwardly over Swenson, holding the red phone. The others around the table in the Pentagon War Room continued the discussion and also watched the board. Black felt a peculiar unreality about the situation. Simultaneously he sensed that this was, somehow, a time for first names, but he could not do it. The half-dozen times he and the President had met in the past few years, the President had always been warm but had called him "General Black" with a grin. But now there was a new tone in the President's voice. Or perhaps it was the old intimate tone.

"Blackie, keep the story of Abraham in mind for the next few hours," the President said. Then he paused. "Are Betty and the family in New York?"

"Yes," Black said. A dread premonition came over him.

"I need your help," the President said slowly. "Get out to Andrews Field immediately. Further instructions will be waiting for you there. Things are not good, Blackie. I may be asking a great deal of you."

"I'll do what you say," Black said. He paused. He knew the President was in some private agony. "And you do what has to be done."

"Good luck, Blackie," the President said.

Immediately Black wanted to call Betty—to talk with her, and with his two boys. But it was out of the question, he knew. Then he felt a wave of apprehension, vague and inexplicable. He remembered—Betty was spending the day across town with a friend. She and the boys would not be together until late afternoon. The knowledge was unsettling to Black. For a brief instant, memory of the Dream flashed back into his mind. No time. He shook the thoughts off and strode rapidly toward the door.

After hanging up, the President sat perfectly still for a full minute, his eyes closed. Then he swung his feet from the desk, and looked at Buck.

"Tell the switchboard to get our Ambassador to Moscow and also the Soviet Delegate to the United Nations," the President said quietly. "Put them directly onto the line which connects us with Khrushchev. The moment that we can talk to Khrushchev open the conference line again."

As Buck talked into the phone he looked at the President. The President's face had undergone a strange transfiguration. Some muscles had relaxed, others had tightened, his eyes were closed. A stranger could not have guessed the President's age. Nor the meaning of his expression. Then Buck identified it: the President's face reflected the ageless, often repeated, doomed look of utter tragedy. A tragedy which is no single person's but the world's, which relates not to one man's misfortunes, large or small, but to the human condition.

For the first time since he was a boy of fourteen, Peter Buck felt the need to weep.

ch. 16

THE LAST EFFORT

On General Bogan's desk was a "touch" phone which had not been operated in all the time that he had been at Omaha. One operated it merely by touching a button, and out of a small square box the voice at the other end of the line came out magnified and enlarged.

This particular "touch" phone was reserved for the possibility of direct communication with any potential enemy military leaders.

A peculiar aura surrounded it. It was like a piece of contaminated equipment, oddly disconcerting, unnerving, contradictory. The men who tested it did so with distaste. While almost every other piece of equipment in the room was associated with some man, was his "personal" equipment, no one wanted to be associated with the touch telephone. It was almost like the physical presence of the enemy in the War Room. Everyone knew that the phone could not actually overhear them, that it had to be passed through a number of careful checks before it was actually operative, but even so it was a totem of the enemy, awesome, ill-regarded.

Some minutes before, General Bogan had received a call from one of the President's aides telling him to activate the touch phone as arrangements were being made for direct radio communication with Soviet tactical officers in Russia. Now the light below the touch button glowed red. General Bogan quietly reached forward and pushed the button. There was utter silence in the room. Even those men who were out of hearing range watched tensely.

"General Bogan, Strategic Air Command, Omaha, here," General Bogan said.

There was a slight static, then a voice spoke in flawless English.

"I am the translator for Marshal Nevsky, Soviet Air Defense Command," the voice said. "Marshal Nevsky sends his greetings. He tells you that reception here on our end is five by five. How do you read us?"

"We read you five by five," General Bogan said. "I have no instructions on what we are to discuss. Have you received instructions, Marshal Nevsky?"

The translator spoke Russian very rapidly. An even, strong voice replied.

"We have received no instructions, General," the translator said. "Only that we should set up communications with your headquarters."

Then there was silence. Colonel Cascio moved his eyes from General Bogan's face to the touch phone. He seemed mesmerized, fascinated, by something enormously seductive, but also revolting. The red phone rang.

"General Bogan, this is the President and I should like you to put this call on your intercom so that everyone in the room can hear what I say," the President said. "I should also like you to open your touch phone to the Soviet Air Command so that they also can hear me."

"One moment, Mr. President," General Bogan said. He turned to Colonel Cascio and gave instructions. The arrangements took only ten seconds.

"Mr. President, when you speak your voice will be

heard by everyone," General Bogan said.

"Gentlemen, this is the President," the President began and his strong young voice rang through the room, drowning out the endless hum of the machines. The men had, quite unconsciously, all come to attention, their thumbs neatly lined alongside the seams of their trousers, their eyes staring straight ahead. "What I am saying can be heard by the Soviet Air Command, Premier Khrushchev's personal staff in the Kremlin, our Chiefs of Staff in the Pentagon, our SAC group in Omaha, our Ambassador to the Soviet Union, and the Soviet delegate to the United Nations. Whatever orders I give to American military or civilian personnel are to be considered as direct personal orders from the Commander in Chief. They are to be obeyed fully, without reservation and instantly."

The President paused. General Bogan looked around the room. He had a sense of unreality, a kind of smoky twisting in his mind, a surrealistic sense of things dissolving. The whole thing was dreamlike, but it was iron hard and inescapable. There was no possibility of awakening to something else.

"We are caught in a desperate situation," the President said slowly and emphatically. Over the touch phone General Bogan could hear small hushed Russian voices translating. "By some sort of error, probably mechanical, a group of American bombers has penetrated Soviet air space. It is our best estimate that they will try to press home an attack on Moscow. Each of the bombers is equipped with two 20-megaton bombs. Though all of the planes are under heavy attack from Soviet defenses, in all probability at least two of these bombers will get through. This is a tragic mistake. It is not, I repeat, not, our intention to engage the Soviet Union in warfare. Premier Khrushchev is, at this moment, en route to a headquarters located outside of Moscow. When he again contacts me I will do everything in my power to persuade him of our sincerity."

Again the President paused. When he resumed speaking his voice was so slow that each word seemed to dangle.

"Those of us on this hookup are the only people who can save the world from an atomic holocaust," he said. "We must all do everything possible to prevent our planes from attacking Moscow. At the same time, we must make it absolutely clear to the Russians that this is an accident and in no way part of or prelude to an American attack. Already I have done everything I can by myself to achieve these two goals. Recall of our planes has proved impossible, but it has been constantly attempted. All other American offensive and defensive forces have been withdrawn from Condition Red. This the Russians were able to verify on their monitoring systems. The Russians now concede that their Air Defense Command may not be able to intercept our Group 6. They have a momentous decision to make: should they order a retaliatory attack against the United States? Premier Khrushchev tells me that some of his military leaders favor such an attack." The voice paused or faltered and then came on again. "This is understandable."

Colonel Cascio listened, immediately understood, and was filled with a terrible confusion. He knew that in the position of these outraged Russian officers he would feel the same way. Cascio glanced around the room. Everyone was immobilized by the strangeness of the situation.

The President's voice continued. "Premier Khrushchev has behaved as I believe I would under similar conditions. He has delayed retaliation. And I think he believes that this is an accident. But we must convince him, and his chief advisers, that it is. I order every American to cooperate fully with Soviet officers in whatever attempts they make to shoot down our invading bombers. This is a firm and unalterable command. You are to give whatever information the Soviet officers may request of you. Let me emphasize that any hesitation, any withholding of information, may have the most tragic consequences. Are there any questions?"

The President paused. There were no questions.

"Gentlemen, I wish you success," the President said. "This is a difficult situation for all of us. I expect you to conduct yourselves as patriots and to carry out my orders without hesitation."

The President's line clicked dead.

General Bogan turned to look at Colonel Cascio. Cascio's eyes were green and they had a hard glow in the dim light.

Suddenly a voice came up on the "touch" phone. It was the voice of the Russian translator in the Soviet Union.

"Does the Bloodhound have both infrared and radar homing capabilities?" he asked. "A number of our fighter planes have been destroyed by a missile which seems to home not on the infrared source, but the radar transmitter. Is that possible?"

"Colonel Cascio will answer your question, sir," General Bogan said. He nodded at Cascio.

Colonel Cascio looked at General Bogan. Even in the dim light General Bogan could tell that the blood had drained from Cascio's face. His eyes rolled slightly in his head. Then his throat began to work as if the muscles were out of control, seized by a convulsion. It was the throat of a man sobbing, but no sound came from Colonel Cascio's lips. He shook his head. His hand reached for the button below the "touch" phone and then, his finger only an inch from the button, he went rigid. His entire body seemed frozen, gripped by a spasm of immobility. He did not tremble, he did not speak, he simply arched into a posture that ached with tension.

General Bogan felt nausea rise in his stomach. He was not an emotional man, he knew he lacked intuition. But he understood perfectly the awful thing he was watching. For years Colonel Cascio had been trained to guard information, to be secretive, to be suspicious of the Soviets. For half his life he had carried in his mind facts that bore the words TOP SECRET, and, with a tireless and unending diligence, he had locked them into a private part of his brain. And now he was asked to reverse all these reflexes, to shatter the training of a lifetime. But he had also been trained to obey orders, any orders which came from legitimate superiors. All of this was too much and Colonel Cascio was locked in a dilemma so cruel and sharp that he could not move.

General Bogan reached out and touched Colonel Cascio's arm. It was like touching marble. With his other hand General Bogan punched the "touch" button.

"Answer the question, Colonel," General Bogan said. He spoke in a firm imperative voice. "The Soviets are listening to what I am saying."

Around the War Room the tension became a pressure on the eardrums.

"That is a direct order," General Bogan said.

Colonel Cascio's mouth opened. The lips came back from the teeth. He swung his unseeing eyes toward General Bogan.

"A direct order," General Bogan repeated softly.

Colonel Cascio made a sound. It was low, primitive, agonized. It was a growl of despair. His body relaxed. He shook his head.

"Marshal Nevsky, the Colonel who is our expert on this subject has suffered some sort of seizure," General Bogan said. The translator spoke and over the "touch" phone there was a muttering of voices that grew in volume as Bogan listened. "We have prepared for such situations. Each of the men in the War Room has a standby who possesses the precise information which the active-duty man possesses." General Bogan paused. He looked around the room. Lieutenant Colonel Handel was there, Cascio's understudy. But Handel's eyes were glued on Cascio. They were close friends.

General Bogan struggled to keep control, to think clearly. He must quiet what he guessed was a rising suspicion in the distant Soviet headquarters. There could be no chancing a repetition of Cascio's behavior. His finger started down a list of names. He skipped over Handel and stopped at the master sergeant who backed up both colonels.

"Sergeant Collins, report to the Commanding General's desk at once," he said.

A door at the side of the War Room opened and a sergeant, rotund and middle-aged, came trotting toward the general's desk. He came to a stiff halt.

"Sergeant Collins, does the Bloodhound have both an infrared- and radar-seeking capacity?" General Bogan said.

"Yes, sir, it has both capacities," Collins said, a cherubic smile on his face.

"Can the radar-seeking mechanism be overloaded by increasing the strength of the signal?" the Russian translator said quickly. The voices in the background of the Soviet headquarters had died away.

General Bogan felt his body sag. Apparently they had decided to believe him.

"Yes, sir, it can be overloaded by increasing the transmission power output and by sliding through radar frequencies as quickly as possible," Sergeant Collins said. He was still smiling his anxious cherubic smile, quite unaware of the other men in the room staring at him, quite oblivious that he was unwittingly playing the role of Judas. "What happens is that the firing mechanism reads the higher amperage as proximity to the target and detonates the warhead."

"Thank you, General Bogan," the translator said quietly. "We have already communicated the information. We have rearranged our communications net so that tactical defensive maneuvers are controlled from this room."

General Bogan realized with a quick simple insight that with the new communication network his War Room was actually directing the defensive operations of the Soviets.

The new information was reflected almost instantly on the Big Board. Two Soviet blips began to move toward one of the Vindicators. When they were five miles distant the Vindicator dropped two tiny blips and the Bloodhounds hung almost motionless as their rockets began to ignite. They had barely separated from the bigger blip of the Vindicator when they were detonated by the information which Sergeant Collins had transmitted. Instantly the green funguslike splotch on the Big Board enveloped the Vindicator. Then the ugly blip exploded into enormousness. The two Soviet fighters were caught in the spreading blast and disappeared.

The light on the "touch" phone went off. Sergeant Collins turned and walked slowly from the room, seeming to deflate as he went.

General Bogan looked at Colonel Cascio. The recovery was unbelievable. The man seemed relaxed, the hard glitter gone from his eyes. He appeared perfectly normal and spoke apologetically about what had just taken place.

"I am sorry, General," he said. "I just could not do it. I don't quite remember what happened. The back of my eyes seemed to turn white and I couldn't see anything or say anything. I think I am all right now."

"Colonel, it could happen to anyone," General Bogan said. He knew this to be untrue, as did Cascio. Actually General Bogan was watching his colonel carefully. He considered the possibility of replacing him with Sergeant Collins. In theory Collins knew as much as Cascio about technical details. But Colonel Cascio, by a combination of training, intuition, and skill, was a much more valuable person. General Bogan knew he would have to keep him on the desk. He was turning away when Cascio grabbed his arm.

"General, I think it is a Soviet entrapment," Cascio said tensely. His voice was tight but under control. "We've known for weeks that they have been fooling around with our Fail-Safe mechanism. I think they wanted this to happen. I think we should tell the President that we think it is an entrapment, that the Soviets are using the time to ready their ICBMs and to fly their bombers to advantageous position for a second strike."

"But we do not have any evidence that they are moving their bombers," General Bogan said sharply.

"But, General, they might be flying bombers in the grass," Cascio said with urgency. "For all we know they might have hundreds of planes, already over the Arctic and heading for us. Also they may have fired ICBMs and put them in the trajectories of the known and identified satellites. Remember, sir, we computed that problem and decided that satellites could be used to mask ICBMs."

"Maybe, but I am not going to report anything that I do not know for sure," General Bogan said.

"I think we should recommend a full-strength strike immediately by all air-borne units to be followed by other strikes as soon as ICBMs and standby units can be activated," Colonel Cascio said.

"That decision rests with the Pentagon and the President," General Bogan said slowly.

"Look, General, those people at the Pentagon don't know the situation the way we know it," Colonel Cascio said. "They have secondhand information, they are not trained to evaluate an enemy who knows every trick in the book. They are in the political game. So is the President. We, those of us in this room, we are in the war business. We know it better than anyone else. If we move now and decisively we can still save the situation. Even though we've backed down from Condition Red we have enough bombers in the air to launch a crippling first strike. As you can see on the Big Board, the Soviets don't have anywhere near the defensive capacity we thought they might have."

General Bogan's head ached. He felt as if the neurons of his brain had begun to burn, like filaments that were overburdened with electricity. He stared at the Big Board and the blips and signs seemed like enormous and threatening mysteries. By a single action, one command, he could simplify everything. He sat down.

Colonel Cascio went on talking, but General Bogan did not hear the precise words, only the sound of persuasion.

General Bogan felt an odd and sudden companionship with Colonel Cascio. He was bitter toward an undefined authority, toward the "they" in Washington who had overburdened him. He turned in the chair. He felt smaller, more secure, more elemental. His fingers knotted into fists, his mouth opened slightly and gasped for air. He felt a terrible self-pity, an infantile sense of being asked to do too much. His body curled in the chair, he felt saliva gather in the corners of his mouth. He had the sensation that he could remember nothing of what he had just heard. His memory stopped and was only a second long. With a sense of relief he felt a sensuous sliding away into irresponsibility, into numbness, into something primordial. He felt a gurgle begin in his chest, a kind of primitive and very comforting voice. He felt warm, enclosed, removed. The sound reached his lips.

Then Colonel Cascio turned and looked at him full face. That look was enough. For a change had taken place. The hard, fixed stare was back in Cascio's eyes. Colonel Cascio was mad, crazy. The heat was gone from General Bogan's mind. Slowly he came to an upright position. He smiled the smile of a civilized man at Colonel Cascio.

"Colonel, you may not be aware of it, but you are talking mutiny," General Bogan said quietly. "One more exchange like this and I will have you taken from the War Room."

Colonel Cascio nodded, but his expression remained rigid.

The President's voice flooded back into the room. "General Bogan, will Group 6 break radio silence as they approach Moscow?"

"Yes, sir, just before they get within lob range of their target they have instructions to open regular radio communications."

"And when will that be?" the President asked.

General Bogan calculated quickly, "Well, sir, it should be just about any time now."

"Very well," said the President, "make arrangements for me to talk personally with the commanding officer of Group 6 as soon as he reopens radio communications."

"Very well, sir." Bogan pointed a silent order to Lieutenant Colonel Handel, who rushed from the room to make the necessary arrangements.

The light on the "touch" phone went on. A voice spoke quickly in Russian, the translator overriding the Russian, translating even as the other voice spoke.

"This is Marshal Nevsky in Ziev," the voice said. "We recently developed a radar-masking device which is installed on all our bombers. It picks up enemy radar signals and automatically distorts them. When your radar signal comes back it has been skewed anywhere from five to one hundred miles. We assume your planes have similar devices. Does your detection apparatus also pick up an incorrect location?"

"No, sir," General Bogan said. "On our plotting boards we have the correct latitude and longitude of our planes because of a compensating device on our radar which automatically corrects the radar signal which comes back from our planes."

General Bogan knew what the next question would be.

"Can you give us the longitude and latitude of the three planes left in the air?" Marshal Nevsky asked.

"We can do that, but we cannot give you their altitude," General Bogan said. "We have not been able to correct our altitude-determining radar to compensate for the distorting signals from the planes."

"Will you please give us the position of the three planes?" Marshal Nevsky asked. "We can fly fighters at various altitudes once we know their approximate position."

General Bogan felt weary. He leaned forward to push the lever which would open the intercom to the appropriate desk-console. Suddenly there was a stunning pain against his skull, a ringing in his ears; the room reeled and he had the quixotic impression that electricity had suddenly poured out of the telephone into his head. He was on the floor staring up at the lean contorted face of Colonel Cascio. And Cascio was talking in a firm and authoritative voice over the War Room intercom, the heavy crystal ash tray with which he had hit General Bogan still in his hand.

ch. 17

THE VINDICATORS

Group Commander Grady flew in total blackness, broken only by a single glowing scope. This scope combined both range and altitude radar results in such a way that it gave a stereoscopic image of the terrain ahead of them. At this altitude and speed the eye could not perceive a hill or tree or power line or smoke stack in sufficient time to take evasive action. But the scope picked out even the smallest raised obstacles and projected them blackly on the screen so that Grady merely had to lift the plane at the indicated spots to clear.

Occasionally when the scope showed fifty or sixty miles of clear terrain ahead, he glanced out of the windows into the quiet Russian night. He could see the lights of villages. Trucks and cars moved along highways. Occasionally the lights of a factory would glow in a great complex. Somehow the sight of normal activity disturbed Grady. He knew that a blackout was no protection against a nuclear bomb but it was also clear that the Russians were making no attempt to go to their bomb shelters.

Grady was beyond the point of rational analysis. The stress of fighting off the Soviet attacks, the bitter and blunt fact of watching his own planes go off in great smears of blast and light—all of this had reduced him to a tough, skeletal, and very single-minded person. He knew only one thing: get to the target.

"How is No. 2 plane doing?" he asked the Defensive Operator.

"She is hard to track so low but occasionally I can catch her," the operator said. "She's about fifty miles away and at nine o'clock. I think she may be losing a little speed and might be damaged."

"In a few minutes we will be at lob range. Let me know five minutes before we get there," Grady said. "We can come up on the TBS and find out what shape she is in then."

At lob point the Vindicators could elevate their noses, turn to afterburners, and "lob" their bombs onto the target. The "lob" distance could, depending on speed and missiles, range up to fifty miles. If they broke radio silence before that time there was a possibility that the Soviets would launch rockets designed to run the reciprocal of a radio beam and home in on the Vindicators. Once they approached the lob range, however, SAC headquarters wanted to know it, for it was virtually a certainty that the bombs could then be delivered and an evaluation made of the American strike. Past the lob-range point the planes were also free to communicate with one another if they desired.

"Six minutes to lob point," the navigator said. On the terrain scope a long, low range of hills came up slowly. They were twenty miles away and they would be reached in approximately forty seconds. Grady began to lift the nose of the Vindicator slightly.

"We are five minutes to lob point," the navigator said triumphantly.

"Turkey 2, Turkey 2," Grady spoke into the TBS microphone. "This is Turkey 6. What is your condition?"

"Turkey 6, this is Turkey 2," a voice said with remarkable distinctness. "We have suffered some slight wing damage because of shrapnel, but all it has done is reduce our speed. We are down to 1,350 miles an hour and the drag seems to be even."

"Turkey 2, our condition is excellent," Grady said. "As far as I know we have not been hit. We are now four minutes to lob point and I am going to report to base."

Grady reached forward and picked up another microphone.

"Ultimate No. 2, Ultimate No. 2," Grady said crisply. "This is Turkey 6. Do you hear me?"

"We read you five by five," a clear voice said in his ear. "We have a message for you."

"I am not authorized to receive messages," Grady said. "I am merely reporting that we are approaching the lob point and are undamaged."

A new voice broke in over Grady's radio. He recognized it immediately. An involuntary shock went through his body. The voice he heard was that of the President. But it could not be. He glanced at the Fail-Safe box. The "go" signal was clear and reassuring.

"Colonel Grady, this is the President of the United States, your Commander in Chief. The mission you are flying has been triggered by some mechanical failure. I order you and the other planes under your command to return to your base immediately."

Grady sat stunned, disbelieving. He did not speak. His hand moved toward the radio toggle switch, stopped three inches short. He looked at it. The hand dropped to his knee.

Grady looked at the navigator and then at the defense operator. They had also heard the message. Their eyes were fixed coldly upon Grady. He felt helpless. He was sinking. He wished he were somewhere else—anywhere else. He wanted to cry. His mind moaned a piteous complaint and abdicated; subconscious emotions were welling up within him and he was in their

control. He reverted to childlike thoughts. He wanted
God. He was a little boy who needed his mother. He
wanted to close his eyes—to close out this nightmare
and open them again as that little boy. He tried. He
closed his eyes. He opened them. No, it was true. The
voice came back over the radio at him.

"Colonel Grady, I repeat. This is the President."

Again the distinctive New England accent bored
into Grady's consciousness. But this time it had the
opposite effect. His mind focused. He saw clearly it
was an enemy ruse. How easy the President's voice
was to mimic, he thought, remembering the many
briefing sessions in which this possibility had been discussed. His nerves steeled. He interrupted the voice
briskly: "I am not authorized to receive tactical alterations by voice once past Fail-Safe. What you are telling
me I have been specifically ordered not to do."

"I know that, damn it, but this is—" Grady had
reached forward and flicked off the radio, leaving the
remainder of the President's frantic plea dangling in
space.

ch. 18

CASCIO'S COMMAND

The War Room was frozen in mid-action like a collection of children stopped rigid in a game of "Statues."

"Gentlemen," said Cascio, ignoring the body of General Bogan at his feet, "I am taking over command of this post at the specific order of the President of the United States. He has long been aware that General Bogan is psychologically unbalanced and he specifically warned me to observe him closely. The negotiations which General Bogan has been conducting with Marshal Nevsky are not authorized by the White House and are the acts of a madman. By the direct authority of the President of the United States I now authorize you to take all orders from me."

General Bogan felt a strange sense of wonderment. It was true, he realized dully, that the madman had a great advantage over the sane. Having only moments before walked up to the edge of lunacy himself, Bogan had an almost fatherly appreciation of Cascio's sure intuition. The colonel was performing beautifully, with the marvelous sensitivity to audience which marked the great actor.

General Bogan climbed to his knees, then carefully came to an upright position. He moved slowly, careful not to provoke Cascio into striking him again. General

Bogan looked around the room. There was a balance so delicate that it was almost palpable. Over the months General Bogan had come to know the personalities of the various officers and enlisted men in the War Room. Some of them already had the red of hatred and rebellion in their eyes. They would be willing to follow Cascio. The middle range, the officers who would serve long tenures as light colonels and retire as full colonels, were vacillating. The brighter of the officers, that small fraction destined for a rapid rise and a generalship, had already started to move. They were moving toward Cascio and against him.

But their movements were unnecessary. Out of the gloom of a far corner appeared two Air Force enlisted men wearing brassards and .45-caliber pistols. General Bogan had known that they were there, he had known it for months, but today he had forgotten them. They had become like furniture. He watched with an awed regard for their capacity to remain silent and invisible for months and then to move with such relentless stalking skill. They came like ballet dancers doing a piece of practiced choreography. They flowed by each chair and desk and person as if this were a daily routine. They came up behind Cascio quietly and with an enormous confidence.

One of the airmen tapped Colonel Cascio on the shoulder. He turned and saw the brassard and at once started to turn his head and to scream into the speaker, but his hand was empty. The other airman, with a blow that was swift and precise, had chopped at Cascio's wrist. The speaker had flipped neatly into the airman's hand. Cascio was screaming into an empty palm.

"Colonel, if you speak another word, our orders are to render you unconscious," the first airman said, and his lips broke into a smile at the extravagance of the language.

"I guarantee you, Colonel, that we can do it quicker than you can speak the next word," the other airman said.

Cascio had already fallen silent. In some way he sensed the end of his brief power. His face went suddenly lax. The sharp aquiline profile which had been rigidly composed for hours now suddenly went idiot. It seemed almost to puff out. General Bogan turned away. He realized that Cascio had gone through the terrible temptation, and yielded—the temptation to which General Bogan had been exposed only a few moments before. The first of the airmen tapped Cascio on the elbow and turned him with a robot docility. Bogan watched the man, Cascio, cave in as he walked away between the two airmen. By the time they reached the first exit Cascio seemed to be a shrunken, monkeylike version of the commanding figure he had been just thirty seconds before.

General Bogan turned quickly back to the touch phone.

"Marshal Nevsky, there has been a slight interruption in our operations here," General Bogan said. The touch phone had been on continuously. "I am now prepared to give you the longitude and latitude of our bombers, in accordance with your earlier request."

"General Bogan, I was aware of your difficulty," Marshal Nevsky said. "We have had one or two problems like that ourselves. One cannot foresee every situation. I await your information."

General Bogan quickly scanned the men in the room. His command was sure now. No need to be concerned about Handel or anyone else. Cascio had, in a perverse way, served his country. He had exhibited what every man—including Bogan himself—felt. His yielding to the insanely mutinous impulse had purged the similar impulses from the rest of them.

"Colonel Handel, I order you to give your best estimate of the longitude and latitude and the heading of all planes in Group 6," General Bogan said.

Colonel Handel read off the longitudes and latitudes and his voice went directly into the touch phone.

Immediately the planes closest to the Vindicators began to regroup, to close in. Now the fighters were flying at different altitudes searching for the Vindicators. The decoys were no longer effective.

Three of the Soviet fighters almost simultaneously linked on to the lead Vindicator. The Vindicator jinked, went into a dive, lost luminosity. So did the Soviet fighter blips.

"Marshal Nevsky, when the group is down to two surviving planes standard operating procedure is for those two planes to dive to the lowest feasible altitude and continue their attack as close to the ground as possible," General Bogan explained. "In this way they hope to escape your radar. The plane which your three fighters are now engaging is a defensive plane only. It has no bombs aboard. It carries only defensive devices."

Bogan's heart sank on hearing Nevsky's voice. He suspected what the changed tone of the Russian marshal meant. The words from the translator were: "Thank you, General Bogan, but we will try for a kill in any case."

Even when filtered through the translator's neutral voice the words carried the impression of mistrust. He knew what Nevsky was thinking. It was what any commanding officer would have to think in Nevsky's position.

General Bogan turned wearily to the Big Board. The three blips of the remaining bombers were easily distinguishable from the Soviet fighters scattered in their path. No. 6 bomber was clearly in the lead. As General Bogan watched, the configuration of Russian fighters changed slightly and veered toward No. 6. Bogan wanted to turn away. He knew the outcome. The fighters converged on No. 6's diversionary run. Suddenly a green blotch supplanted the No. 6 Vindicator as well as the fighters around her. She was gone, but she had served her final diversionary function. She had feinted the Russian fighters out of position. The remaining two Vindicators were now almost certain to make it. As General Bogan watched they had shifted to maximum speed. At their present reduced weight they could approach 2,000 miles an hour and slip through for the Moscow bomb run.

The sound of a commotion came over the touch phone. Muffled voices in Russian were interrupted by a louder noise. Then a single Russian voice came over the line. The translator's flat English explained: "Marshal Nevsky has just collapsed. It appears to be—I don't know. He is being carried out of the room. General Koniev is now in command."

Simultaneously the voices of the President and Swenson interrupted, demanding an explanation.

"I think I can explain," General Bogan broke in. His voice was sympathetic and full of understanding. "Marshal Nevsky sent his fighters after our No. 6 plane, though I told him it carried no bombs. This final diversion let the other two planes through. But he did what any good officer would do. He followed standard safeguarding procedures. He went after all three. Our final approach tactic is based upon the assumption this will occur. Moscow will shortly receive

80 megatons. Marshal Nevsky realized this almost immediately."

The Big Board quickly verified General Bogan's prediction. The two remaining Vindicators went into a steep dive and fifteen seconds later they disappeared. The Soviet fighters began to disperse again in a random pattern.

"The two Vindicators have gone off our screen," General Koniev said. "Do you still have them?"

"No, General, we have lost them too," General Bogan said.

General Koniev paused. General Bogan sensed that he wanted reassurance. General Bogan also sensed that the best way to give it was to remain silent.

"Can you raise them by radio?" General Koniev asked.

"No," said General Bogan. "The bombers resumed silence after the President's recall attempt failed. However, we're still trying."

"What defensive capacity do they still have?" General Koniev asked.

General Bogan pushed a lever and the thin mechanical voice from the appropriate desk said, "We are not sure of their defensive capacity. Things got a bit confused for a few minutes there. We estimate it as no less than fifty per cent and no more than seventy-five per cent. They have almost one hundred per cent of their decoy and masking devices, but these are not very great."

"We are unable to pick them up on radar and they are traveling so fast that visual sighting by antiaircraft cannon is almost useless," General Koniev said slowly. "I must assume that the two planes will get through."

"I think you are correct," General Bogan said.

"We have only one chance left," General Koniev said. "That is to focus all our remaining rockets in

their estimated path and fire them simultaneously at
the right moment in an effort to set up an impenetra-
ble thermonuclear barrier."

"It has a chance," General Bogan admitted admir-
ingly. "Let us pray that it succeeds."

"I am trying it, but I'm afraid your estimate is right.
Two planes will probably get through. And then, however it goes, whether just your four bombs or our thousands of bombs and your thousands of bombs, it is all
over. We will have devoted a lifetime to assuring our
own destruction."

General Bogan rocked back in his chair and looked
at the empty seat that had been Colonel Cascio's. He
thought of the other room and the empty chair of
Marshal Nevsky. They had both been honest and patri-
otic craftsmen. Each had worked with courage and
determination to win. Each had lost. Everyone had
lost.

"Are there surprises that you have left for us?" General Bogan asked.

"None, General Bogan," General Koniev said. "Your
people," he paused, "have been honest with us. The
simple fact is that they were also better than we
thought. Six hours ago I would have guaranteed that
we would have shot down one hundred per cent of a
single wing of your planes. If you had sent a massive
first strike, we knew our record would not have been
so good. But I could not have believed that our forces
would prove incapable of handling just six planes, as
they seem to have been."

There was a heavy silence between these two professional soldiers. Each roughly knew what the other was
thinking. They had never met. They had never talked.
They had known of one another's existence, but only
as names in an "order of battle" schedule. But each
had a sense of how identical the careers, the risks, the

chances, the ambitions, the losses, the gains, and, most telling, the ignorance, on both sides had been.

"General Koniev, how many minutes do we have?" General Bogan asked.

"I should say about eighteen to twenty minutes, depending on how much decoy and masking capacity your two planes have," General Koniev answered. "We are shooting off everything we have. Our antiaircraft rings are having a field day. One of our fighter-bombers fired a rocket into a forest and it has lit up the landscape for miles around. He fired at a short-range radar station which had not turned on its IFF and he thought it was a Vindicator although it was completely stationary. Tomorrow I will have to pass judgment upon the pilot of that plane. If there is a tomorrow."

General Bogan mused. This was like the idle conversation that truck drivers used to exchange when he was a college undergraduate and drove trucks during his vacation. The crisis was over, the long haul made. They were engaged in shoptalk. It was a way to pass the time until the final decision.

"General Koniev, what is your location right now?" General Bogan asked suddenly.

It had occurred to General Bogan that General Koniev might not be in the equivalent of Omaha. He felt a sense of alarm for the man on the other end of the phone.

"I am several hundred miles from Moscow," General Koniev said. "It was not an orderly dispersion. When Premier Khrushchev left he ordered a handful of us to leave. I was among the handful."

General Bogan was about to speak and then he fell mute. He wondered if General Koniev had left his family in Moscow. But he did not want to know.

"It is a hard day," General Bogan said to the translator.

There was a long pause.

The word came back from the translator. General Bogan knew the response before it was translated.

"This is a hard day, General Bogan," General Koniev said. "Good-bye, comrade," General Koniev said.

"Good-bye, my friend," General Bogan said.

The translator paused, hesitated, and then knew it was unnecessary to translate. Everyone waited.

ch. 19

THE LAST MILE

The two remaining bombers bored on through the night, each man doing his little drill. A curious cool lankness came over Grady's mind. He felt outside of himself, as if he were watching himself from a few feet away. He *was* an automated man, under the rubber and nylon suit and the pressure helmet. There was only flesh and bone; there was no heart. There was intellect, but it lay inert, unmotivated by emotion. The intellect stared at the scope, altered the altitude from time to time, acknowledged reports from the navigator and the defense operator.

It was fear that brought Grady back within his body.

"Jesus Christ, sweet Jesus Christ," the defense operator said. Then the old controls reasserted themselves.

"Colonel Grady, the infrared indicator shows that a large number of rocket engines have been ignited approximately twenty miles in front of us. They should start showing up on radarscope in a second," the defense operator said.

Fifteen years of training whirred through Grady's mind. In intelligence briefings he had been informed that there would probably be this last belt of rockets. He also knew that the rockets were designed to fire at high-flying targets. To avoid having the rockets fly at friendly heat-producing installations like steel factories, most of them were designed to be inoperative until they reached a very high altitude. Then they could, by a number of devices, seek out heat-producing engines.

"How many Bloodhounds do we have left?" Grady asked the defense operator.

"Two," the defense operator said.

Now Grady's mind, challenged by this technical problem, was turning over rapidly, evaluating and re-checking various alternatives. Yet he knew that he would find an answer only by intuition. And then it came to him: the Soviets intended to launch all their remaining rockets simultaneously. They would deto-nate at an altitude high enough to spare the country-side but the huge fireball and the thermonuclear bar-rier spreading out in all directions might knock down the Vindicators.

He knew it was a Russian gamble. For no one was certain what a thermonuclear screen would do to nu-clear devices. Shock, heat, neutron bombardment, or all three together might abort the attack. Grady had his decision.

"The second that they start to rise on the radar-scope, fire the two Bloodhounds, one to port and one to starboard, and guide them for a maximum elevation straight up," Grady ordered.

"Straight up, sir?" the operator asked. He had never heard of such a tactic. His voice froze with skepticism.

"Straight up, the instant you see the enemy rockets start to rise," Grady rasped.

There was a pause of two seconds.

"There," the operator said. Instantly Grady felt the Vindicator dip as the Bloodhounds took off. He saw the twin rush of their rockets. A brilliant burst of flames lit up the night, a private spectacle provided by the two gigantic roman candles which sped out before the Vindicator prior to turning on the upward arc

which sent them flaming dramatically into the black
night sky. Grady turned to the defense operator.

"How much more speed can you get from the Bloodhounds by putting them on fullblast?"

"Five hundred miles an hour, but it will increase the
fuel consumption," the operator said quickly. "At that
angle they would probably get no higher than 120,000
feet before they ran out of fuel."

Grady was doing his calculations by eye and intuition. He estimated that when the Soviet missiles
reached 20,000 feet the two Bloodhounds would be
2,500 feet above them. He was gambling that although
they had probably been set to explode at 20,000 feet
there was also an "overriding command" built into
them that if they perceived a target within range that
they would pursue it. He knew that they would be
keyed to detonate at something less than 2,000 feet
from the target. If he could keep the Bloodhounds
2,500 feet above the wave of Soviet missiles, there was
the possibility that they would all start to home automatically and senselessly on the Bloodhounds.

"Give the Bloodhounds just enough extra boost, in
little shots, so that they stay at least 2,500 feet above
the enemy missiles," Grady said.

The operator's face swung toward Grady and the
eyes were full of a savage admiration and a gleam of
understanding. His long, sensitive, musicianlike fingers
reached for the controls.

"They're at 18,000, now 19,000, now 20,000," the
operator sang out. This highly unorthodox procedure
seemed to fill him with delight.

Then they both fell silent and stared at the scope.
The wave of missiles was now directly overhead and
Grady's hand, without thought and quite by reflex,
went to the lever which controlled the lob device. If
the rockets exploded in the next second, he would have

time to lob the two bombs toward Moscow—just before the Vindicator was beaten to earth by the blast.

The line of missiles came to 20,000 feet and then passed 20,000. Then the perfect line began to angle off as the outer missiles turned toward the Bloodhounds. Instantly Grady recognized that the tactic had succeeded. The missiles were now chasing the two Bloodhounds and those that were the farthest away were losing some altitude as they angled toward the two decoys. The operator was whispering to himself as he watched the instruments. He reached for control, pulled it down for a moment, and the two Bloodhounds leapt up ahead. They were still responding to signal.

The Soviet missiles also automatically boosted their speed. At one end of the line there was suddenly a bright eruption of light. One of the missiles had misfired. The blast wave was picked up by the scope and it temporarily obscured several dozens of the blips around it.

Grady shook his head and yelled into the intercom.

"Pull her back! Go for altitude!" He had also pushed the button for TBS so that Turkey 2 would hear him. "Stand by for a ram." Four seconds later the blast wave hit the Vindicator. It seemed as if the air had suddenly turned hard. The plane was pressed down as if by a giant's steady smashing power. Grady looked at the altimeter. In the four seconds they had gained 1,200 feet of altitude and now they had been battered back down 1,000 feet. Then the blast passed. The plane shot upward, shuddering as tiny rolling waves hit it.

The operator turned and looked at Grady. He winked. His eyes were alight with success and a hard pride. Also, there was something else in the eyes, a kind of dread knowledge. He knew that the three of them would soon be bombarded by a lethal dosage of neutrons. They would die, but not before their mission was accomplished.

The scope cleared. The Bloodhounds were now at 100,000 feet and the converging pack of Soviet missiles had taken the form of a vast arrow of pursuit. A few seconds later the Bloodhounds would reach 150,000 feet.

The defense operator chuckled to himself. "They're getting more range than I thought," he said. "Maybe they'll go 200,000 feet."

In fact, they went to 220,000 feet. Then abruptly they began to slow down and the great pursuing arrow of missiles streaked toward them. Suddenly the entire scope seemed to erupt in an enormous explosion as all the Soviet rocket warheads went off simultaneously.

Without orders the navigator had fought for altitude ever since the first blast wave had passed. They were now flying at close to 10,000 feet. When the shock wave from the explosion came it was much less severe than the first one. The awful physics of time and distance had weakened its thrust. The Vindicator was shaken savagely and the wings dipped. But when the pressure passed, although an ominous groan came from where the wings joined the fuselage, they held.

"We're making like a fat-assed bird," Grady shouted. Through their masks the navigator and defense operator eyed him cautiously.

"How many minutes to Moscow?" Grady asked.

"Seven minutes," the navigator replied.

There remained only one decision for Grady to make. At the present altitude, their chances of being shot down by orthodox antiaircraft were negligible. But when they dropped the bombs, even if they made an abrupt rise of 1,000 or 1,500 feet they would be destroyed by the blast. If they climbed to 25,000 or 30,000 feet, a safe altitude, they would simplify the problem for conventional antiaircraft and increase the chances of their being shot down. But in a real sense the decision had been made. Grady felt a kind of mild euphoria. His mind raced back to the old informal days of flying where pilot and crew knew, and sometimes even loved, one another. There was no reason under current procedures why he had to talk to the other two men in the plane at all. If he wanted, he could carry out the mission completely by himself. They would, he knew, not even look at him as he gave the order to drop the bombs. But every man should have some say in the matter of how he is to die. Anyway Grady wanted to talk.

"Look," Grady said. "We're not just walking wounded, we're walking dead men. That first blast must have given us enough Roentgens to shrivel the marrow in our bones. We'd have a couple of days at best. So I intend to take her in at 900 feet and then when we are over the target to climb to 5,000. The bombs are set to detonate at 5,000 so we'll go with them."

He glanced at the two men. The two pairs of eyes stared levelly at him. Then Thompson spoke.

"O.K., skipper," he said. "There's nothing to go home to anyway." He laughed.

ch. 20

THE CONFERENCE LINE

The American Ambassador and the Soviet delegate to the United Nations reported on the conference line before Khrushchev came on.

"Where are you, Mr. Ambassador?" the President asked.

"On the top floor of the American Embassy in Moscow in my library," the American Ambassador said.

"Where are you, Mr. Lentov?" the President asked the Soviet delegate.

"In the UN building in New York," Lentov replied.

"Whatever happens I would like both of you to stay precisely where you are until I release you or Premier Khrushchev releases you," the President said.

Then, slowly and calmly, he told them what had happened. When he had finished both of the men were silent for a moment. Buck glanced at the President. He knew what all of the men on the line were thinking: the American Ambassador was exposed, without protection if the Vindicators got through. All of the men on the line except Buck were experienced diplomats. They had run risks before. They were calm.

Buck could hardly believe what he heard next. The Soviet delegate began to discuss baseball scores. He was surprisingly knowledgeable. He confessed that his favorite team was the New York Yankees.

"I know that it is somewhat like rooting for the aristocracy," he said with a laugh. "But I cannot resist them. The first year I was here was the year that Mantle and Maris tried to break Babe Ruth's home-run record. It is a question of the power and the grace. I admire both qualities."

"In that case, if you had been an American you would have become a Wall Street lawyer," the President said.

"Oh, now, Mr. President," the Soviet delegate answered, "remember I said power *and* grace. Your Wall Street people have the power, but they are still lacking in grace. No, if I had been an American, I would have been a designer, probably of cars. The only thing in America which equals our Communist party in naked power, grace, and the ability to take adversity is the American car. Its exterior is often hideous, as is our Communist party, but inside it is rugged and durable."

"I agree with you, Ambassador Lentov, about power and grace." It was the American Ambassador speaking. A voice from the grave, Buck thought, casual remarks from a man about to be burned alive. A clear and steady voice, not a tremor in it. Buck's hand began to shake violently as it clenched the phone. He could not bring himself to look into the President's face. The voice went on. "It is a combination of power and grace which makes for top success in baseball as in politics. In both games the very best are a class apart. You can tell them from the first day in a training camp. Their objective is beautifully simple. It is the top. Once they have made the decision, their energies, their intelligence, their muscles, everything, give their naked power the additional virtue of grace. The multitude of the second-best often have as much power drive, but they lack the thing that Mr. Lentov calls grace."

"But no, Mr. Ambassador, it has little to do with natural endowment," the Soviet delegate said. "I once served in Mexico and came to love the bullfights. Often the best *torero* would be a scrawny, chicken-breasted fellow. But once in the ring, there he would possess what you call grace."

There was a long silence. The American Ambassador was well-bred, wealthy, married to a beautiful woman, was reputed to be a good father, and a tremendously hard worker. But it was not until this moment that Buck realized he lacked a single quality, "grace."

"There is a grandeur about such a life," the President said. "But there is also a desolation about it. Take Babe Ruth. I never saw him in action but I saw him after he had retired. He was like the husk of a man. Once the husk had been filled with a desire and a will and a pride of accomplishment. When I saw him there was a dullness to the eyes, a flaccidness to the muscles. I remember my father had a collection of pictures of people like Herbert Hoover, John Nance Garner, Bernard Baruch, Eisenhower, and Truman, which he kept in fine oak frames in his study. He regarded them as tragedies. Men cut off from power while they still had the grace and the desire to exercise it. They were somehow like puzzled old bulls."

"Maybe our way is better," the Soviet delegate said dryly. "In my country there are old cows and there are old steers, but there are no old bulls who still have potency. As long as the old bull has power he fights, he is useful. There is only one kind of retirement for the virile old bull: death. In a way it is better."

The connection with Khrushchev was made in utter silence. Buck jumped when he heard the voice come up on the conference line.

"Comrade Lentov, you have become a philosopher," Khrushchev said. Instantly all of Buck's mind and intuition went into alert. There was a marked difference in the voice.

"Mr. Premier, this is a time for philosophy," the Soviet delegate said.

They all waited. Khrushchev did not respond. Then he spoke on a different matter.

"I was told that you had invited your Ambassador to Moscow and my delegate to the UN to join us," Khrushchev said. "I assume there is a reason."

Buck found the word he wanted to describe Khrushchev's tone—finality. He reached over and scrawled on the President's pad: "Finality. Tone heavy, final. K. has decided."

The President read the message without change of expression.

"There is a reason," the President said. "First let us know how it is going with the Vindicators."

"My experts tell me that two of them will probably get through and will bomb Moscow," Khrushchev said heavily. "Your estimate was correct, Mr. President."

"I take no pleasure in it, Premier Khrushchev," the President said.

Buck thought suddenly of Khrushchev's family, the daughter and the wife with her baggy clothes and plain face who had somehow endeared herself to Americans when the Khrushchevs had visited years before. Were they in Moscow?

"Let's get on with it," Khrushchev said roughly. "In a few minutes the bombs will be falling. I have brought my whole retaliatory apparatus to full readiness. If we cannot satisfy one another in the next few minutes I must release that apparatus. What do you propose, Mr. President?"

The President sat straight in his chair. With his left hand he held the phone to his ear. With his right hand he drew a straight black slash of a line down the precise center of the note pad in front of him.

"First I will tell you what will happen, Mr. Premier," the President said firmly. Suddenly the flesh around his mouth turned white, but his voice did not falter. "Then I will tell you what I intend to do to demonstrate our sincerity."

"Proceed, Mr. President," Mr. Khrushchev said. "But make it as brief as possible, if you please."

"The two planes will drop four 20-megaton bombs on Moscow. There is a possibility that our Ambassador will hear the sound of jet engines a moment or two before the bombs drop," the President said. "In any case, he will be aware of antiaircraft fire from your guns and, perhaps, the sound of your defensive missiles blasting off. A few seconds after he hears this noise, the bombs will explode. When they do, even if our Ambassador cannot say anything, his telephone will give off a distinctive shrill sound as it melts from the heat of the fireball. We know; we have tested. When we hear that sound we will know that the American Ambassador to Moscow is dead."

A grunt came over the line, as if someone had taken a hard blow in the stomach. Buck thought it came from Khrushchev but then he was not sure. For a moment there was silence on the conference line.

"Do you understand, Mr. Ambassador, that you are to stay precisely where you are?" the President asked.

"Yes, sir," came the Ambassador's voice.

"Mr. President!" Khrushchev's voice fairly exploded over the telephone. Involuntarily Buck winced and looked at the President. There was neither sorrow nor sympathy in the voice now, only rage. "Is this your grand plan? To sacrifice one American—the good Ambassador—for five million Muscovites?" The voice literally choked with anger, then rumbled on. Buck wrote the word "rage" on the President's pad and watched his hand shake as he did so. A simple scene swam into Buck's mind and it was captioned "End of the World." It was, he realized, the way he had always pictured it. There were rows of buttons on a board—blue, green, and red buttons—and a thick peasant hand with stubby fingers hovered over them, seemingly about to plunge. At that moment, with Khrushchev's voice babbling now incomprehensibly in his ear, the hand started on its final murderous downward arc. A terror, pure and simple as anything Buck had ever felt, clawed at his guts.

The President's voice, high-pitched and urgent and barely under control, snapped him out of it. Buck's translation rode over Khrushchev's voice and he found he was shouting, repeating phrases, banging the table with his fist. "No, no, Mr. Premier. That is not what I had in mind. You must listen to me, *listen to me*. At the moment that we hear the shriek of the melting telephone in Moscow, I will order a SAC squadron which is at this moment flying over New York City to drop four 20-megaton bombs on that city in precisely the pattern and altitude in which our planes have been ordered to bomb Moscow. They will use the Empire State Building for ground zero. When we hear the second shriek over the conference line we will know that your delegate to the United Nations is gone and along with him, New York."

"Holy Mother of God," Khrushchev said. His voice seemed almost like a pant.

Then there was a deep silence. Suddenly, like a mechanical mockery, there was a flare-up of static on the line. It sounded like some macabre laugh, something torn from the soul of the mechanical system.

"There is no other way, Mr. Premier, that I could think to demonstrate to you our sincerity," the President said softly. "We will each have lost our largest city. But most of our people and our wealth and our property and our social fabric will remain. It is an awful calculation. I could think of no other." He paused and his voice dropped low. "Unless, unless you think it unnecessary. Unless you feel the offer itself is enough. Showing our intentions—" He stopped in mid-sentence and Buck saw cross his face a look of physical pain, of some kind of extreme agony, and in his eyes the last flickering hope.

There was silence on the line for a full ten seconds.

"I would like to say that this is unnecessary," Khrushchev finally said. "I cannot. We have worked ourselves into a position of suspicion and hatred so great that the only way out is to proceed with what you suggest. My people would liquidate any leader who allowed the destruction of Moscow to go unavenged. My successor would be forced to take a greater vengeance. More than just New York would be destroyed. Then you would retaliate. . . . No, this is tragic, but it must be so."

"We must sacrifice some so that the others can survive," the President said and his voice was weary. "I do not know how the Americans will take my action. It may be my last. I hope they will understand."

There was another pause. Each of the men on the conference line realized the weird inappropriateness of mere words. Also, each was in his own particular kind of shock. They sat quietly.

"Jay, I am grateful," the President said to the American Ambassador. "I am also grateful to you, Mr. Lentov."

"I thank you both," Khrushchev said. He paused, "I also admire you."

"Thank you," the Ambassador and the delegate said almost simultaneously.

They waited quietly.

"I must tell my people at the Pentagon and Omaha of my decision," the President said finally. "I will speak so that you can hear what I say."

ch. 21

NO OTHER WAY

It took only a few seconds for the White House switchboard to make the phone connections. When the President spoke, the War Room in Omaha and the Big Board room in the Pentagon had been added to the conference line. In those two rooms the President's voice came over the loudspeaker system.

"Gentlemen, I have had to make a terrible decision," the President said. "It is the hardest I have ever made. I have not asked your advice because this is not a decision on which one needs or can use advice. I want the responsibility to be entirely mine."

General Bogan listened to the words with his body tensed. He knew fatigue in every bone, but he also knew that in the next moment he might have to direct the attack of hundreds of SAC bombers against the Soviet Union. He felt a basic and immense confusion. He could not conceive of how general war could be avoided. Yet in all of the hundreds of conferences he had attended no situation just like this one had ever been anticipated. He felt crippled, oddly disabled.

In the Pentagon Groteschele whispered to Stark as the President paused.

"He's going to send in a full strike," Groteschele said. "He has to. There is nothing else he can do."

Stark looked at Groteschele and then he licked his

lips, cleared his throat. Groteschele realized that Stark was frightened. The fact amazed him. It also started a tiny root of fear twitching in Groteschele. Suddenly it was no longer an elegant and logical game. Real men in real bombers and real missiles carrying real thermonuclear warheads would soon be in motion. Their targets would be millions of unprotected people. Long ago Groteschele had stopped thinking of war in terms of flesh and blood and death and wounds. He thought in terms of neat strategies and impeccable rules. Now, quite suddenly, in a physical way, he understood what might happen. His mind resisted, but his body trembled with a series of small shocks.

"Two of the Vindicators will, apparently, get through to Moscow and will deliver four 20-megaton bombs on that city," the President said. "Moscow has not been alerted. Premier Khrushchev estimates that it would cause panic and would not save lives in any case. When the bombs fall on Moscow we will know that fact because our Ambassador's phone will give off a distinctive sound as it is burned by the explosion."

The President paused. Buck felt that he should look away, but he could not. The President was about to outline the most sweeping and incredible decision that any man had ever made, and it was a decision which he hated. But he was boxed in, cornered by some accident of history, trapped by some combination of mechanical errors not even fully understood.

"I have attempted to persuade Premier Khrushchev that this was a mistake, a tragic error," the President said. "I have made available to him all of the classified information which his defensive forces required. Premier Khrushchev has not launched his retaliatory forces but he will unless he receives some dramatic evidence of our sincerity. The scales must be balanced—

and right away. The discussion we had is not important. The result is. If Moscow is bombed by our bombers, I must order a group of Vindicator bombers now circling over New York to deliver four 20-megaton bombs on that city. That is all, gentlemen."

Congressman Raskob was the first person at Omaha to respond. For a long moment he was as rigidly uncomprehending as the rest of the men in the room. Like them he stared at the loudspeakers, not sure that he had heard correctly. Then Raskob got to his feet and walked over to General Bogan. He still had the walk like La Guardia, but the cockiness had gone.

"He can't do it, General," Raskob said in a quiet voice. His eyes were blank, like something painted on marble. "You can stop him. Even if they call it mutiny you can stop him." He paused and seemed to be talking to himself. "Emma, the kids, the house, all gone. The whole 46th Congressional District. All gone." Raskob's voice took on a lilting, persuasive, hectoring tone. It was the voice he used in the House. "Congress will support you to the hilt, General. You will go down as the most famous patriot of all time."

General Bogan sensed that by some peculiar psychological quirk the shock had simply turned Raskob's inner thoughts into words. He was talking to save his sanity.

"I'm sorry, Congressman Raskob," General Bogan said. "My God, I'm sorry! I know your family lives in New York. But eighty or ninety or a hundred million lives in America and as many more in Russia are at stake, Congressman Raskob," and General Bogan realized he was using the title deliberately to bring Raskob back to reality. "Congressman Raskob, think of that. And even if I did not understand his decision, I would not disobey the President."

Raskob's eyes came back to life and the look in them

made General Bogan turn away. It was a look of pure desolation.

"I can understand the decision if I forget it's my home, if I just think of politics. The power balance must be reestablished or the world will explode—I can see that. An eye for an eye, a city for a city. It is the way justice works when it rests on power. We sacrifice a city to save the nation," Raskob said and his voice was gentle and rational. "But my city—my home—my family—mine—mine—" Raskob lowered his head to the table. Both hands were palm up and he buried his face in them. It was a brief reversion to a gesture of sorrow as old as man himself. But Raskob raised his head quickly. His face was composed. "It must be done," he said simply. "An eye for an eye. There should be some other way, but there isn't." His eyes, that had been marble-dead a moment before, were filling with tears, but his voice was controlled. "Politics is filled with hard decisions, but this is the hardest one ever made. And it is correct."

"I think it is correct, sir," General Bogan said.

"General, would there be time for me to fly to New York?" Raskob said. "I would like to be with my family."

"No, sir, there would not be time," General Bogan said. "And even if there were I would not allow you to leave this room until the situation was resolved."

Raskob nodded understanding. He walked over and sat down at a desk.

"The machines and the men and the decisions got out of phase," Knapp told General Bogan. "We knew that something like this could happen in theory, but no one wanted to take it past that. No one knew how to turn it into diplomatic terms without seeming to be dealing from weakness."

General Bogan listened, but aside from a sense of

respect for Knapp, he did not follow Knapp's words. He was thinking of Raskob.

He sensed somehow the disbelief that must be gripping Raskob. It was almost beyond grasping that all of the skyscrapers, the scores of office buildings, the tenements, the housing developments, the bridges, and the millions of people would, in a few minutes, be gone. It would be a place of fire, dust, great winds, and a landscape of black mounds of melted steel, carbonized flesh.

Would Raskob ever go back to New York, General Bogan wondered? For no apparent reason he was sure that Raskob would. Not out of morbidity, but out of curiosity as to what the ruins would look like. And out of love for what had been. The ancient image of the Wandering Jew came to Bogan's mind and under it a kind of caption: politician without a constituency.

The General shook his head to clear it of another man's sorrow, only to find that it was his own.

In the Pentagon the heads swung toward Swenson when the President had finished speaking. Most of the people around the table knew that Swenson's family lived in New York and that the headquarters of his business was also located there. Swenson's face did not change expression.

"Are there any papers or documents in New York which are absolutely essential to the running of the United States?" Swenson asked. "And would there be time to get them out of New York, General Stark?"

"No-no, sir, there would not be time," Stark said. He was having trouble with his voice. "There are a number of irreplaceable documents in New York, but none of them are absolutely crucial for the running of the country. Of course, the records of a large number of private companies—"

"They will be able to rebuild without those papers," Swenson interrupted. He looked sharply around the table for signs of revolt, cracking nerve, a break in the chain. What he saw he found reassuring.

Because time must be passed and the group might be called upon for further decisions, Swenson forced a discussion of steps that would be taken by companies to reconstruct the records that would be destroyed in New York. The conversation was bizarre. It was led by a man whose entire family might be burnt to death in a very few minutes and carried on by men who had not the slightest interest in the subject matter. But Swenson forced them to it, snapped roughly at the CIA man once, caught Stark in an error in logic.

Groteschele when he had heard the President's words thought first of his family, but only briefly. Chiefly he thought of them because he had always heard that in emergencies men thought of their families. In Scarsdale they would probably escape the effects of the fireball and direct blast. If they survived that they would be able to go to the bomb shelter which Groteschele had had built in their back yard.

Then, having done his duty toward family, Groteschele thought of his future. If both Moscow and New York were destroyed it would be the end of his present career. After such a catastrophe, triggered by an error which no one could identify, the world would not tolerate further discussion and preparation for nuclear war. Surely the great powers would disarm to a point below the level where such an accident could be repeated.

For a moment he felt a pang of theoretical regret. He really would have liked to see the thermonuclear war fought out along the lines which he had debated, expounded, and contemplated. It was not true, he told himself, that one fears death more than anything. One might be willing to die to see one's ideas proven.

Then Groteschele swung his attention to what his future work would be. If there were drastic cutbacks in military expenditures many businesses would be seriously affected; some of them would even be ruined. A man who understood government and big political movements could make a comfortable living advising the threatened industries. It was a sound idea, and Groteschele tucked it away in his mind with a sense of reassurance.

He threw himself into the discussion about the reconstruction of records with zest. Swenson eyed him carefully and guessed almost exactly what had gone through Groteschele's mind.

"Mr. Secretary, will there be any effort to warn the people in New York about the bombs?" Wilcox said.

Swenson looked sharply at Wilcox. When he spoke his voice was cold.

"That is the President's decision, Wilcox," Swenson said. "I assume he has discussed it with Premier Khrushchev and taken whatever action he considers appropriate."

Stark looked at the Big Board. At one side of it there was a line of buttons, all of them glowing green. One of those buttons would have turned red if an air-raid alarm had been signaled or the Civilian Defense agencies had been alerted. Stark knew that Swenson also knew that, but that Wilcox probably did not.

"A lot of lives could be saved if people had even a few moments to take cover," Wilcox said stubbornly. He was not a man who frightened easily. His voice was controlled and Swenson knew that he had nothing to fear on the score of Wilcox becoming hysterical. But the mood of the room was becoming what Swenson had anticipated but not found a few minutes before—that of an unbelievable tension, an eerie overcontrol.

Wilcox reached in his brief case and took out that day's copy of *The New York Times*. He threw it on the table so that it slid to a stop in front of Swenson. Squarely in the center of the front page was a picture of the President's wife. She was in New York for the opening of a new art center.

Everyone at the table except Swenson stared rigidly at the picture. The President's wife was a beautiful woman who had captured the imagination of the American public as few other women in public life before her. With a simple elegance, she did a great many things: painted, dedicated children's hospitals, wore handsome clothes, entertained the great and the powerful, traveled around the world representing her husband, and cared for her children.

Swenson looked sharply at Wilcox, then at the other men around the table. He had read a great deal about how people behaved under stress. One thing emerged from the studies: a group could stand a very high level of tension, of terror even, if they were certain that everyone in the group was equally exposed. Allow even the suggestion of preferential treatment and a composed group would disintegrate into a chaotic melee of desperate individuals.

Was Wilcox trying to suggest that the President's wife would or should receive some sort of preferential treatment? Even officers as magnificently trained as those gathered in this room could be shattered if they thought that the President might be calling New York to get his wife out of the city.

"I don't quite understand you, Wilcox," Swenson said. "Make yourself clear and quickly."

Wilcox's finger went past the picture of the President's wife and pointed at a story in the left-hand column of the *Times*. "CIVILIAN DEFENSE CHIEF STATES SURVIVAL RATE WOULD GO UP GEOMETRICALLY WITH TIME OF WARNING." It was an article in which the Civilian Defense Director had issued a reassuring statement that with a few hours warning casualties in an all-out war could be cut drastically.

Swenson realized that Wilcox had not even considered the fate of the President's wife. It had never occurred to him that the President would do such a thing as give prior warning to his own family.

Groteschele, Stark, and the CIA man all laughed simultaneously. It was a short, mirthless but relieving laugh. Swenson looked at them and smiled. Wilcox looked at the others in astonishment, then growing irritation.

"On very short notice an alert to a big city would probably do more harm than good," Swenson said. "A couple of hours and people can be dispersed and moved. But with a couple of minutes warning all you would do is produce an enormous amount of panic, crowding of the streets, a frantic searching of parents for children, and the rest. Statistically, more people are in protected spots just before the alarm than they are right after it."

Stark started to say something and Swenson looked at him and shook his head silently.

He knew what Stark was going to say: if four 20-megaton bombs are dropped on Manhattan no one is going to survive even if they are in the strongest bomb shelter made for civilian use. Of course, there would be a few exceptions—some technician at a hospital who happened to be in a room supplied with oxygen and surrounded by stout walls, some janitor in a deeply buried basement in which by some quirk he could

suck in the sewer air and subsist on that for a few
hours. But it would not be more than twenty or thirty
people, Swenson felt sure.

Some old reflexive control kept Swenson from thinking of his own family. It could do no good. And at the
core of his personality was an almost fierce love and
sentimentality about his family. Once exposed, once
allowed to express itself, this torrent of love and an-
guish would render him worthless as a leader. So his
cool mind reminded him over and over in an endless
subconscious chant: there is nothing you can do, nothing you can do, nothing.

His job was to keep this group of men intact, in
command of the situation, ready to move in whatever
direction the President ordered. It was still possible
that the Vindicators would not get through, it was possible that the Soviets might not believe that New York
was actually destroyed, it was possible that some third
power might panic and start to launch nuclear
weapons.

Swenson's neat prudential mind sorted out the alternatives, weighed them, thought ahead to which man
should be entrusted with what tasks in the alternative
situations.

ch. 22

THE CONFERENCE LINE

The conference line connecting Moscow, Khrushchev, the United Nations, and the White House was open, but there was very little conversation.

Buck no longer felt confusion or embarrassment. He merely felt that during the course of the last few hours he had been greatly toughened. The pressure and tension, so sudden and immense as to be incalculable, had first bewildered him, turned him soft with contradictory moods. But now he felt weathered and sure. Without looking ahead he knew that his life would be different after this day.

He found himself looking at the President and running over different ways of approaching the situation. If the situation had been reversed, if Soviet planes had accidentally been launched toward the United States, would the President have demanded the sacrifice of a Soviet city?

Probably, Buck thought to himself, although a part of the American tradition and political character would have allowed for time to see if the Soviet attack had been accidental. But how else could it be proved to be an accident? No way, he thought. The Soviet mentality, however, steeped in its own version of Marxist toughness, would not afford the time to wait, must always make its interpretation on the basis of utmost suspicion of its opponents.

"Mr. President, the activity here in Moscow seems quite ordinary, just like any other day," the American Ambassador said.

Buck sensed that the Ambassador wanted to say something and was asking for permission. The President leaned forward, understanding in his eyes.

"A general alert would be useless, Jay," the President said. "With the amount of time left it would only cause a mass hysteria and probably not save a single life."

"That is correct, Mr. Ambassador," Khrushchev said. His voice was quiet. "I have activated only those parts of our defense that have a chance of shooting down the Vindicators. Our ICBMs have already begun to stand down from the alert. I want no chance of some hare-brained lieutenant getting excited and taking things into his own hands."

It was the opening that the Ambassador wanted.

"What steps will you take to make sure that this most terrible of tragedies is not repeated, Premier Khrushchev?" the Ambassador asked.

"This is not the most terrible of tragedies," Khrushchev said, but his voice was not belligerent. "In World War II we lost more people than we will lose if the two planes get through and Moscow dies. But what makes this intolerable is that so many will be killed so quickly and to no purpose"—he paused, took a breath, and then went on—"and by an accident. The last few hours have not been easy for me, Mr. Ambassador. They are not made easier by the fact that I am talking with you and Ambassador Lentov who will probably be dead in a few minutes. I have learned some things, but I do not have the time to tell them all to you. One thing I can say: at some point in the last ten years we went beyond rationality in politics. We became prisoners of our machines, our suspicions, and our belief in logic. I am willing to come to the United States and to agree to disarmament. Before I leave I will take steps that will make it impossible for our armed forces to repeat what has happened today."

"Premier Khrushchev, I will welcome you and I shall also take the same steps that you have mentioned in regard to our armed forces," the President said. "You have put your finger on something that has been gnawing at my mind during these last few moments."

The President paused. A calm fell on the line.

"Premier Khrushchev?" There was a tentative note to the President's voice.

"Yes, Mr. President?"

"This crisis of ours—this accident, as you say. . . . In one way it's no man's fault. No human being made any mistake, and there's no point in trying to place the blame on anyone." The President paused.

"I agree, Mr. President."

Buck noticed the President nod, receiving the agreement as if both men were in the same room talking together. The President continued, in part thinking aloud: "This disappearance of human responsibility is one of the most disturbing aspects of the whole thing. It's as if human beings had evaporated, and their places were taken by computers. And all day you and I have sat here, fighting, not each other, but rather this big rebellious computerized system, struggling to keep it from blowing up the world."

"It is true, Mr. President. Today the whole world could have burned without any man being given a chance to have a say in it."

"In one way," continued the President, "we didn't

even make the decision to have the computerized systems in the first place. These automated systems became technologically possible, so we built them. Then it became possible to turn more and more control decisions over to them, so we did that. And before we knew it, we had gone so far that the systems were able to put us in the situation we are in today."

"Yes, we both trusted these systems too much." A new grimness crept into Khrushchev's voice. "You can never trust any system, Mr. President, whether it is made of computers, or of people. . . ." He seemed lost in his own thoughts and his voice faded.

"But we did trust them," said the President. "We, and you too, trusted our beautiful Fail-Safe system, and that's what made us both helpless when it broke down."

Buck was translating quickly. The President's thoughts came tumbling out, were arrested for a moment, then started again. He had been speaking as if long-pent-up worries were suddenly being released. A thought flashed through Buck's mind. These two men seemed to understand each other now even before their words were translated. Out of the crisis shared they were developing an intuitive bond. Buck watched the President's face as he was thinking, searching for his next words, and Buck realized a strange fact. There were some things, some profoundly important problems, that the President could communicate to only one other man in the world: Premier Khrushchev. Buck sensed that both men felt this and were grateful for the empty moments now available to them. It let them make a breach in the awful isolation of their positions.

The President was still talking. "Today what we had was a machine-made calamity. And I'm thinking that today you and I got a preview of the future. We damn well better learn carefully from it. More and more of our lives will be determined by these computerized systems."

"It is true," Khrushchev said simply. "I wonder what role will be left to man in the future. Maybe we must think of man differently: 'The computer proposes; man disposes.'"

"Yes, that may be the best we can hope for, but we can't even be sure of that today. Somehow these computerized systems have got to be brought under control. They represent a new kind of power—despotism even—and we've got to learn how to constitutionalize it."

"Mr. President, that would be a kind of constitutionalism I could approve. But this is a problem for politicians, not for scientists." He laughed. "Computers are too important to be left to the mathematicians."

There was another silence, lasting no more than twenty seconds. The President stirred in his chair.

Then it happened very quickly.

"Mr. President, I can hear the sound of explosions coming from the northeast," the American Ambassador said. "They seem to be air bursts. The sky is very bright, like a long row of very big sky rockets. It is almost beautiful, like a Fourth of July—"

And then his voice was cut off. It was drowned in a screech that had an animal-like quality to it. The screech rose sharply, lasted perhaps five seconds, and then was followed by an abrupt silence.

Buck's ears could hear the silence broken by a strange sound. It was, he guessed, made by the throats of approximately fifty men who simultaneously remembered that they must breathe. Somewhere there was the sound, discreet and isolated and perfectly audible, of a single sob.

"Gentlemen, we can assume that Moscow has been destroyed," the President said. He paused, looked at Buck, seemed to be waiting for a miracle, unable to talk. Then he spoke. "I will contact General Black, who is now orbiting over New York City."

ch. 23

THE SACRIFICE OF ABRAHAM

It was a beautiful flying day. Black was flying his "hold" pattern, an effortless oval 46,000 feet above Manhattan. At 15,000 feet there was some small puffy cumulus which gave the firm lines of the Hudson and the East River silvery contrast. Manhattan stood out in clear-cut blocks and rectangles. Even from this height one could make out the soft greenness of Central Park, the odd enclave of grass in a forest of cement. Black had taken the boys there recently with ball and bat—abruptly his mind pulled away from the whole subject. He completed his final check. Everything was in order. The bombs were armed, the crew had been briefed. He had done that first in a very preliminary way over the squadron intercom net.

Black liked the operation of the aircraft, the moving of levers, the pull of the yoke and the sense of control over tons of intricate machinery. There had, he acknowledged to himself, even been a thrill of power when thermonuclear bombs were added to the plane. It was some primordial sense of strength, some childish love of a powerful toy. But above this, and justifying it, was some superior notion of duty. For years Black had thought he was defending his country and he had been right. Again and again he had been assured that either the bombs would not be dropped or they would be dropped only after an aggression against the United

States had commenced. In either case Black would have flown toward the enemy with all the skill and confidence and intelligence he possessed and without a qualm. And he had been assured that there was no third alternative: war by accident was impossible. It was here that Black was in torment. For he had known that it was possible and he had done nothing about it. Now he was being used as the instrument to right the balance. There was a kind of ironic justice in it that appealed to Black. . . .

All was quiet readiness. He turned on the squadron intercom net, asked for and received a check-back signal from each member of the crew. He began speaking quietly and slowly.

"I may not have a chance to finish this, I don't know. But I have to say a few things. You have been briefed on the mission. But I want to add a few personal comments. I think you all know that I'm from New York. My family is down there now." The leader to the last, Black mocked himself. He had told them of his family only to make sure that no one held back, that all knew that he was making the biggest sacrifice and was willing to go ahead.

"I have one last simple order for you. That order is that no one else is in any way to have anything to do with the release. I have set this thing up so that I can handle it entirely by myself."

Black paused. He felt a dullness creep over part of his mind, or perhaps it was his soul or heart. It was an anesthetic sensation. His impressions and memories of New York and of his family were blunted, then almost extinguished. It was a relief. With part of his mind he realized that this was the way the human animal protects itself.

"To repeat. I will fly the plane and launch the bombs," Black said. "No other person will touch an instrument during the release. You may look up or you may close your eyes. You are accomplices and I would be dishonest with you if I said otherwise. But the ultimate act is mine. I think it is worth it, for it is a chance, the only chance, for peace. Please confirm by stations."

He waited for the confirmations before resuming. As they came in he looked down for the last time at the great magnificent sweep of familiar landscape. It seemed more beautiful because of its utter innocence. The millions of people went about their tasks and pleasures unaware. It's better this way, Black thought.

Another voice broke in. It was the President's.

"Blackie, this is it. The bombs have just fallen on Moscow. Release four bombs according to our pre-determined pattern. Report back in three minutes."

Black turned, looked at the men around him. Slowly they raised their eyes toward the heavens. He wheeled around into the final course, checked his sights, opened the control panel in front of him, moved his index finger steadily toward the button by the numeral 1, pressed it firmly for three seconds, removed his finger, moved it down to the button by the numeral 2, pressed it firmly for three seconds and straightened up. His left hand found its way to his side pocket. He knew now who the matador was, what the final sword would be like. The Dream was over. Carefully his hand felt out a small object nestled in his pocket. The hand jerked sharply. At the same instant his right hand grasped the left arm of the copilot beside him. Black slumped forward in his seat.

Major James Callahan was startled out of his prayer as his left arm was grabbed by General Black seated beside him. He looked to his left to see Black slump down in his seat.

Black's eyeballs rolled in his head, deep in their pits

and pure white. The strong unfinished head rolled back on a loose neck.

Major Callahan knew without thinking what had happened. Tears formed in the corners of his eyes. He reached over, took Black's lifeless right hand in his own, bowed his head, held it tight to his tearstained cheek, then placed it on Black's lap. He composed himself, straightened, looked steadily ahead, and reached forward to turn the bright red key which controlled communications with the White House.

"Mr. President, this is Major Callahan. The mission has been accomplished. The four bombs have exploded 5,000 feet over New York. General Black has killed himself with his suicide kit."

"Thank you, Major, it is something I—expected."

The President's voice was still audible but he had apparently turned to an aide by his side.

"Prepare immediately for the consideration of Congress the Medal of Honor in the name of Warren Abraham Black, Brigadier General, United States Air Force. Have the citation read simply: for the highest act of courage and the most supreme conception of duty to his country and to mankind."

Don't miss these
ROBERT LUDLUM
bestsellers!

Superb plots filled with exciting chases, double crosses and secret codes... worlds without scruples... brutality without restraint.... For rollercoaster action, heart-stopping suspense and international intrigue, nobody does it better than Robert Ludlum!

☐ **THE GEMINI CONTENDERS**
   12859-5 $4.95

☐ **THE MATLOCK PAPER**
   15538-X $4.95

☐ **THE RHINEMANN EXCHANGE**
   15079-5 $4.95

Special Offer
Buy a Dell Book
For only 50¢.

Now you can have Dell's Readers Service Listing filled with hundreds of titles. Plus, take advantage of our unique and exciting bonus book offer which gives you the opportunity to purchase a Dell book for *only 50¢.* Here's how!

Just order any five books at the regular price. Then choose any other single book listed (up to $5.95 value) for just 50¢. Use the coupon below to send for Dell's Readers Service Listing of titles today!

 DELL READERS SERVICE LISTING
P.O. Box 1045, South Holland, IL. 60473

Ms./Mrs./Mr. _____

Address _____

City/State_____ Zip _____

DFCA - 12/87